Martyn Harris was born in Swans........ .... University of Kent. He now lives in north London, is married and has
three children. He has written for many newspapers and magazines, including *New Society*, the *New Statesman* and the *Spectator*,
where he is currently television reviewer. He writes the 'Odd Man
Out' column for the *Daily Telegraph*, for which paper he has
recently reported on the Kurdish refugee crisis and the break-up
of the Soviet Union. His first novel, *Do It Again*, is also published
by Penguin.

MARTYN HARRIS

———————

THE MOTHER-IN-LAW JOKE

PENGUIN BOOKS

PENGUIN BOOKS

Published by the Penguin Group
Penguin Books Ltd, 27 Wrights Lane, London W8 5TZ, England
Penguin Books USA Inc., 375 Hudson Street, New York, New York 10014, USA
Penguin Books Australia Ltd, Ringwood, Victoria, Australia
Penguin Books Canada Ltd, 10 Alcorn Avenue, Toronto, Ontario, Canada M4V 3B2
Penguin Books (NZ) Ltd, 182–190 Wairau Road, Auckland 10, New Zealand

Penguin Books Ltd, Registered Offices: Harmondsworth, Middlesex, England

First published by Viking 1992
Published in Penguin Books 1993
1 3 5 7 9 10 8 6 4 2

Printed in England by Clays Ltd, St Ives plc

For Flora and Gwyn Harris

Characters and events are as fictitious as I could manage, but for their contributions, witting and unwitting, I would like to thank Frank Muir, Frankie Howerd, Bob Monkhouse, Ivor Dembina, Caroline Heler, Paul Fisher, John Phillips, John Sessions, Stephen Fry, Jo Brand and the Red Rose Club in Finsbury Park. Especial thanks once again to Max Hastings for generosity well beyond the call of moral blackmail.

Martyn Harris

A difference of taste in jokes is a great strain upon the affections.

George Eliot

Everything can be funny so long as it happens to somebody else.

Will Rogers

The fundamental property of a novel is that by the last page some change of character or circumstances has been effected. In situation comedy this is impossible.

David Nathan, *The Laughtermakers*

PART ONE

... Our dog bit her on the leg and it came up all red and swollen – and my mother-in-law's leg didn't look too good either ... So I phoned the doctor – I know he enjoys a good laugh ... She was rushed into hospital where her condition has been described as critical. She's critical of the food, the bedclothes, the wallpaper ... She needed a blood transfusion, but they couldn't find her a tiger ... She was eating her heart out, but she broke a tooth ... They wanted to put her on a drip, but she said she'd had years of that with her husband, and couldn't they find her a proper man ... When we went to see her she was sitting up in bed, teeth out, curlers in, knitting herself a crash barrier ... She said that when she goes she'll leave me everything she's got, so I said, what have you got? And she says Hepatitis B ...

CHAPTER ONE

'Oh yes, you're the one,' she told me, doing her mad parrot squint across the hospital counterpane. An armful of gold bangles crashed as she beckoned me closer to the bed. A waft of patchouli; a generous and greasy cleavage; a Greek peasant headscarf with a row of coins across her brow. There might well have been a crystal ball on the bedside table.

My mother-in-law was playing the deathbed of Madame Blavatsky that season, her voice a meaningful croak, her shoulders hunched beneath the weight of ancient foreknowledge.

'The moment Diana telephoned I knew she had found her man. We're very close, you know. A golden child.'

Her first words, and me still shuffling bashfully down the bedside towards my boyfriendly peck, parting the plastic lianas of drips and drains and breath-dewed ducts. Monitors beeped and ECG screens scribbled radium lines of electronic alarm, as she seized my wrist and did her lasering-of-the-soul routine. Diana, in Kickers, hovered anxiously behind.

'Mum, I'd like you to meet –'

'You're Welsh of course, I can see that.' She read my hand, fingered my phrenology, checked my teeth and playfully prodded my navel. 'Dark gods of the Celts with a dash of Kenneth Griffith. Untrustworthy but interesting. And you're an actor too, like me.'

'Oh, not really. Just college stuff. Revues and things. I don't –' But modesty never interested my mother-in-law.

Abruptly the Sibyl departed and she rummaged in her hand-bag. 'You can go out and buy me a packet of fags in a minute so Diana and I can dissect you *minutely*.'

'*Mum*...'

'Push that glass nearer, dear heart.'

A brown hand, clawed and ringed, felt its way to the Lucozade bottle on the bedside table and slopped out a quavery glassful. A vigorous slurp and a labourer's back-handed swipe at the lips. It was an operation for ingrowing toenails, I think. She was forty-eight years old, and fit as a butcher's dog, so what was in all those glugging drips and amber drains? Lucozade? But the old cow never skimped on props. She'd have computer-aided tomography for her tonsils and a defibrillation unit standing by when they descaled her teeth.

I would find out, in years to come, that doctors fell apart for my mother-in-law. Grim-faced GPs, icy with pro-fessional rectitude, would hand over bricks of blank pre-scription slips to get her out of their waiting rooms. Starchy staff nurses went limp and gave her the keys to their drug cupboards. Whole hospital wings were cleared, rotas rescheduled and consultants choppered in from the Mayo Clinic when my mother-in-law's colon cramped. Now hang on. Just wait a minute. I'm calling her my mother-in-law and we'd only just met.

But it was all decided you see.

Outside the hospital a NUPE picket was huddled around a brazier. Pickets, braziers, we don't seem to have those any more: all faded into the sepia of social history like the Cat and Mouse Act and the Match Girls' Strike. But this was *that* winter and so I dropped a ten-pee piece into their bucket, and wandered off, down Pond Street to Thresher's, to buy my mother-in-law the sixty king-size and two minia-tures of White Horse, as instructed.

'You really think you should, Mum?' Diana asked her.

'Doctors just want you to expire miserably, Didi. Not you of course, dear heart. I've been out on the balcony and seen that consultant snouting away in his Volvo when he thinks that nobody's looking. And he pongs of brandy on the morning ward round. Liver like a Brussels pâté past its sell-by. Just make sure it's the Silk Cut, there's a ducky. Give him the Sinking Fund, Diana.'

And the Sinking Fund was tucked away in my donkey jacket pocket: a greasy, pigskin purse, bulging with twenties. Outside the hospital I ran a furtive thumbnail down the notes and reckoned I was carrying three hundred pounds. More than I had seen in cash, in one lump, in my life. A flight to Barbados? A new motorbike? Six weeks dossing in Greece? You could buy those things for three hundred pounds in 1979, but I went to the off-licence and bought the cigarettes.

The Sinking Fund Purse or SFP, regularly replenished from some mysterious source, paid for booze, fags, food and drugs, I gathered. Big bills, like Diana's grant, were fed from another upper-crust, upper-case entity, known as The Trust.

'But who *put* the money in The Trust?' I once asked, with my plodding, lower-class literalness.

'My great-grandfather made a lot of money in South Africa,' said Diana vaguely. 'But I think his father may have been rich too . . .'

I knew the area around the hospital already, from literature if not yet from life. On the corner of the little green was the bookshop where Orwell had worked, now a chess café, and the model for the Chestnut Tree Café, in *1984*. Further up the hill, where the road widened out under weeping willow trees, was the small white house where Keats wrote *Ode to a Nightingale*, and higher still, behind a fold in the Heath, was the Vale of Health, where Lawrence once lived with Frieda.

At university in Cardiff my friend Reg, London lad and

worldly wise, had schooled me in the subtle snobberies of the metropolitan postcodes. 'South of the river, forget about it. Nobody lives there but blacks and bank clerks. E3 to E8 is all sawn-off shooters, soccer yobs and Paki sweatshops. Stamford Hill, Golders Green, Hendon is Jews and Jags. W3 to W8 is big mick boozers, small-time TV people and Sikh sweatshops –'

'Hang on, hang on,' I stopped him, bewildered. 'Does everyone walk about *knowing* these things?' The Welsh town I came from had an ordinary bit and a posh bit. There were tidy people and people who were common. I'd learned the English categories of working, middle and upper class by now, but these new complexities seemed overwhelming.

'It's what London *is*,' Reg told me patiently. 'SW3 is better: Sloanes and Kensington crocodiles. NW5 and NW1 are trying hard: Alan Bennett, Jonathan Miller, Hunter Davies, A. J. P. Taylor. But the real colour supp. country is N6 and NW3. That's where you want to be.'

And that was where I was, stamping up East Heath Road against the wind, fingertips digging for warmth in the fluff and grit of pocket seams. I turned right, across a cinder car park that was piled high with black plastic bin bags. There were rats in the streets of London that winter the tabloids said, but only their photographers seemed able to find them. I crossed a dam between two ponds, where narrow gardens filled with wet furniture and mossy statues ran down to the water. Behind a picture window a man was working at a typewriter. Novel, poem, play? He glanced up, and from behind his desk I watched myself, a dark figure in denim and shoddy moving across the shining water, rubbernecking the swans and gentry gardens. He looked down again at his typescript and I was switched off.

I started up a dim tunnel between dusty evergreens, sensing space and light beyond. Over the hill ahead I could see coloured kites flying; scraps of simple geometry on Fuzzy-Felt blue. I climbed a steep asphalt path towards them, keeping my eyes left to the big red-brick houses which fringed the Heath, saving the view which I knew would be there until I reached the top.

It was one of those winter days when the sky lifts its lid on London and floods the city with a hard, splintering light which shrinks distances and pulls into focus the blue ranges of downland which define its limits. In the shallow bowl of the Thames Valley the lava flow of the city had halted. Brown and massy, it was still smoking lightly, hardening here and there into the cubes of office blocks, firing light off their new-formed edges, and the crystal spikes of churches, stabbing through the brown slurry of terrace and traffic.

The noise of the city was a vast and muffled grinding, like the shifting of tectonic plates, which I heard through the feet rather than the ears, as I stood there feeling the new geography form around me. The river ran from right to left, which meant I must be looking south. The pale slabs marching leftwards were the East End. An airliner sinking towards the gleam of the river on the right signified Heathrow Airport. Beside the path was an etched steel panorama, scribbled cockandballs with felt tip. Leaning over it I located the Telecom Tower, St Paul's, St Pancras, St Bride's, St Clement Danes.

Among the kite-flyers a late hippy type in black cape and pantomime boots was building some kind of Black Mass set-up on the ground. There was a sheep's skull painted silver, and a circle of copper bowls filled with rice, grains, peas. He was trying to light a black candle on the skull, and muttering gibberish to himself as he fiddled with a box of kitchen matches. All very tacky and pretentious, but on the windy hill over London, with black cape flying, he had a certain theatrical menace you had to admit. The kite-flyers, and dog-walkers, and mothers with push-chairs were giving him a wide berth.

I was shy in those days, I really was, and the last thing I wanted to do in the world was talk to this twat, so I decided I'd have to talk to him.

'Would you like a light?'

He looked at my Clipper lighter and then at me with the usual, pitying, I'm so fucking far out, why don't you just drop dead look. So I squatted down beside him, very friendly, and started picking up grains of rice from one bowl and dropping them in another, watching the irritation gather in his shoulders.

'Don't do that,' he said at last, his cover broken.

'Oh, sorry mate. I was just wondering if you'd like a light.' I held out the Clipper again, and reluctantly he took it this time, and lit his stupid candle.

'Ta.'

'You don't know what this place is called, do you?'

'Parliament Hill,' said the hippy, grudgingly re-enlisted to the draggy world of kite-flyers and dog-walkers and baby-buggies.

I said the words over to myself as I walked back to the hospital. I'd found the first bit of London I could call my own, and won a stake in it too. Parliament Hill. Parliament Hill.

It was afternoon when Diana and I left the hospital. We walked arm in arm, up Pond Street and across Haverstock Hill into an area of ponderous oxblood houses, and avenues of big trees with the bark flaking off.

'Are they all diseased or what?'

'They're plane trees,' she told me. 'They're supposed to look like that.'

'Why do they want trees that fall to bits?'

'They grow new bark all the time. And they have very shallow roots. They don't dig up the drains and sewers.'

I liked the idea of trees bred for cities, and I liked that she knew what they were called. It was one of the things about being rich. Even if you grew up in the city, you knew the names of trees and flowers and birds. It made you sound knowledgeable, but also unaffected, if you could talk about hornbeams and gillyflowers, jays and grebes. I thought that I'd like to be able to do that.

'She liked you very much,' Diana told me.

'I liked her. I don't think I've ever met anyone like that.'

'My mother's mad.'

'No she's not,' I said, with new loyalty to this stranger who had said she liked me. 'She's a bit eccentric. Interesting. People who are really mad are just boring.'

Diana squeezed me gratefully through the donkey jacket and pushed her head into my shoulder. An untidy mass of hair that tickled my nose.

'She really is mad though. She wants to be old, like one of the old ladies that she visits. Crackers, incontinent, a house full of cats.'

'How can anyone want to be *old*?' I asked her.

We had turned off the street of suburban villas and were entering a narrow mews, when Diana shouted something suddenly and yanked my arm hard. A giant red axe-blade swung through the air past my face, sucking the skirt of my donkey jacket in its backdraught. A lion's breath of exhaust fumes licked our ankles, and a bellow of fractured air, and the axe-blade was 100 yards gone, hoovering up the cobbles with its foot-wide radials.

'God,' I said stupidly. 'That was a Maserati.'

A girl half my size had saved my life, or at least my legs, and I felt even more foolish, provincial, off balance. I couldn't read an *A–Z*, couldn't make sense of a tube map, and couldn't even, apparently, cross a London street on my own without being run over. I reached unsteadily for a saving scrap of knowledgeability.

'Nice car.'

'Bloody idiot,' said Diana. 'There's this silly sports-car garage and they like testing their little skateboards down our street.'

The house was at the end of the mews, older than all the terraces around it, and skewed to the street plan, as if it had once stood in open country and been overwhelmed by the steady creep of nineteenth-century suburbs northwards from the Euston Road. It was Georgian, white stucco, and four storeys high with only one doorbell. Some kind of creeper had climbed half-way up the front and obscured the ground-floor windows. There were dustbins in the front garden and a litter of motorcycle carcasses. 'They used to belong to Saul,' Diana explained. 'Mum calls them the garden gnomes, because they never go anywhere.'

'God, it's *huge*.'

'They don't use half the rooms these days.'

I pulled her back from the gate a few yards and kissed her for a long time. We had only been together about six weeks, and I could foresee a guarded, family evening of careful conversations and single beds. Diana didn't like necking in the street, but she stuck her tongue in my mouth first, which surprised me, and ground her pelvis against mine. After a while I put my hand inside her sweater, to make her make me stop, and she trapped it efficiently with her elbow.

'We'd better go in now,' she said, and fished for a key in her shoulder-bag. 'Ready?'

I was after her money, of course. I'd better make that clear now. My own family wasn't poor, they had a house, a car, washing-machine, all that stuff, but it wasn't the right kind of money. They had a TV set, for instance, but it was too big. They had decent furniture, but it all matched. They bought a good carpet, but it went all the way up to the walls, and nosed its way into the corners like spilled gravy.

They weren't without cultivation the Em and Pee. There were some books, but they came from book clubs instead of shops, and lived in a glass-fronted case with a key. There was a stereo and some classical records, but they listened to them too self-consciously, as if hoping someone might come in and find them at it. My mother had some 'pieces' she was going to leave to us when she'd gone. A silver-plated

Victorian tea service and some Swansea china, but I didn't want it. I used to look around their house when I went home on holiday and there wasn't anything I wanted at all.

My first girlfriend was rich. Her father was a builder and drove a custard Rolls-Royce with his initials on the number-plate, but they were the same sort of people as my parents really. They had a bed with a brown velour console at the head, where Louise and I would go when we were babysitting her brothers. There was always a packet of Fetherlite in the bedside drawer, and a copy of *Lady Chatterley* that we would read together while we slowly frigged each other to a state of chaste exhaustion.

Louise's parents ate breakfast, dinner and tea like mine, but they liked to go out for a good meal. Her father took us out for a good meal once and ordered Mateus Rosé wine, which I'd never had before. He showed us how to sniff the wine and hold it up to the candle flame, swirl it around the glass. Then he said it was so good he wanted to buy a crate from the restaurant and the waiters had to load it in the back of the Rolls for him right that minute. I was very impressed, but I thought they probably had the wrong kind of money too.

I went out with another rich girl at university. Her name was Sophie and we used to screw all the time, but she had a large stubbly bottom which I couldn't stroke without losing my erection. Her father was something called an equerry in the Royal Household. I imagined him in shining leather boots, holding the bridle of the Queen's horse at the Trooping of the Colour. In bed Sophie used to like me to do it to her from behind, and once she asked me to tie her hands together.

One weekend her brother came down from Sandhurst in an MG TC with leather straps on the bonnet. He was going to Northern Ireland with the Green Howards when he finished his training. He showed me how to kill someone with the edge of my hand, and talked about it being a great life in the mob. Unlike university you learned to mix with all sorts, and acquired a practical training that stood you in good stead for the rest of your life. When he left he looked me in the eye and shook my hand very hard and said I should be careful. Their family seemed to have a lot of money, but I didn't think it was the right kind either.

The hallway of Diana's house was a kind of trench, its sides made from packed strata of coats, books, cardboard boxes, carrier bags. Diana led the way – around a buttress of bicycles, a firing step of stacked newspapers, a reeking rampart of paraffin cans – and I followed, an anxious subaltern in his first day at the front. The trench wound through a living room, where its walls were made from pianos and dust sheets and blinded television sets. More twists and turns, and then the strata of the sides began to include frying-pans and fish-finger packets, and I realized that we were in the kitchen.

'This is Cahill,' said Diana. A bald man in a pink tweed jacket materialized from the complex background, like a number from an optician's colour card. He swarmed over Diana with noisy exclamations of joy, and then turned to me, offering a very hairy hand.

'Brendan Cahill.'

'Phil First.'

'Would that be one of these fine new made-up names?' said Cahill. 'Like Dinah Lone and Stan Fast?'

'And Tim O'Mortice and Peter Rout? No, I'm afraid it's on the birth certificate.' I thought I might as well give him the standard line. 'I'm the last in a long line of Firsts.'

'Oh, that's very good,' said Cahill. 'I expect you'll be wanting a drink.'

'I'll get them,' said Diana, and began poking about among the army of bottles on the dresser.

'You've met Diana's mother, Philip? My own ticker plays me up, but that poor woman is a martyr to her body. Not that you'll ever hear a breath of complaint.' He spoke with one ear cocked, as if taking his cue from a voice somewhere in the ceiling. His accent was Dublin posh, and there was a puff of silk cravat at his neck between frayed wings of Tattersall check.

'She's coming out tomorrow,' said Diana, pouring small splashes of amontillado into cloudy mustard glasses.

'They'd never put her out on the street in her condition,' said Cahill indignantly. He drained his glass and refilled it himself.

'It's only her bloody toenails, Cahill.'

'Well, we must be making preparations. Sheets, food for the invalid, flowers, a drop of wine . . .' He trailed off vaguely. 'Did she by any chance give you the SFP, Diana? We do seem to be running a little low.' He waved a hand to a cupboard spilling tins and packets on to the floor; among them I noted an Instant Whip with its price tag in old pence.

'I can get some shopping in.'

'No need, dear girl. No need at all. One of the small ways I can make myself useful. Philip shall come with me for the walk.'

Diana peeled a single twenty-pound note from the roll in the purse and stuffed the SFP firmly back in her shoulder-bag. 'Phil's probably tired.'

'Nonsense. A twenty-minute expedition. And we boys must get to know each other.'

'Well, all right. I'll just show Phil where he's sleeping.'

Upstairs the house went on and on, through long-abandoned categories of domesticity. A breakfast room, a music room, a telephone room, a day nursery, all dust-draped and dim in the winter twilight.

'This is Saul's room,' said Diana, 'and this was Gran's. Mum's sitting room is on the next floor, and then mine above that. And Henrietta's in the nanny bedroom at the moment.'

'What about me?'

'We're sleeping together,' said Diana firmly.

It would have taken a year of tense negotiations to sleep with a girlfriend in my parents' house. Arguments, threats, counterthreats, blackmail and boycott.

'You're sure they won't mind?'

'Don't suppose they'll even notice,' she said. 'You want to see the attics?'

We dropped our bags in her bedroom, small, neat and lavender scented, then climbed the last flight of stairs. One great loft was a junk room, crammed with mahogany tallboys and stacked picture frames, impassable beyond the dust-swept quadrant of doorway. The other rooms were only slightly less full: vistas of tumbled bedding, tea chests, dulled mirrors and bursting cartons of crockery.

'There's a lot of good stuff amongst all this junk, isn't there?'

'What sort of things have you noticed?' said Diana.

'Oh, um, those old lamps and things.'

'Those are John Lewis,' she said. 'Mum buys an awful lot of rubbish. When we've got more time I'll show you the Pipers and the Palmers and Grants.' The names meant nothing to me. They could have been brands of biscuit, but I made appropriately grateful noises.

'And who's Cahill?'

'Well, he used to run a restaurant in Barcelona, and he says he's an architect, but I've never known him actually build anything.'

'I meant what is he doing here?'

'He's Mum's boyfriend,' said Diana. 'And I've got this awful feeling that she's going to marry him.'

It was getting dark when we left the house and the air was already stained with the orange glow of the first street lamps.

'You like the car?' said Cahill.

I had noticed it when we arrived. A new Mercedes saloon, gun-metal grey, and glittering coldly as it squatted in the gutter outside the gate.

'That's yours?'

'The Krauts know how to make a car,' said Cahill. 'Drove this one from Frankfurt in a day and I stepped out of it feeling like I'd just had my morning bath. Take my advice, and never buy a cheap automobile.'

I told him that I wouldn't.

'We could drive to the shops, but it's only ten minutes and petrol's such a wicked price.'

Cahill was swinging a carrier bag, a green loden coat draped over his shoulders, while I pushed an ancient wicker trolley which jibbed and snatched at the worn pavement. I seemed to be falling into the role of professional shopper to the Schondler family, but it felt like a safely neutral one for the time being.

'So you're a comedian,' said Cahill.

'Not really, I just –'

'I heard a very good one the other day about these two Irishmen who wanted to rob a bank ...' It was a long, involved story, and I spent it looking at the windows of the shops we passed. The butcher's was called The Village Butcher, the wine shop was called The Wine Shop and the baker's was called The Baker's.

Neatly bobbed women in tabards and Biggles boots were loading Volvo estates with crates of wine and boxes of French bread. There were still Christmas lights in the window of the greengrocer's, and a smell of oranges and damp earth that reminded me suddenly and sharply of home.

'So the bank manager said, "You've sawn off the wrong end of your shotgun."'

'Oh yes, that's very good.'

Cahill was yawing and sawing with laughter on the pavement, and clutching my arm for support. 'I shouldn't really with this old ticker of mine but you do have to laugh, don't you?'

'Yes.'

'I was thinking we should pop into the Haywain for a quick one before dinner.'

'Well, I haven't got much . . .'

Cahill straightened himself up and assumed a purposeful air. 'We have twenty pounds, and if a man can't buy dinner and drink for twenty pound . . . What do you say we go and see if they're still running at Ludlow?'

So I followed him into the betting shop, or rather The Betting Shop; a plasterboard pit with a green aquarium light. Around the walls were burst bar stools decorated with the decomposing remains of beached whales. Crusted lips; barnacled ears; and spiritual eyes that swam with television and whisky tears. The sportsmen of Hampstead.

'What would you say to Comic Turn in the 4.45?' Cahill demanded. 'Attractively weighted, wouldn't you say? And she's good in the mud. Seven to one and an auspicious name in the circumstances.'

'Well, I don't know much about . . .'

Cahill seized the twenty and poked it through a slot at a jazzed lobster of a girl behind the smeared glass.

'That's all the money we've got.'

'Nothing ventured,' said Cahill. 'But as a concession to the conservatism of youth we'll put it on each way.'

It was a strange list of shopping that we bought. A dozen packets of Instant Whip, four tins of smoked oysters, twenty-four of Whiskas, a dozen bottles of Tuborg Royal Brew, three of amontillado, a packet of Scotchbrite, a Romeo Y Julietta cigar, a box of prawn crackers, a bunch of gladioli and a bottle of lobster bisque.

'What are we actually going to eat?' I asked Cahill in the pub afterwards. He tossed back his third large Bushmills and listened again to the ceiling.

'That young woman of yours is a marvel in the kitchen,'

he told me, and I noticed his accent was sliding from Dublin towards Belfast. 'Though where she gets it I do not know. Her mother is a firecracker in bed, but that shopping trolley would cook you a better meal. D'ye know what Joan Collins wears behind her ears to attract men?'

'Her ankles,' I told him, and he looked so disappointed that I had to be conciliatory.

'You used to run a restaurant?'

'The best steak restaurant in Barcelona,' said Cahill. 'Politicians, film people, painters. English beer from the wood. Lobster from Cadaqués. Beef from Japan.'

I stole a look at his face, but it was solemn, his ear cocked to the promptings of those inaudible voices.

'Why Japan?'

'Because the Japanese *care* for their beef cattle, Philip. Beautiful plump little bulls with shining coats and gentle eyes. Fed every day on warm mashes steeped in molasses and rice wine. Dressed at night in little woollen suits to keep them cosy. Each one with its own geisha girl to oil its soft little snout and to groom its silken hide.' I was giggling by now, but Cahill's face was grave and dreamy. 'Those lovely geisha girls, they massage their little bulls every day, squeezing and teasing with their gentle fingers until they're so soft and tender, you could carve them where they stand. People would drive from Gerona, Calella – the Caudillo himself would fly from Madrid to taste my Japanese beef.'

'*Franco* used to eat at your restaurant?'

Cahill tapped the side of his nose with an air of enough said, and took from his pocket the roll of greasy bills, flattening them on the table between us. He counted out eight fivers.

'Here's your winnings.'

'But I didn't –'

'Psssht. 'Tis only fair.' And he glanced at the ceiling once again. 'But mum's the word.'

CHAPTER TWO

Reg was leaning over the bar when I found him, reading the *Guardian* crossword puzzle upside down. On the public side an old soak with a roghan josh complexion and a blue Barbour jacket was wheezily sub-vocalizing the clues beneath a trembling purple forefinger.

'A torque twisted into a fancied circle. Seven letters.'

'Try "equator",' said Reg, raising a hand to me in greeting. Muttering ungratefully the soak filled in the clue with a frayed Bic, its point rucking the damp newsprint. Reg was wearing vast black magician's trousers with silk braid seams, and a breezy Dan Tempest shirt which blazed in the treacly twilight of the pub. For the sake of effect he jabbed at a few optics, crashed a wire tray of pint pots into the dishwasher and whisked an invisible droplet from the bar with a spotless towel.

'Right then. What will you have?'

'Gin and tonic, please.'

'Large Gin and It for the young man with the cheekbones, Eugene,' he sang out to his non-existent assistant. 'You like our little *estaminet, Philippe*?'

At eleven thirty in the morning the saloon bar of The Jar was almost empty, apart from a few shaky livers-on-legs, drinking their hangover cures two-fisted out of Duralex tumblers. The colour scheme was phlegm and nicotine, smoked haddock and used teabag. Golden plumes of cigar smoke spiralled through the rays of winter sun that filtered through the frosted glass. The smell of frying sausages floated from the kitchen. No music and no machines. I approved.

'They're *all* bent in here,' Reg explained. 'The customers are queer, the pot boy's a pouf and the barmen are all bum bandits. Even the drayman's horse has a funny look in his eye.' As he talked he squirted gin, topped tonic and tonged ice in a single balletic blur. Reg had been *practising* at this.

'Landlord came back from Piccadilly last night with a little tart called Sid. Blond Mohican haircut and leopardskin bondage trousers. Took him to bed and he squealed the place down all night like a Gloucester Old Spot. Landlord's a dead spit for Miss Piggy, by the way. He comes home with a different one every night, I gather. There's talk of putting him up for the Queen's Award for Industry. Cheers.'

He slid the glass across to me, choked with ice, and brimming with clear alcohol, a bottle of Schweppes on the side. From beneath the bar he produced a wooden chopping board with a half of lemon, freshly sliced. 'Ice'n'lemon? Ice'n'lemon? These silly tarts behind the bar waste half their lives asking people if they want ice and lemon. I mean, has anyone ever drunk gin and tonic *without* ice and lemon? It's like asking if you want bread with your fucking sandwich.'

I handed him one of Comic Turn's fivers, and after a busy flourish at the cash register he gave me the change for a ten. 'Don't count it and don't worry about it. They're coining it in this place. At closing time the piss-artists come in here will trade you their BMWs for a carry-out of barley wine.'

Did I tell you Reg was queer? My London friend from university with the penchant for posh postcodes? Reg kicked down the door of his closet when he was fifteen, and traumatized his Golders Green family with an affair with the school swimming-pool attendant. At seventeen he eloped with the father of his French penfriend on an exchange trip to Rouen. At nineteen I met him at the student pub in Cathays Park, a dour place that lived off keg beer and crisps but pretended to sell cocktails. Reg was waving a lot of money at a buttock-faced barman, and demanding 'a pint of stout with a dash of advocaat and a cherry on top, *garçon*.'

'It's a disgusting drink,' he told me confidentially. 'Looks like somebody's spunked in the bathwater. But it creates such a wonderful *stir*.'

He had a long, mournful, pastry-coloured face and eloquent hands with filthy fingernails. He read *Liberté* ostentatiously, took taxis everywhere and threw away his underpants when he had worn them once, his father being in the wholesale clothing trade. He was jeered at by the rugby players, and in his second year seduced the lock forward of the first fifteen. 'Splendid gluteal development,' he told me wistfully, 'but the smell of *wintergreen*.'

I loved him, and waited in trepidation for the pass that never came. 'You don't have to worry, Philippe. You're such a fucking *het*. All those gloomy androgens coursing about your veins, giving you pitstink and blackheads and bad temper.' So we ran the campus newspaper together, and did the all-male production of *La Belle Hélène*, with Reg's lock forward in the title role. We did hospital radio, and we did the Red Lion Revue, and we did an awful concept piece called *Bitz* that we took to Edinburgh. He was so much cleverer and better read than me that naturally he failed his degree, while I got a decent 2:1 and stayed on a year, and met Diana.

With another gin and tonic in hand I ordered sausage and chips, and collected the change for another tenner.

'So what's it like, Diana's place?'

'Sort of Gormenghast,' I told him. 'Mad mother, Irish con-man boyfriend, lots of hangers-on. Diana said you could come to dinner tonight if you like.'

'I shall steal a bottle of Miss Piggy's best bubbly. No, I shall steal a brace of bottles.'

'Because the best things always come in braces.'

'Fuck off my lines,' said Reg.

The roghan josh gave a rusty groan and rattled his newspaper at us. 'This twelve down is a real bastard. D'you think there's a misprint?'

I studied the clue from over his shoulder. 'It just says HIJKLMNO. Five letters.'

Reg made a show of polishing a glass and staring abstractedly into the distance. 'Try "water",' he said finally.

'How d'you reckon that?'

'The clue is H to O and H_2O is water, geddit?'

'How the fuck does he do that?' said the soak.

By spending two hours over the crossword in bed every morning I might have said, but didn't.

'There's a Comedy Store type of place down the road in Camden Town,' Reg told me later. 'Went down there the other night with Miss Piggy.'

'You think we could play there?' I asked him.

'We'd have to write a lot of new stuff. Audience full of heavy-metal headbangers and off-duty nurses from the Royal Free. I don't think smart-arse little Sartre spoofs would go down too well.'

'What were the acts like?'

'Not much cop. There was a girl doing menstruation stuff, and a bloke doing toilets.'

'D'you laugh?'

'Course I didn't laugh,' Reg told me indignantly. 'Most of them were so boring the paint was watching them dry.' He refilled my glass, and gave me the change for another tenner. 'Mind you I did hear a good one from Miss Piggy last night.'

'What was that?'

'It was about the two Irish queers who couldn't tell the difference between Vaseline and putty.'

'What happened to them?'

'All their windows fell out,' said Reg. 'It's a pity we can't do jokes like that.'

*

My mother-in-law arrived home at the same time as me, but in a Royal Free ambulance with light and bells going full clap. She stepped straight out of the rear door and into the path of a Porsche 921 which was hoovering up the cobbles of the mews at a good sixty miles an hour from its standing start some forty yards away. It's a 24-valve, fuel-injected, quadruple OHC, turbocharged engine and they'd left the mufflers in the oil-pit, but it sounded like a skylark's tweet beside my mother-in-law's wall of righteous wrath. '*You fucking fucker fucking fuck your fucking fucked up fucking fucks* . . .' Or words to that effect.

But she didn't move an inch from the ambulance door and though, as I say, the Porsche was doing sixty minimum I'd swear the thing *flinched* in its trajectory as my mother-in-law seared its cocky scarlet paintwork with her fusillade of fucking fucks – and the driver's face went white behind his smoked glass and hand-stitched wheel – and that whole self-important, pumped-up pod of power bulge, airdam and spoiler seemed to lose its tumescence suddenly and sort of flop and slither and slide to an apologetic stop in the smoking track of its own tyres. Diana had appeared in the doorway of Aberdare House and Cahill at an upstairs window. There was a rattle of window sashes going up half-way to Highgate, and the Porsche driver flapped his hands apologetically, as birdsong and insect life shakily resumed across north London.

'She never *looks*,' said Diana.

When I had carried her case upstairs, and been shooed away by Cahill, I went down to the kitchen where I found Diana sitting at the table, opposite her brother Saul, with family conference in the air.

'Wholly inappropriate,' he was telling her. 'House in condition. Man Cahill totally unsuitable. Lodgers everywhere, nothing about . . .' He glanced suspiciously at me as I edged my way out of the trench, and into the room, and Diana went into a nervous flurry of introductions.

'Saul. Phil. Meet. This is –'

'I was just wondering if I could get myself a cup of coffee,' I told them, humble with afternoon hangover, 'and then I'll get out of your way.'

'No, stay . . .'

'All means,' said Saul, who seemed to have an aversion to the lesser parts of speech. 'Pleased meet. Heard lot course. Diana tells very talented. Monty Python, ha, ha.'

I poked about in the sugar-crusted midden beside the cooker, searching for kettle and coffee jar, and taking him in through my shoulder blades. A business suit on a Saturday afternoon; a green silk tie with crossed sculls on it. He was a big bastard, with apple cheeks and cleft jaw, his reddish hair laid back flat across his pink scalp, like bacon rashers on a Christmas turkey. Four or five years older than Diana.

'Essential move place more suitable,' he was saying. 'Reasons economy, practicality, mention *hygiene*.' He took a pained sniff at the complex odours of the kitchen, which at that moment included chip fat, cat pee, rotting linoleum and the scorched-tin miasma from the nest of dog ends in the scullery plughole. 'Street outside Brands Hatch good as.'

'Mum would never agree to live anywhere else,' said Diana. 'I mean, what would she do with all her *stuff*. And there's all the cats to think of. She's got at least eight at the moment.'

Saul glanced irritably at the fat tabby, then nesting in a silver sugar-bowl on the dresser. 'Put a few down: nobody needs eight cats.' It was his first complete sentence.

'It's babies, isn't it?' said Diana, and Saul snorted.

'Actually told me other day wanted have child *that man*. Woman fifty years old.'

I sat down between them with chair slightly back from the table, the neutral observer.

'So you don't actually live here then, Saul?'

'Flat Wapping,' said Saul, cheering up. 'Currently

unsuitable City-based operations, major investment opportunity 1980s.'

'Saul's a banker,' explained Diana and I studied him again. Growing up in Wales I had been taught to feel sorry for bankers and businessmen and accountants, and others who had been too thick to get proper jobs in teaching or medicine or law. But Saul did not look unhappy or apologetic about his calling. Indeed, he positively glowed at the appellation.

Over the next hour or so I deduced that Saul had some especially close relationship with The Trust, which he referred to with approval as an entity of great sagacity and insight. The Trust held strong views on the unsuitability and inappropriateness of current arrangements at Aberdare House. The Trust approved of restructuring, liquidity, sensible fiscal controls. It disapproved of cats, lodgers and lovers. In its heart of hearts The Trust believed that Saul's mother would be much happier in a sensible little service flat.

'Somewhere *appropriate*. Maida Vale. St John's Wood,' said Saul finally.

'Mum hates St John's Wood,' said Diana. 'She says that it's full of cabinet ministers' mistresses and Toyota executives. There's no proper bookshop and the vicar is Low Church.'

The doorbell rang and I went to answer it. On the step was a tall girl with a beehive of soot-black dreadlocks, mountainous white breasts and sticky-jampot lips. 'Would you mind awfully?' she said, and stalked past me into the hallway, leaving a stack of Harvey Nichols carrier bags behind her. I managed to lodge them in a niche in the wall of the trench, between a birdcage and a gas mask, and returned to the kitchen, where the new arrival was running two-inch purple talons through Saul's rashers.

'This is Hon,' said Diana, rhyming it with 'don'. 'Saul's er . . .'

'You're getting frightfully *bald*, baby,' said Hon, ignoring me. 'You might just as well shave the whole lot off like Terence. And that's a fucking awful suit.' Saul blushed crimson and hee-hawed in a hell of a girl but what can you say kind of way.

She embraced Diana warmly: 'Your *skin*, sweetheart.' I noted that in spite of the breasts, her buttocks, in tight black leather trousers, were boy-sized Smarties. She uncorked a bottle of Barolo one-handed, filled herself a glass, waved it about her in general benediction, and disappeared upstairs.

'Is Hon short for something?' I asked.

'Her real name's Henrietta – Hattie,' said Diana. 'But her father was an earl or a duke or one of those things. Hon is a kind of joke from when we were at school.'

'Lloyd George peerage,' said Saul, smoothing his rashers, and recovering his colour. 'Pennies to rub together really.'

'She's your girlfriend?' I asked him.

'*Exactly*,' said Saul, apparently meaning the opposite. 'Flat Wapping unsuitable. Separate ways. Mutual amicable perfectly.'

With an air of purposeful distaste Diana had begun scouring saucepans and stacking crockery in the sink. Family conference seemed to be over and I began stuffing piles of rubble into black bin-liners. But Saul seemed determined to continue extolling the merits of service flats and St John's Wood.

'Have you thought about splitting the house into flats?' I suggested in the end. 'Then your mother could carry on living here, and you could sell the other floors.' Diana winced, but Saul beamed. An ally in appropriateness and suitability at last.

'Bad idea,' he told me, meaning the opposite again. 'Bad idea at *all*.'

Dinner as I've said, was something that came between

breakfast and tea at my parents' house. It was a big, uncompromising meal of floury potatoes and meat cooked to rags in a swamp of thick gravy. There were sprouts, simmered for an hour, to the texture of toothpaste; fluffy swede; and Surprise peas named, I supposed, for their surprising colour.

It wasn't just a dinner, but a *proper* dinner, which contained some deep, unalterable symbolism among its constituent parts: a sacred trinity of meat, potato and veg, unified in sauce. All dinners, even salads, followed the same basic pattern, with tinned ham replacing the roast meat, lettuce and tomato for the vegetables and salad cream in place of gravy.

I liked my mother's meals, but an atmosphere of agonized planning and desperate hazard always accompanied her cooking. For Sunday dinners she had to get the vegetables out of the way on Saturday, and for Christmas the sprouts were peeled, cross-scored and soaking in salt water by Guy Fawkes Night. Meat went on low, well before chapel, and vegetables were keeping warm in foil-covered ovenware dishes an hour before we sat down to eat.

When we did sit down her migraine would arrive, and she would hover a tense half-inch above the arm of the sofa, nibbling a banana, while we troughed ourselves and bickered around the table. As soon as my father had lit his inter-course cigarette and poked his spent match out into his last, uneaten potato, she was off and up again, clearing the way for the apple tart. 'Just get these things out of the way.'

The first course would be washed up and out of the way before we had eaten our seconds, and the seconds before we had sat down to our cup of tea. The whole thing never took more than twenty minutes. 'And now we can relax properly,' my mother would say, as she began to worry about teatime.

Once, when I was over at a friend's house, his father, who was a lecturer in Russian at the university, offered to make us tea. He fried Manx kippers in a big iron skillet, made doorsteps of brown bread and butter and drank a glass of white wine while we ate. I gaped at the sophistication, and worried about inviting them back.

My parents never ate out. My father had a highly specialized digestive tract which could not deal with other people's food, and though they were kindly people, they never invited others to a meal. They wouldn't have been able to see the point. Dinner was the climax of one process and the beginning of another: it demarcated preparation from digestion, morning from afternoon, but it was not something to be made an event in itself. The idea would have seemed slightly indecent.

That evening at my mother-in-law's house was the first real meal I ever ate: a meal that was a celebration of itself rather than a punctuation mark or a refuelling stop. Twelve years on, and I still remember what we ate. There was a dish of cold meat and pâté, not very much. Then Diana served up some baby broad beans in butter, about twelve each. And Cahill made a little bit of pasta in creamy sauce. Very nice, but I was beginning to get worried. After all, it was getting on for ten o'clock. When was *dinner* going to be? And who was actually cooking it?

The salivary glands in the corner of my jaw ached. I drank a lot of red wine to numb them: slippery Italian stuff that came in plastic flagons from Oddbins, and gobbled bread. The girl called Hon produced some tiny lozenges of lamb in pink juice, with a teaspoonful of mashed potato each. Cahill made an oily salad of unfamiliar leaves, and we ate it with little triangles of soft cheese. I drank more wine, reached for more bread and realized I was very full indeed, and that I'd been eating for four hours.

'Mumsie always hated sex, of course,' my mother-in-law was saying. 'Poor Daddy had to go to a Negro woman in Cricklewood every Wednesday afternoon. She had a son called Boniface – I suppose they were Catholic – who Daddy sent to Charterhouse where he was bullied terribly.'

'Don't think *actually* Negro,' said Saul.

'She had a parrot called Solti,' my mother-in-law said indignantly, 'and *all* her family came from Swindon.'

'What happened to Boniface?' asked Reg.

'He joined the Portuguese navy as a tank calibrator, so I suppose he must have been a pacifist. After the war he came to work for us as a gardener, and then he won the football pools and asked me to marry him. It was out in the garden by the compost heap. I couldn't of course, though I don't suppose he really was my brother. It was the year I was in *Separate Tables* at Liverpool. Could you top me up, Philip?'

For dinner she had changed her outfit from fortune-teller to African Queen: a crusty gold kaftan, with a chunky coral necklace and a wooden skewer through her topknot. There were old stage photographs of her around the house: roguishly laughing, or meditative, with chin cupped in palm. She was much heavier now, with a shadow of razor stubble on her upper cheeks, but for the first time I could see her looks for myself. From my place of honour on her left I trickled wine into her glass from the cumbersome flagon, then took it around the table again, for the sixth or maybe seventh time. Only Diana put her hand over her glass.

There were eight people besides myself: my mother-in-law, Cahill, Saul, Diana, Reg, the girl called Hon, an Arab lodger with a name like an angry wasp and an elderly Japanese woman I never saw again. Cahill did some of the talking, and Reg too, but it was my mother-in-law who carried the evening: teasing, bullying, telling stories, singing nursery songs. Was it really possible for someone's mother to talk about sex and Gielgud and abortions and Bacon and illegitimate half-brothers, and a mad aunt who danced naked on the garden path while playing the banjo?

Apparently it was, for my mother-in law talked about all those things. And as I sat there listening, in the hot kitchen, at the edge of the circle of smoky candlelight and green silver, it was with a sense of the doors to a new, adult civilization creaking gently open.

'It was Mumsie being Swiss, I expect,' she was saying now. 'Mumsie said she would never have another one after your uncle Gerald. She did the last abortion herself in the downstairs loo. She kept the knitting needles afterwards and used them to make a pair of mittens for Daddy, which I always thought was some sort of *comment*.' She waved a cheese-smeared knife at Reg, who she had already identified as a likely ally in outrage. 'Don't *you* think it's awful to hate sex, Reginald?'

'Oh, we didn't have sex at all in Golders Green,' said Reg promptly. 'Though it was spoken of in Hendon, and some say even practised in north Finchley.'

My mother-in-law regurgitated a mouthful of wine into her glass.

'There were relations of advanced views who ordered their sex in from John Lewis,' Reg went on, 'but my parents preferred strict parthenogenesis, like the pussy willow.' I recognized my cue.

'So how did they account for you?' I asked him.

'As the nearest thing to an Immaculate Conception in the Jewish faith,' said Reg. 'The product of a brief encounter between my mother and an imperfectly disinfected toilet seat at the Euston Station ladies' loo.'

'And what about the rest of your family?'

'Well, there's my brother of course, who's the offspring of a Terylene hand-towel at the Golders Green Orthodox synagogue. A sister who springs from an unwiped doorknob in Peter Jones. And several grandchildren now, who can trace their ancestry back to flush chains, sports-car seats, borrowed handkerchieves and even a casual puff on a scrounged Silk Cut.'

They were all laughing by now, which is the time to change tack if you need to, because once you've got them like that they'll never notice a caesura. I switched my voice to breathless *ingénue*.

'So, I mean, like, well, how *are* babies really made then, Reg?'

He leaned forward, arms on the table, and lowered his voice to a conspiratorial whisper. 'Well, it's like this, see, Phil.' A glance to either side. 'Girls have all got this little trampoline thing inside them called a hymen. Now there's all these eggs that bounce up and down on the hymen and what you have to do is get one of your little seamen . . .'

'Your what?'

'Your seamen. These microscopic little blokes what swim around inside your John Thomas. You have to get one of them to like poke a hole in the trampoline, and catch one of these bouncing eggs and then run off with it.'

Pause for puzzled silence.

'What for?'

'Dunno,' said Reg, 'but it's called an organism. Then when you have your organism you wrap your seaman up in a tissue and put him down the toilet. That's called Le Petit Mort. Little dead man, right?'

'Right. And then you make love do you?'

'Nah, nah, nah. You've already *made* love. What you do then is have a smoke and stare at the ceiling. It's a deeply pleasurable experience.'

It wasn't one of my favourite routines. Too much willy and toilet. But Reg used to do it very well, with his long, solemn, Jewish face and earnest oik's accent, and it worked all right on the night. Diana knew it already of course, and smiled dutifully. But Cahill was coughing into his wine glass; my mother-in-law was hooting like a tug boat; Saul was purple and damp about the eyes. Only the girl Hon was cool, gazing up at the Scotch airer on the ceiling over the tip of her cigarette, ostentatiously unimpressed.

'Is that part of the act then?' my mother-in-law asked.

'Was once,' said Reg, reaching for the grapes. 'Phil wrote most of it, though some of it's nicked of course.'

'So why doesn't Phil do it?' said Cahill.

'I'm the Wellma boy,' I told him.

'The what?'

'The feed, the straight man. In the old double acts like Eric and Ernie or Mike and Bernie, he's the one you clap on the shoulder and say "Wellma boy, and what have you been up to?"'

'I thought you were supposed to be New Wave comedians or something.' It was Hon speaking, her cigarette pointing at me.

'Oh that. It's just a label really. New Wave. Alternative comedy. It's just a matter of trying to get away from stuff like Jimmy Tarbuck and Bernard Manning. You try not to do nig-nog jokes or Jewish jokes or sexist jokes. Don't do jokes at all really.'

'Isn't it sexist to make fun of a woman's genitalia?' said Hon. There was a silence, and I caught Reg giving me a right-one-here look.

'With respect, um, Henrietta, I don't think we were actually laughing *at* women's hymens. It was more a piece of –'

'Typically pathetic schoolboy smut,' said Hon. 'Trying to overcome male fear of female sexuality by making it ridiculous.'

In the longer silence which followed I carried out a quick mental reappraisal of this woman. Subtracted the preposterous heavy-metal-chick hairdo, the black leather bitch-goddess get-up and the Lloyd George lineage. Added fifty points or so to her IQ. All I'd done to Hon so far was humbly to hump her Harvey Nichols carrier bags, but she was out to get me all right.

'You don't think you're making a teensy-weensy *category* mistake here do you, dear? Confusing the comic with his comic persona? Of course you've read Henri Bergson, *Le Rire*? Well no, perhaps they don't do that at the Harrods bookshop. Or how about Freud on *Jokes and their Relation to the Unconscious*?'

There was a flush at the base of those milky breasts, and the pressure of Diana's hand on my knee. '"The smutty joke",' said Hon, with that quoting-from-memory tilt to her chin, '"was originally directed against the woman, and is comparable to an attempt at seduction."' Reg clapped, I added another ten points to the IQ, and decided to forget about Freud.

'I think what Reg and I were trying to do there in our confessedly clumsy way was parody the person who has learned their sexual anatomy off a cigarette card. Though it might just as well have been someone who'd acquired their sexual attitudes from *Cosmopolitan*. Stereotyped, cliché-ridden: the mechanical man – or woman – who substitutes prefabricated prejudice for ordinary intelligence. It's the basis of most humour. I suppose you see what I'm driving at?'

My mother-in-law was grinning, Cahill and Reg uneasy, Diana frankly embarrassed. 'Of course I see it now,' said Hon, still flushed, but unfazed. 'But at the time I somehow got the impression you were just being a patronizing little prick.'

'Anyone for coffee?' said Cahill.

I knew already from working on stage that one of the rules of the put-down is that it's not the wit which matters so much, as the speed. Another is that if you can't be clever, be crude. If in doubt, lash out. Go for massive retaliation, total overkill, and Hon's torpedo, though clumsy, had been terrifically well timed. Its echo rolled on, and the evening was slightly off-kilter now. My mother-in-law and Cahill went to bed at midnight, and we young things stayed on, with Reg rolling joints, Diana doling out nips of Metaxa, and Hon and I avoiding eye contact.

'You ever see Tommy Trinder?' said Reg.

'Old chap, hat,' said Saul. 'You lucky people!'

'That's the bloke. Jewish jokes, black jokes and a lot of totally filthy jokes, but one of the best backchat artists of all time. Hardly worked from a script at all.' We sat back, grateful for the anecdote whatever it might be. Reg the diplomat was doing his stuff. 'One time he was performing at the Palladium, while round the corner at the Empire Leicester Square was one of his films. Terrible schlock thing called *The Bells Go Down*, where he played this fireman in the Blitz.'

'I saw that on television one Sunday,' said Hon. 'He gets hit by a bomb or something.'

'Exactly. He gets killed at the end,' said Reg. 'Well anyway, Trinder was always delighted to see people coming in late to his shows. "Hope the lady enjoyed herself, sir. Glad you could fit me in too, madam. Hope you didn't mind us starting without you?" All that kind of thing.

'This particular night a couple arrive late and Trinder says, "You're very late, sir. This is a live show not a cinema. But if you want to see a good film you could go round to *The Bells Go Down*, at the Empire Leicester Square." And the man says, "No thanks. I prefer to see you die here."'

'And what happened?' asked Hon.

'He died,' said Reg.

CHAPTER THREE

I know, I know. I should have told you about Diana by now. My girlfriend of six weeks' standing; my wife to be; the mother of my children, unconceived; the reason we are here, doing what we're doing. But Diana is more difficult than the others, perhaps because she is nearer. Like a newspaper photograph held too close, when I look at her she dissolves into the dots of meaningless detail.

I know that she's pretty: hair the colour of blackberry jam; long grey eyes; sanded-down Nordic nose. But I don't think she's beautiful. You need self-absorption to be really beautiful and Diana is too external. She visits old ladies in hospital, remembers birthdays and believes in the *Guardian* women's page. She wears seated Levis and Guernsey sweaters, defeated underpants and beaten bras. She hates shopping for clothes: her best frocks are sprigged cotton Laura Ashley numbers with lacy collars and no waist. The Englishwoman's battledress, in which she can materialize, ready for action at a moment's notice, from the nearest wallpaper or herbaceous border.

Diana has good teeth, but unloved toenails, like tiny, ragged cockleshells. I suspect she has no sense of humour, but she laughs a lot, out of friendliness. She's training to be a doctor, has a wicked little case of scalpels, and a skeleton in her college bedroom, name of Sid. All day Wednesday my Di cuts up dead people, then comes to my bed smiling, smelling faintly of pickled eggs.

It was in hospital that I first met her, on the children's ward at St Fagan's in Cardiff, where Reg and I were running a kind of two-man panto in the week before Christmas. Diana was going out with this stiff-necked ginger registrar, who Reg called Dr Dick, and I saw her around from time to time and said hello. We'd been doing a hospital radio show for a year or so. Some Pythonesque stuff and bits of politics, but mostly nicked from *Round the Horne*, so it went down quite well with the hip replacements and prostates.

The kids' pantomime was *Goldilocks and the One Bear* (health service cuts, we explained), and was the usual outrageous botch of assorted fairy tales. So far as I can remember, the plot was that Goldilocks (me) goes into the Three Bears' cottage to use the loo (an excuse for lots of farting from behind the sluice-room doors). She is surprised by Reg dressed as a kind of wicked Noël Coward bear, with cigarette holder and watered-silk dressing-gown. The other two bears are in jail for being 'cottagers' – a joke lost on everyone I think, apart from the knot of doctors, watching from the doorway of the ward. There were a few girlfriends, Diana among them, and they all had that expression of tolerant amusement which grown-ups wear for this sort of idiocy.

Goldie is rescued from Noël Bear by a butch Peter Pan, played by Reg again, 'flying' down the ward on a hospital trolley, and they escape together to Never Never Land, where Coke comes out of the taps and children carry out surgical operations on doctors. This was all done in shadow-play behind a sheet of course, with terrible sounds of hammering and sawing and squelching, and false legs made from old wellies being amputated and tossed aside.

The kids were all howling at this, and jumping up and down on their beds, but some of the doctors didn't look too happy at all, and when Reg started to pull yards of hosepipe out of the patient's stomach Dr Dick came marching down the ward saying, 'Look here . . . I really think . . . upsetting the children.' But Reg is far too much of a trouper to be bothered by a little audience participation, and he simply grabbed hold of Dr Dick's stethoscope and tossed it to one of the kids, who started crawling under his white coat 'to listen to his goolies', so that Dr Dick was standing there sheepishly with kids squealing and prancing around him. And in the row I heard Diana say to another girl, 'Honestly, Richard is a prat sometimes.' And I fell in love with her on the spot.

She'd had a wicked adolescence compared to mine. At least six men before me; three experiments with coke, two with acid; and one minor orgy. This excited me and I wanted her to tell me about it, but she wouldn't. She peed with the bathroom door locked, and undressed with her back to me. I loved the firm, buttery hemispheres of her rump, but she wouldn't let me do it to her from behind because it hurt. How can it hurt Doctor Di? This is the way half the human race does it. The way we were designed to do it. But it didn't hurt her in the crotch, I knew. It hurt her in the head, where her body was a pale neat ethereal envelope: nothing to do with the meat machines she sliced up on the slab on Wednesdays. A step down from the angels rather than a step up from the apes.

Listen, after six weeks I'm already an expert on Diana. Go on, you can test me now. Mother's name? Adrienne Wallis. Occupation? Failed actress, successful invalid. Father's name? Cornell Schondler. Occupation? Jazz sax-ophonist. Whereabouts? Since the Divorce – some fifteen years before – Chicago. Diana's favourite food? Shepherd's pie with ketchup. Brand of tampon? Lillet. School? Pro-gressive Beddington, where pop stars' sons do pottery, and divorcees' daughters do pop stars' sons. Shoe size? A dinky little three. Smoker? Ex. Drinker? No head for it, but will occasionally get tiddly. Books? *Lord of the Rings* (ouch), *Emma* (predictable), *Steppenwolf* (double ouch). Can't pat-ronize her though, because she knows about aquatints and opus numbers; béarnaise sauce and Bordeaux wine.

Can you see her more clearly now? I don't know if I can.

Reg says the big question about Diana is how come she's so sane when her mother's so crazy? I say that's exactly why she's so sane. If you came home from school at fourteen and found your mother in bed with an Irish layabout at lunchtime, both of them stoned out of their heads and the kitchen floor awash with cat pee, you'd be sane too, because someone has to be. It's no big deal being sane.

She loves me because I told her that I loved her. Women are very grateful like that, especially women without fathers. I'm almost sure I do love her in fact. I've tried out the images of shipwrecks, train crashes, drownings and so on. I'd risk my life for her, I'm certain of it. I've tried out other pictures, of prams and high chairs, supermarket trolleys and sandcastles, and I'm almost sure I'd risk my self as well. Reg says to me that men always marry women they don't quite love, and love the women they can never marry. It's a way of keeping love separate, uncompromised and inviolable. But what does Reg know? He's just a fucking queer.

When you do the sums it all looks pretty good really. She's clever, not like a clever man maybe – but she has better A levels than me and you can't be stupid with three As now can you? She's definitely good-looking, all my friends have said so, even if she's not my usual type. What's my usual type? Gold-dusted breasts and legs like swords; raspberry-nippled and satin-basqued; bruised eyes and painted toenails; a pornographic pout with no knickers – the type I've never had and never will have because they don't exist. Diana exists, and she's obviously good, kind, caring – all the stuff which comes in useful later on when you're old and sick. You have to consider these things.

What's love anyway? The thrill of spite I felt when Diana snubbed her Dr Dick? The tenderness you feel for the nape of someone's neck when they're asleep. The image of a face remembered on a train, in the passing flicker of reflections on the carriage window. The ache in a sleeping arm flung out across the empty bed. Now you see me now you don't.

Love is what you feel for someone who's not around, and Diana isn't going to be around much for the next few months. She's going back to Cardiff, to her last year of medical school. To the scalpel case and to Sid the skeleton. And I am staying here in London, in this house of strangers: the latest lodger in a long line, deciding what to do next.

The night of the dinner party, the night before she left, we lay awake a long time, restless with red wine. I was on the outside – I'm claustrophobic, I always sleep nearest the door – with Diana in the crook of my right arm. Her hair was tickling my nose, though I didn't like to say.

'You think you'll be all right here on your own? Mum says it's fine and everything, and they all think you're great but . . .'

'I don't think your friend Hon liked me very much.'

'She's not exactly a friend these days,' said Diana, and I allowed myself to bask briefly in her loyalty. It's one of the most chilling, but also enchanting things about a woman, the way they will discard their previous lives for love.

'We were best friends at school,' she told me, 'but I've hardly seen her since I've been at Cardiff. I think she was just frightened by you.'

'Oh, come *on*. I mean, I was absolutely terrified of her. I'm petrified of practically everyone here at the moment.'

'I don't think you realize the effect you have on people sometimes, Phil. You can seem very intense, very intimidating.'

I savoured this information, but it seemed sensible to disbelieve it for now. My right arm was sliding its hand slowly down the far side of her body, to rest palm-down in the soft valley between belly and thigh. That was as far as it could reach, but its fingertips were on the edge of exciting fuzz, its purpose unmistakable. Diana turned affectionately towards me, nuzzling more hair up my nose. Somehow the exploring hand had been forced back to the neutral territory of her flank.

Hon had been coming to stay with the Schondler family since she was small, Diana said. There was a shared nanny, lifts to primary school, joint holidays in Cornwall. 'Her mother split up with the earl when she was little, and she doesn't get on all that well with her stepfather. I think she found it very secure here.'

'I can't really imagine her going out with Saul.'

'Saul wasn't always like he is now. He used to wear his hair long. All those motorbikes in the front garden. And I think Hon saw him as a way of staying in touch. She's always thought of this as her home really, her own was so weird.' I boggled silently at the image of Hon's home life that was suggested, while my hand tried another tack: sliding gently over the curve of her hip to rest carelessly across the buttock cleft. A fingertip was drifting over the puckered rim of her anus when suddenly Diana rolled on to her back again, twisting the fingers into a painful knot.

'Oh, Phil, I'm terribly sorry, are you –?'

'Yes. No. I'm all right. It's just. Ow . . .' I massaged the crippled digits tenderly, while Diana stifled a giggle. It was becoming a bit of a joke between us, this sort of thing. A curious kind of accident proneness that seemed to haunt our sex life. Teeth that clashed painfully on kissing; skin that became terribly ticklish in the middle of a clinch; limbs that went inexplicably into cramp. Just the clumsiness of two bodies that had yet to synchronize with each other, I supposed.

'It's going to be a very early start for me in the morning,' Diana said. 'First lecture at eleven.'

'I'll make you breakfast.'

'I love you.'

'I love *you*.'

I lay staring at the blood fireworks inside my eyelids for a long time, listening to the slowing oarstrokes of Diana's breathing, bearing her away into sleep. My brain, full of red-wine tannin, was rattling along like a tin train. After an hour or so I gave up, and slid out of bed. There was a light shining faintly two floors below, and I walked on the outside of the treads, as I used to do when I was a child, creeping downstairs to listen outside my parents' sitting room. I would sit there on the stairs for hours sometimes, muscles tense with incipient flight, though there was never anything to hear. Just the sea-breaking sound of the television, and the muffled hoot of my parents' conversation. I think I used to like the small sense of private power it gave: of hearing them when they couldn't hear me; of feeling my life separate from the great current of theirs.

On the first landing I bumped into Hon, in crêpe de Chine dressing-gown and red ballet slippers, her fingers on the handle of Saul's room.

'Oh, hello. It's me,' I said, idiotically.

'So I see,' said Hon.

'I was just going down to the kitchen to get a drink or something.'

'I was just seeing if Saul wanted one,' she said. She turned the door handle with the appearance of confidence, but it was clearly locked, and she paused, baffled.

There were stirrings inside the room, and then a bleary voice.

'Will you please leave me alone, Hon?'

'He doesn't seem to be thirsty,' I said happily.

'No.'

She flounced away into the shadows, and I carried on down the stairs, walking in the centre now, and creaking as much as I could.

'Is that you, Diana?' My mother-in-law's voice from the open bathroom door.

'It's Philip.'

'Won't be a minute, dear. Just pull the door shut would you? I'm completely starkers in here.'

I pulled on the door handle, with averted eyes, but in the mirror inside the door I glimpsed her back, strong and brown and shockingly nude. One large thigh was propped on the edge of the washbasin as she soaped between her legs with a flannel. As the door grated shut over the gritty linoleum, she looked up into the basin mirror, and for a second our eyes met in that tricky rhomboid of reflected light.

'Naughty, naughty, Philip. Time you was beddy-byes,' and I felt my face grow hot and my lips form unvoiced apologies.

On the ground floor, light was flowing in a sharp vee from the door of the kitchen. I pushed it open, blinking in the brightness. Cahill was sitting at the table, polishing a silver candlestick, and also naked except for an alarmingly small cache-sexe in a violent shade of fuchsia.

'I was just looking for a drink . . .'

Cahill cocked his ear to the ceiling: 'Done your duty then, Philip? The old woman won't get off to sleep without a good stuffing. But I swear it's wearing out the lead in my pencil.' I was in no mood for Cahill's locker-room complicities, and my ears declined to understand him. I started rummaging purposefully in the fridge.

'It's absolutely vital to polish fine silver immediately after use, Philip.'

'Is it?'

'And you know the finest polishing cloth on earth?'

'No.'

'The human hide,' said Cahill, rolling the candlestick fondly across the furry bag of his belly.

I poured myself a glass of milk and bolted.

When I woke, very late the next morning, there was an ache in the arm lying across the empty side of the bed, and a note pinned to the pillow. I didn't have my contact lenses in, but I didn't have to read it anyway, because I knew the gist of the thing. I was loved, I was wanted and I was going to be missed, but for the next three months or so, I was on my own.

*

It was going to be a purposeful period. Get some serious work done on my doctorate; get a job of some kind; work on the stage act with Reg. I unpacked my clothes and hung them in a corner of Diana's wardrobe, which took about three minutes. I set out my books in stacks on floor and dressing table. I laid out the folders of my dissertation on her writing desk: 8,000 words so far on 'Comedy and the Conservative Spirit', and only 32,000 to go. I was ten minutes into the three months already.

Downstairs in the kitchen all eight cats were sitting around on the worktops like furry, complacent caryatids, and the smell of ammonia brought tears to my eyes. I chased them into the garden, and dumped the cat trays on to a weed-clogged rosebed. I put a kettle on to boil, scoured the algae stains off the old butler's sink and started work. I'm good at this kind of blitzkrieg housework. The everyday stuff of dusting, polishing and putting away is depressing in its connotations of eternity, but show me an Augean stable and I'll cleanse it.

I filled and emptied the sink six times, wiped down the worktops and table, washed the tall, schoolroom windows and scrubbed the floor. A pleasing nineteenth-century kitchen, with cast-iron range and painted wooden cupboards, began to emerge. I was using an ivory-handled dessert knife to slice cakes of congealed crud from the bottoms of the table legs when the phone rang.

'Miss Piggy has got some shifts for you at The Jar if you want them,' said Reg. 'I told him you used to mix cocktails on the *QE2*.'

'Because I couldn't tell a port and lemon from a gin and tonic?'

'You should stop listening to Jimmy Tarbuck, *Philippe*. It's Monday, Wednesday and Friday. Start at seven and finish when Miss Piggy has got round to buggering you in the beer cellar. Eight pounds a night and all you can nick from the till.'

'What did you make of the dinner party?' I asked him.

'The old bat with all the ironmongery round her neck has you marked down as resident house eunuch, and general support for her declining years. I should watch out for her. But Saul was heaven. I shall unseam the little *chou-fleur* as soon as there's a window in my diary.'

'You don't think Saul is queer, do you?'

'As a chocolate teapot. And the Honourable Henrietta has got the raging hots for you.'

'She hated me.'

'Poor Phil,' said Reg, and hung up.

My mother-in-law came down for breakfast at around two – a three-pint pudding basin piled with muesli, yoghurt and four dessertspoons of brown sugar, which she stirred steadily for several minutes with a noise like a rusty concrete mixer, and then swallowed in what seemed to be one vast, engulfing mouthful, like a boa-constrictor with a guinea pig. The glittering African Queen of the night before was now playing the trembling Hangover Hag, in a blue, balding, candlewick dressing-gown, with Dr Scholl sandals on her bandaged feet. Layer upon geological layer of corn plaster and bunion pad, yellowing lint and frayed Elastoplast. I'd always thought the expression was medieval, or perhaps purely metaphorical, until I came across my mother-in-law's collection of toerags.

I was basking modestly in the miracle of hygiene I had worked in her kitchen, but my mother-in-law was oblivious: her eyes unfocused and her jaw rotating steadily on the massive bolus of roughage. I glanced around complacently at swept-clean surfaces, the scoured hob, the pristine cat-litter trays. She'd notice when she'd woken up properly . . .

'Where's Daddy's teacup?'

'I'm sorry?'

'My father's teacup. On the dresser.'

'Oh, I washed everything up. It's all right. It'll be in the cupboard . . .'

'You stupid, stupid boy.' Her face was fractured with fury, a worm of milky phlegm wriggling down one side of her chin. She was actually beating her spoon on the table.

I was on my feet, shakily casting about for the wretched cup in the shining ranks of washed crockery. 'Look, I'm sorry Mrs Um, I don't . . . What does it look like? I'll get it out again.'

'My daddy left that teacup there the day he went into hospital for the last time.' She was hissing. 'The last thing in this house that touched his lips. It's never been moved, never been touched. And *you washed it up*.'

I could feel shameful tears prickling my eyes and a heat in my chest that wanted to become a sob. 'There were cups and dishes all over the dresser. I'm sorry, I really am, but . . .'

The Hangover Hag's face was glistening with righteous rage, her knuckles braced on the table, as she gladly surrendered herself to the seduction of cliché.

'Just exactly who do you think you are? Some little Taff yobbo from Llantwit Minor who moves into my house without being invited. Sleeps with my darling daughter, without a by-your-leave. Starts meddling with precious things which don't belong to you. Get out of my kitchen. *Get out*.'

And I got.

I sat shakily on Diana's bed for a long time, listening to the noises downstairs. My mother-in-law storming about and slamming doors; a long and furious conversation on the telephone. In the kitchen I'd just felt frightened and guilty. Any woman, however insane, can make any man, however reasonable, feel guilty if she gets angry enough. But I was angry now, and mostly with myself for not bawling back at the old bag.

I didn't know my way around metropolitan manners yet, but I suspected the laws of hospitality might rule out raving at a relative stranger for rinsing a teacup. Reconciliation was obviously out of the question, and a good shouting match would make me feel better, but what was the point? I was washed up and washed out before I'd even begun. I could live with the irrational loathing of Diana's best friend, but hardly a hate campaign by my hostess.

Drearily I started pulling clothes off hangers while I contemplated the options. I could go back to Cardiff for a while. My room in the flat in Pontcanna was still empty, but I thought of the farewell party we'd thrown there a week ago, and abandoned the idea. I might be able to doss down on Reg's floor at The Jar for a couple of nights, then find a room somewhere cheap, but where was going to be cheaper than here? Outside there was the sound of a car pulling up, a key in the lock, and then Cahill's voice in the hallway. I had repacked my clothes, and was stacking my books in their tea chest when he knocked softly on the bedroom door.

'I was thinking you might like to come out for a drive with me, Philip.'

I didn't trust myself to look at him in case of any treacherous redness about the eye. 'That's very nice of you, Cahill, but I'd better be off soon. Diana's mum, she . . .'

'Ach, she's never at her best first thing in the morning,' said Cahill. 'Come downstairs with me. She wants to have a word.'

We found her in the chilly, dust-draped drawing room, playing the *Crossroads* theme one-fingered on the Chappell baby grand. 'Mumsie was a pianist before she met Daddy,' she said, without preamble and without turning around. 'Quite a good one. She did broadcasts on the Third Programme and some concerts at the Wigmore Hall.'

There was a silence, while I cast about for the right things to say. Cahill had faded into a corner, where he was looking through an old *Britannica*. While he turned the pages I told my mother-in-law she was a filthy-tempered old slag. Dirty, slovenly and with disgusting table manners. Clearly neurotic and quite possibly certifiable. She had exploited the dependent position of a guest in her house, and I'd be thankful never to have to visit it again.

Or at least that was what I told her in my head.

'I suppose she gave up music when she married your father?' I said finally, grudgingly.

'Oh no,' said my mother-in-law. 'She carried on for some years after that. When I was a child she would still come in here to practise, three or four hours a day. She didn't like people to watch, but I used to sit listening to her on the stairs with Nanny. When she gave it up she said it was because Daddy made her, but really I think it was because she knew she would never be the best.'

I grasped that I was listening to something in code, but it was a cipher I would not understand for years yet.

'I thought it would be best if I left,' I said stiffly. 'After this morning. I've cleared up my things from Diana's room . . .' But she wasn't hearing me.

'When Mumsie stopped playing she wouldn't let anybody use this piano. So when I wanted to annoy her I used to come down here and bash away on it. That's me over there.'

She was pointing to the small bronze of a girl's head on a corner cabinet. Tangled curls were pushed back from a high forehead. The eyes were part closed; the full, almost Negroid lips were set in an insolent half smile. It was a beautiful, arrogant thing, and I said so.

'It's Jacob Epstein,' said my mother-in-law. 'Done before I was born of course, but Daddy always said it was me.'

'You must have been terribly fond of your father. His teacup . . .'

'He was a bit of an old fart really,' said my mother-in-law. 'A weekend painter who always wanted to be a proper artist, but never had the balls.' It wasn't an apology. She didn't deal in apologies, but it was better than that. And I was her captive once again.

Against one wall was a large inlaid chest with dozens of

shallow drawers. My mother-in-law began pulling them out, and laying drawings on the table behind her: dry and flimsy as giant butterflies, mounted on heavy boards, with tissue-paper shrouds to protect their colours. 'He bought well, but he had good advice. Some Pre-Raphaelite stuff. That's a Holman Hunt, and this is a Rossetti sketch. The pastels are mostly later: Sickert and Grant; but there are some more modern prints you might like.'

She pulled back the tissue paper from a sketch of some sheep in a field. They were small, fat sheep, which managed to look both solid and purposeful but also slightly comic, in the way that real sheep do.

'You like that?'

'It's funny.'

'It is, isn't it? You can have it if you like. But it's a present for you, not you and Diana.'

It seemed wildly generous but not insane. Not until I peered at the scribbled signature in the right-hand corner, and reeled. I didn't know much about art, but I knew that Henry Moore wasn't a brand of biscuit.

Cahill's Mercedes smelled like a cigar box inside: cedar, tobacco and leather. There was no wear on the brake-pedal rubber, and 8,000 miles on the clock. We drove south, through St John's Wood and Little Venice, then west towards Kensington. Outside the car the afternoon rush hour was building up: the grinding steel ropes of the traffic, plaiting and unplaiting; the grey torrents of pedestrians, swirling and piling down into the tube stations, like bathwater.

On the pavements letter-box mouths mimed rage and grief; in lorry cabs grimy fists beat upon noiseless horn buttons. But inside the squashy, black-leather interior of the Mercedes it was quiet as a church. I sat admiring the doorways of shops and office buildings. Twice as high as a man, built by optimistic Victorian architects for the race of giants they knew would succeed them. I was in *London*.

'History,' Cahill was saying. 'Tradition. Heritage. There's a lot of history in Diana's family. Her great-grandfather built that house when there were still cows in Highbury Fields; and they hunted the fox over Belsize Park.'

'I can't accept that picture from her, Cahill.'

'F'why not?'

'Well for one thing, on present form she's perfectly capable of asking for it back tomorrow morning, or telling the Hampstead police that I've stolen it. And for another thing it's a *Henry Moore*. A drawing like that must be worth thousands.'

Cahill snorted. 'It's an etching, Philip. One of seventy-five or a hundred. Very nice, but you'd be lucky to get fifty pounds for it down in the Cork Street galleries.'

'Oh.'

I reappraised my mother-in-law for the fourth or fifth time in the two days I had known her.

'High time they sold some of that stuff anyway,' said Cahill. 'Realize some assets; develop some liquidity. Things are changing in this country, Philip. A new government soon, and a new decade. Chains are being broken and cobwebs swept aside. Restrictive practices, institutional inertia. The mangy old lion is stirring in its sleep.'

We were in the far west of London now, somewhere near the river, and Cahill was steering the Mercedes down a rutted bank towards a field where cars were parked and fires blazed in old oil drums.

'Where are we?'

'The market place, Philip. The free play of market forces. Capitalism in the raw.'

He braked the car next to a dilapidated caravan with a serving hatch chopped roughly in one side, and poked a fiver out of his window. A hand-lettered sign read 'Hogarth Car Autcions'.

'Had my eye on a little wine bar in Chalk Farm d'ye see, Philip. Cocktails are the coming thing. Some pretty girls in miniskirts for the fellows. A sparkler and a paper umbrella in the drink for the ladies. Pinacoladas. Harvey Wallbangers. The Slow Comfortable Screw against the Wall. A lot of mucky fruit juice with a dash of liqueur is all it is, but the mark-up is tremendous. They have them all over the island of Manhattan. But I'll be needing something a bit more substantial than the Merc.'

We wandered down the lines of rusting wrecks, with Cahill taking the odd, speculative kick at a fender. Small men in leather jackets, with iron-filing haircuts and mouths full of glottal stops, scampered beneath the cars like monkeys. 'A big estate car like the Volvo or the Peugeot 505, I thought,' said Cahill. 'Something to take a dozen crates from the cash and carry.'

'Do you get a guarantee or anything with these things?'

We had paused in front of a white Range Rover, four years old, with a mossy tailgate and a crumpled offside wing.

'You get two thousand pounds minimum off the show-room price,' said Cahill, 'which will cover an awful lot of repair bills. The market has its own logic, Philip.'

We joined the gaggle of monkey men around the caravan, and there was a half-hour or so of confused shouting, from which Cahill emerged smiling broadly.

'You got the Range Rover then?'

'Too expensive,' said Cahill. 'But I got four thousand for the Mercedes.'

'You *sold* the Mercedes?'

'Liquidity,' said Cahill. 'A depreciating asset.'

'That car must have been worth at least ten thousand pounds.'

'Only the market can know the true value of the commodity,' he said as we began walking back up the ramp from the field.

'Look, Cahill. I'm working at the pub tonight. How the fuck are we going to get back to Hampstead in an hour without a car?'

He peeled a twenty from the roll in his pocket, and whistled, and possibly the only taxi which had driven down that road, that day, pulled up beside us.

They came to The Jar that night, Cahill and my mother-in-law, to give me moral support they said. There was a crowd of LSO musicians, still in white tie, in the public bar, and in the saloon a bunch of actors. I recognized John Hurt, Robert Powell, Peter Barkworth, a ruddy man who'd been in the *Onedin Line*. My mother-in-law seemed to know most of them already.

Miss Piggy knew her too and raised his eyes despairingly to the ceiling in greeting. 'I had a premonition, Adrienne. One of those little shivery feelings you get when somebody steps on your grave.'

'Perhaps one of your boyfriends just crossed you out of his address book, Clive,' said my mother-in-law.

He gave her a large gin and orange on the house, and I gave her eight more. 'Clive was a wonderful Bottom at St Albans Rep with me,' she explained. She poked her face through a snob screen at him.

'Oh Pyramus, Oh Pyramus . . .'

'Oh Thisbe,' said Miss Piggy. 'Will you kindly get your tired old tits off my bar?'

Clive threw them out at midnight, but when I left with Reg, fifteen minutes later, Cahill was teetering about in the alley, singing 'The Wearing of the Green', while my mother-in-law was lying supine in the gutter, an unlit Silk Cut in her mouth.

'Would you like a hand up, Mrs Wallis?' said Reg, kindly.

'I'm perfectly at ease, thank you, my dear.'

'Then perhaps you'd like a light for your cigarette?'

'Reginald,' said my mother-in-law, with enormous dignity. 'A lady never smokes in the street.'

And then she passed out.

CHAPTER FOUR

The girl comic was dying on her feet out there on the tiny stage. She was doing this routine about her house, meant to be one of those intimate, observational, New Wave things. Trouble with my toaster; crisis with my cat flap – all that sort of stuff. But she was falling to pieces before our appalled eyes. Her timing was shot, her eyes were searching the audience for a friend.

She was pretty, blonde, with a whacky hat like a cake tin. But the club crowd was fed up with her; shuffling its feet and lighting its cigarettes, the throat-clearing and coughing winding up towards a chest-clinic concerto.

Waffle waffle. Gabble gabble. We were sitting in the third row back, Reg and I, but I was with her there on the stage. My knees were locked with embarrassment: Reg, sitting beside me, was perspiring, his eyes fixed on the toecaps of his chukka boots.

'Well, it's not a house exactly, it's a flat ...' she was saying.

'You're flat!' shouted a voice from the floor, and you could see her shift into superpanic. Ohmigod a heckler. Whatdoido? She peered helplessly into the glare of the tawdry string of coloured spots.

'I beg your pardon?' she stammered.

'Oh *no*,' said Reg.

'Flat as a pancake!' roared the heckler. And as she glanced down involuntarily at her chest, the audience tittered. Oh fatal move. 'Oh God, get her off,' said Reg.

'Flatter than your jokes!' bellowed the heckler ruthlessly

and you could practically hear her praying. Bring on the undertaker. Nail down the lid. Get me off this stage. But there is no way off a stage. A million miles from mike-stand to steps. A light year from steps to dressing room. You have to go on.

She had begun quavering on about television programmes. It's a laugh every seven seconds if you want to survive, the old hacks say, and she was setting up a joke that was whole laborious minutes away. 'You see a lot of sex on telly, but they always cut out all the good bits. Have your ever noticed that?'

'No,' said the heckler crisply, and the girl staggered visibly, as if shot. The sweat stains were black on her T-shirt and her blonde fringe was plastered to her face.

'Please remind me, Phil,' Reg whispered, 'never to ask a question to which I don't already know the answer.' The crowd around us was beginning to form queues for the lavatories now. Handing pints back over the scrum at the bar, checking the programme for the next act. They'd forgotten about her. She was alone and lost out there: a child nagging for attention in an adult hubbub; switching hopelessly from house jokes, to television jokes, to holiday jokes. 'I went on a cruise last summer . . .'

'You're a queer,' said a new voice from the audience.

'What?'

'A lesbian.'

'No I'm not.'

'Don't fucking *argue* with him,' Reg was hissing.

'You look like a queer,' the heckler insisted.

'Oh . . . um, where was I?' said the girl, lamely.

'Unfortunately, here,' said the heckler, and the girl covered the million-mile gap in two strides, her face wet with tears.

We covered a lot of clubs that spring, me with my pocket cassette recorder and Reg with his notebook, and we saw a lot of deaths. The blonde girl who bombed in Camden

Town; a skinhead stand-up who died pitifully in a Soho cellar; a musical double act they crucified at a club down in Croydon. We taped the acts and took them apart line by line as we worked together behind the bar of The Jar. We filed the best gags and the sharpest put-downs. Wrote out lists of rules in Reg's notebook.

1. Comedy is honesty – be yourself.

2. Don't rely on hackneyed stereotypes – comedy is honesty.

3. Don't resent the heckler, welcome him – he's part of the act.

4. If you can't hear his heckle then make one up which you can deal with. The audience probably won't have heard him either.

5. If he's a bore or a real psychopath turn the spotlight on him. Make him repeat himself. Give him a silly name. Ask where he got his jumper. Embarrass the bastard.

6. All purpose put-downs: (a) I used to be like that after my first pint. (b) You shouldn't drink on an empty head. (c) Just sit down on the chair and we'll plug it in later. (d) I see the school holidays have started. (e) (in desperation) I've sucked better-looking things than you out of my cat's arse. (f) (in real desperation) Is that really your head or has your neck thrown up? (g) (in total despair) Fuck off, cunt.

There weren't many rules, though. We saw the blonde girl with the cake-tin hat a second time, at a club in Finsbury Park. Same act and practically the same audience, and she was great. She killed them, blew them away, knocked them dead, and we couldn't say why.

I was reading comedy books all the time. Biographies, comic theory, joke books, music-hall histories. Reg said you might as well take *The Road to Serfdom* as a blueprint for running a sweetshop, but they helped to put off the fateful moment. There was Freud on *Jokes and Their Relation to the Unconscious*; Bergson on *Laughter*; Harold Nicolson on 'The English Sense of Humour': 'Well *he* clearly never had one,' said Reg, after skimming the essay in three minutes.

'Have you noticed how much the old hacks talk about death?' I said to him. 'The audience they murdered in Birmingham. The crowd they killed in Crewe. They're always socking them with punchlines and slaying them with put-downs. Knocking them stiff, laying them out and stopping the show.'

'Just like pornography,' said Reg.

He was lying on his bed in the attic bedroom, his hands behind his head, gazing complacently at his newly painted ceiling. Reg moved in to Aberdare House a month after me, but he fitted in a lot faster. He had charmed my mother-in-law, made Hon laugh and Saul hoot. My clothes had never quite made it out of the suitcase a second time, but Reg had painted his room white all over – ceiling, walls, floor and furniture – so it had lost its shadows and perspectives, like the inside of a ping-pong ball. All around the walls his breezy shirts were hung on the picture rail, freshly ironed and stirring in the draughts like spinnakers.

'Why pornography?' I asked him.

'Because, *Philippe*, comedy is the only form of communication apart from the stroke-mag that has an actual physical effect on the audience. This cheery chappie up on stage is effecting a physical change on the people out there. You're taking charge of their bodies. It's intellectual assault, verbal rape.'

'And the audience are just victims?'

'Not at all,' said Reg, 'because if you're not a very efficient rapist, then they're going to kick you in the balls.'

He had more ideas than me: the mime of a couple having sex in the lavatory of a jumbo jet was his, and the idea of re-enacting the crucifixion in a suburban launderette: 'You see people don't notice fucking *anything* in a launderette, not even a couple of Roman soldiers nailing somebody to a cross.' One day, working behind the bar at The Jar, he started on the affectations of Cockney rhyming slang: 'It's so *tedious* all that stuff, isn't it? Boat Race – face; whistle and flute – suit. So fucking *obvious*. What we should do is *blank* rhyming slang. Apples and pears – fruit; merchant banker – financial executive; butcher's hook – an implement for hanging meat on.' As a comic idea it was gold, but it was me that wrote it down, cast it into the ingots of dialogue and made him rehearse them.

He brought boyfriends home to the ping-pong ball all the time. A Polish antique dealer in a rabbit-fur coat; an Indian newsagent from Dollis Hill; an Irish labourer in clay-caked Levis, who I bumped into on the stairs one morning, and who bashfully called me 'Sorr'. At night, in my celibate bed, I would listen to the sounds of sex, stirred, envious, disturbed. Bachelor-balled, I dreamed of sex with Diana, with Hon, with Reg, with the knickerless pornographic pout with the gold-dusted breasts. You do, don't you? In that dreamy suspension of consciousness and conscience, between wakefulness and sleep, your body can take you anywhere. Prostitutes; massage parlours; friends; enemies; relations. It took me even to my mother-in-law's bed, where I would find her, oily-breasted and tobacco-tongued, silent and intent as she pumped me to orgasm, and I would wake shamed and sticky between my own damp sheets.

I believed then that all men fostered dreams of orgy in a corner of their hearts. We orbited out on the cool margin of sexuality, always a little detached from the hot centre of procreation, and so we dreamed of utter detachment. The anonymous encounter in the alley, the zipless fuck with the stranger, the tumble of nameless bodies in the firelight. It was why some men chose to be homosexual, but the homo-sexuals denied the whole idea of having a choice. It was central to their dignity, and so I kept my theories from Reg.

One night, after the pub shut, I walked with him up Heath Street to Jack Straw's Castle. There were cars scattered along the road across the Heath, with the courtesy lights on, and single men, reading newspapers. Other men loitered aimlessly around Whitestone Pond, setting off now and again into the darkness of the woods beyond Jack Straw's.

'Plenty of custom about,' said Reg. 'Want a snort?' He produced an aspirin bottle from his pocket.

'What's that?'

'Poppers. Amyl nitrite. Old chaps use it to keep their tickers turning over. It's only a little vasodilator, *Philippe*: nothing *illegal*. You can buy the stuff in a sex shop.'

I sniffed it timidly, but the hit was strong and almost instantaneous, like a sock of sand on the back of the neck. A surging heat and thickness in the ears. A thudding of the heart.

'What does it do?'

'Gives you a completely indestructible stand. Chrome-vanadium cock. I shall have to bid you farewell before I turn into a pumpkin.' His eyes were shining and his teeth very white in the sodium flare of the street lamps.

'You're going in there?' I looked incredulously at the trees and darkness behind the pub. The furtive figures of men drifting towards the shadows.

'There's a place down there called the orgy bush, Phil, and you never know who you're going to meet. Priests, policemen, pickpockets. Very exciting. Just think, in five minutes from now I could have my cock down a cabinet minister's throat.'

I tried to laugh, but failed miserably. And then I watched him go.

The mountains of black bin bags had disappeared from the London squares by June, and the makeshift braziers from the forecourts of fire stations and hospitals. A housewife with a cast-iron perm and teeth like Stilton appeared on television, quoting St Francis of Assisi, while Cahill toasted her in Bushmills, and Reg moaned faintly into a sofa cushion. 'I don't fucking believe it. I just do *not fucking believe it*. Sadie Stern. Discipline and deportment a speciality. And they've made her fucking *Prime Minister*.'

'You could have bothered to go and vote against her,' I pointed out.

'Well, at least she's *committed* to shortening these awful dole queues,' said my mother-in-law, who always voted Liberal, and was therefore a political illiterate.

'She'll make them line up four-deep,' I told her.

'It's about time we had a woman running things in this country,' said Hon. 'All these *men* messing things up for the last fifty years.'

'Oh yes, you can see she's brimful of feminist zeal,' I said. 'We'll probably have a Trident submarine named after Simone de Beauvoir; crèche facilities for the Special Patrol Group; a Well Woman clinic at MI5 . . .'

Hon scowled, and I chalked up one to me.

'A fine-looking woman,' said Cahill, studying the pale, lightly marbled features on the television screen. 'A definite sexual presence.'

'She's got a face like a well-kept grave,' I said stubbornly. 'She drips sanctimony and oozes cant, and she's got a voice like a perfumed fart.'

'I think she's going to provide us with a lot of material,' said Reg.

I was writing steadily now, nine to two every day, but outside my own room I had given up on the tides of crud and chaos which flowed into Aberdare House, and mounted steadily up its mildewed walls. The kitchen was back to the state it was in before I blitzed it, and worse. I scalded my plate and cutlery under the hot tap before I ate, and breathed through my mouth in shallow gulps when I entered the kitchen in the mornings.

As in Gibbon's declining Rome, food, drink, furnishings and costly merchandise of every kind poured ceaselessly into Aberdare House, but only garbage came out. Paperboys called with six newspapers a day, three weeklies on a Friday, and they piled up, unread, in the hallway. The Devon Laundry called on Wednesdays with hampers of fresh linen that were never opened, while unchanged sheets grew slippery and pungent with body oils. Coal arrived for walled-up fireplaces, and gas cylinders for electric heaters. The social services dropped in bales of incontinence pads for the grandmother who had died eight years before. The Oakeshott's van delivered crates of choice meats and fresh vegetables that were piled into the great General Motors fridge, where they grew green and hairy, and were thrown away.

There were whole feudal castes and sub-castes of menials and retainers who nominally supported this tottering domestic fabric: serfs and boyars, churls and guildsmen. A window cleaner who never cleaned the windows; a gardener who never gardened; a daily who sat in the kitchen, complaining about her womb, and smoking my mother-in-law's Silk Cut. Bills arrived – from vets and vintners, Harley Street dentists and Harrods food hall – and were all despatched, unopened, to The Trust, which dealt with such things.

The only letters my mother-in-law opened were the circulars from the mail-order book clubs, and she answered all of those, greedily chiselling out the forms in biro, with the tip of her tobacco-stained tongue clenched between her teeth, like a flap of orange peel. The house was crammed with the remains of past collecting manias. The eight unspayed queens of the cat craze; the crucifixes and icons of the religious era; the Victorian tinsel pictures of the kitsch phase; the mountains of viscose blouses from the British Home Stores parsimony period; the fifty-odd carriage clocks, maddeningly unsynchronized, whose staggered chiming through the night drove an enraged Reg to sabotage their works with wads of toilet paper.

But it was books these days: Books that have Changed Man's Thinking; Books of the Month; Books of the Year; the Connoisseur Club; the Classics of the Ancient World; the Complete Works of Nevil Shute; the Collector's Alastair Maclean. She filled forms for all of them, and each form spawned spin-off forms, each special offer new special offers.

'You don't need to *buy* all this stuff,' I told her. 'There's Swiss Cottage Library round the corner.'

'It's made of *concrete*, Philip,' said my mother-in-law. 'There was a very nice little chemist's where I used to get hot water bottles for Diana and Saul before they knocked it all down.'

'You know you've already *got* a lot of these books upstairs. There's complete sets of Dickens, Thackeray, Melville . . .'

'Melville,' she said. 'Daddy liked Melville, so Mumsie always used to think there must be something indecent about sperm whales.'

'You could sign up for an Open University course.'

'I took the train through Milton Keynes once. Do you know they have cows made out of cement? And the television programmes always clash with church.'

'You don't *go* to church any more . . .'

But it was no use. There was some deep obliquity about my mother-in-law in these kinds of arguments. An inspired incapacity to see the point. And though she read all the time, five or six books a week, they seemed to pass through her whole, like seeds through the body of a bird.

'*Great Expectations* is a masterpiece, I think,' she would announce over dinner, and I would fumble for an adequate response.

'Well, I think it's interesting the way Dickens gradually undermines the position of Pip as narrator –'

'Would you say it was a greater masterpiece than *A Sentimental Education*?'

'Well, I –'

'I think *Scarlet and Black* is *definitely* the greater work.'

She was reading all night and sleeping all day, but her consumption was arithmetic and the book expansion geometric. The cartons arrived two and three a day, bubble-wrapped, gilt-tooled and hand-bound in gleaming Skivertex. They filled the brick and plank shelving I built for her, and spilled out on to the piano lid and sofa table. They marched up the stair-treads and stacked themselves on the landings. Burgess burgeoned and Murdoch multiplied; there was Loos in the loo and Barthes in the bath. 'What am I going to do with this lot?' I asked Reg as I took delivery of the latest carton, and Reg simply carried it out the back and dumped it in the bin, thus short-circuiting a process which was, as he said, inevitable in any case.

One Sunday morning Saul turned up from Flat Wapping to take us all to lunch. My mother-in-law had just gone to bed, and Cahill was on one of his mysterious errands to do with cocktail bars and market forces.

'God for that,' said Saul, who had become obsessed with Cahill, and was forever phoning me up for information on his movements. 'Quite sure about Franco and Japanese beef, Philip?' he would demand. Or 'How much exactly did the Mercedes fetch?' And I told him wearily why didn't he hire his own bloody detective, and leave me out of it.

And so it was Reg, Hon and I who squeezed into his potent little hatchback. The horn played 'Don't Cry For Me, Argentina', and the Blaupunkt quad system played Dire Straits at maximum volume. 'Turn it up a bit, Saul,' said Reg. 'They can't hear it in the bus behind us.' And so Saul turned it down a bit.

We drove very fast through the echoing canyons of the Sunday morning City, then further east, past roaring street markets, jittering over cobbles that were slick with vegetable goo. Ancient Jews with furry hats like millwheels leapt like gazelles for the shelter of bagel bakery doorways. Withered Bangladeshi elders scattered like leaves before the blast of Andrew Lloyd Webber. 'Spitalfields,' said Saul, snatching for his jumping gear stick, and executing a showy double de-clutch. 'Whitechapel, Brick Lane, Commercial Road . . .' Could Saul conceivably be gay? I glanced sideways at the apple cheeks and firm jaw and dismissed the idea as typical Reg whimsy.

I tried to stop my thigh pressing too suggestively against

Hon's as the car bucketed along a potholed alley between warehouses, with the rusted jibs of hoists overhead and glimpses of river to the right. 'David Owen's house,' said Saul. 'Six kay when he was still at medical school. Man of the future Owen . . . David Lean's place there. Old banana warehouse. Two hundred kay min. Very smart move.' As we went further the sky started to open out around us, the air began to smell of tar and salt and cinnamon, and the list of names grew more exotic. 'Limehouse Basin, Gunpowder Wharf, Tobacco Quay, Muscovy Street . . .' And then we stopped.

'Docklands,' explained Saul, and we painfully unpacked ourselves from his tiny projectile. We were on the edge of a great wasteland, clasped in a five-mile loop of the river. Acres of rubble and silvery, poisoned soil. Shining rectangles of silent water a mile long. Idle cranes like black question marks against a boundless sky, the colour of damp salt. Vistas of craters and crumbled walls, twisted iron and smouldering trash fires. A vast and careless army had fought and camped in this place, and then moved on.

'Beautiful,' said Reg.

'Be an Urban Development Corporation soon,' said Saul with a proprietorial air.

And already we could see, up river, the old warehouses yielding to the red-oxide paintwork and acid-scrubbed brickwork of London gentrification. Already the little estates were springing up with their high-camp, proletarian pastiche architecture, of fake loading bays and stick-on crane jibs and Dutch gabling and pointless portholes.

'Major investment opportunity,' said Saul. 'In on the ground floor.'

'Baby,' said Hon, 'I'm bloody starving.'

So we drove back to Flat Wapping, which was a sixth-floor penthouse carved from the top of a spice warehouse. The sanded oak floorboards were eighteen inches wide, and the view ran from Tower Bridge in the west to Greenwich in the east. In the Scandinavian glare of his tiny kitchen Saul tentatively pressed various buttons and stood back hopefully.

'Do a great deal of cooking,' he said, meaning he didn't.

'What have you actually got to eat?' I asked him.

'Squid thingies in the freezer. Summer pudding, no need to cook that.' I mixed gin and tonic and crammed the glasses with semicircular chunks from the ice-making machine in his fridge. Out on the balcony Reg and Hon were admiring the view.

'Hear you've got your first booking,' said Saul.

'Next Saturday night,' I told him. 'A little club in Camden Town.'

'Money?'

'Only twenty quid between Reg and me,' I said, apologetically. 'If there's anything left of us by the time we've finished.'

Saul frowned over the task of comprehending this minuscule sum, but with an effort his brow cleared.

'Must regard *investment*,' he said. 'Great future potential your line of business. Entertainments and leisure. Service economy.'

Was it possible that Saul was really only two years older than me? He emptied a packet of frozen calamari into the hatch of what looked like a surgical sterilizer, closed it, and then opened it again.

'Think they need oil, fat, sort of thing?'

'I think they probably do.'

He poured a bottle of cooking oil into the hatch and pressed another button, seemingly at random.

'Man Cahill,' he said suddenly. 'Been making inquiries.'

'Oh, really?' I found a withered lemon in the salad box of the fridge and started slicing it.

'Hired that detective you recommended.'

'Saul, I didn't reco –'

'No record of this restaurant of his in Barcelona. One

deportation order Madrid name of Cahill, Brendan. Two registrations for bankruptcy at Carey Street, one still undischarged.'

'Is that bad?' The drinks were finished and I lined them up on a glossy black tray.

'Continuing investigations,' said Saul, 'but rely on your cooperation, discretion, so forth.'

'Right,' said I, meaning wrong.

We had lunch out on the balcony overlooking the river, watching the odd sailing boat and kayak skimming across the flood tide. The outsize rings of calamari, lightly stewed in oil, were still rubbery and streaked with blood, 'Like elephants' arseholes,' Reg murmured, making me choke. The summer pudding was vast and grey, and almost all bread, its white sliced flanks mottled with stains of fruit juice and thumbprints, ('An enormous Tampax' – Reg). The food was inedible, but Saul's wine was wonderful, and I memorized the labels. A Blanchot Chablis 1978 and a Château Latour 1966.

'What's all that scrap down there?' asked Reg.

'Old bargemaker's yard,' said Saul. 'Scheduled for redevelopment.'

'And is that lead foundry still working?'

'Until next April,' said Saul.

And as we sat drinking on the balcony over the river, listening to Saul, the whole of the wasteland around us was swept away. Derelict docks became yacht basins; corporation dumps became tennis courts; tower blocks were razed and planning inquiries set aside. New financial centres sprang up, new railways, roads, towers, bridges, temples. Every house doubled in price overnight; every site was snapped up as it was released; and everyone must hurry before it all faded away, like Prospero's Island.

'Is that your phone?' said Hon, and Saul went to answer it.

'Why didn't you come down to live here?' I asked her while he was gone, and she looked at me curiously.

'Mostly because it's such a bloody horrible place. Flat, windswept, miles from anywhere, and full of National Front psychopaths with Dobermann pinschers. No proper transport, shops, cafés, restaurants, theatres, schools, pubs – and for the twenty years it takes for them to arrive you'll be living in the middle of a fucking building site.'

I decided that I might like her after all.

'Man Cahill on the phone,' said Saul, reappearing. 'Mother's at Haverstock Hill police station.'

'Oh God,' said Hon. 'Another robbery.'

'Manner of speaking,' said Saul, bashfully. 'She's been arrested for shoplifting at Camden Lock market.'

'I thought Cahill handled the police very well,' I said to Reg much later, as we were washing up the last glasses at The Jar.

'I should think he's had a lot of practice,' said Reg. 'But it was a good idea to get the vicar to come round to the station.'

My mother-in-law was back at Aberdare House, all charges dropped, by the time we returned from Flat Wapping. There had been an attack of absentmindedness in the market at Camden Lock. A foolish misunderstanding. Cahill's seedy gentility, a twenty in the stallholder's hand for his trouble, and the presence of the Vicar of St Barnabus's had done the trick.

'You know Saul has hired a private detective agency to investigate Cahill,' I told Reg. 'He thinks he's just a straightforward con man, out to get his mum's money.'

'While you'd just like to get it the old-fashioned way, by marrying her daughter,' said Reg.

And I tried to look wounded, but Reg only laughed.

CHAPTER FIVE

The scene was a barber-shop, and I was in the chair with a sheet draped around my neck, while Reg danced behind me, snapping a large and cruel pair of scissors.

'So, as I was saying, sir, I goes back home the other night to the trouble and strife –'

'Your wife.'

'Beg pardon, sir?'

'Your wife,' I repeated. 'The old trouble and strife.'

'My wife is a very fine woman,' said Reg with great dignity. 'Never a cross word. It's just that we have a lot of domestic problems these days, what with the mortgage and the kids and this James Hunt what lives next door –'

'A cunt.'

'You what, sir?'

'You said you've got a cunt living next door?'

'No, we've got James Hunt living next door. The famous racing driver and television personality. Very nice chap as it happens, only a bit noisy on the apples and pears, what with his great plates of meat.'

'His feet make a noise on the stairs?'

Reg surveyed me with an air of bafflement. 'Did I mention feet on stairs? Mr Hunt eats a lot of fruit and steak. Good for his Boat Race.'

'They're good for his complexion?'

'No, no, no. Mr Hunt likes to race *boats*,' said Reg despairingly.

'Now look,' I said. 'This is stupid. You're using rhyming slang aren't you? Arbitrary signifiers which happen to rhyme with the signified item.'

'I don't get your Torvill and Dean.'

'There you are, you're doing it again. Torvill and Dean – know what I mean.'

'I was simply telling you that I can't get the ice skating on the old rubber welly.'

I became cunning. 'We weren't *talking* about ice skating . . .'

Reg clasped a hand to his brow in mock despair. 'I'm terribly sorry, sir, but I've had a lot of trouble with my memory lately.'

'When did it start?'

'When did what start?'

'Now look, I'm not a complete idiot you know.'

'Why, what part of you's missing? ... Oh look, I'm terribly sorry, sir, but I seem to have cut your ear off.' He produced a bloody pig's ear from my collar and tossed it into the audience, bringing squeals from the front row.

There were about two hundred people in the audience, and somewhere among them were Diana, my mother-in-law, Cahill, Hon, Miss Piggy – not that I wanted to see them. It seemed to be going all right, or at least there were no hecklers yet, and no chest clinic in the front row. I'd been worried about the rhyming slang, with its talk of signifieds and signifiers. It was small-scale, university stuff, which was why Reg had stuck in the business of pig's ears and sheep's eyes and fake blood. There was a whole pile of offal growing warm in my lap beneath the sheet. We'd spent more on props than we were getting paid for the gig, but what the hell.

'Any problems with the Lionel Blair, sir?' Reg was saying.

'You mean my hair?'

'I meant the famous dancer and *Give Us A Clue* celebrity, but since you insist on raising the subject of hair, there does seem to be a little thinning here at the temple.' He wrenched a handful from my nylon joke-shop rug, to more squeals from the audience.

His manner now was detached, professional, the Harley Street trichologist: 'Touch of root follicle problem here, perhaps a hint of alopecia. Can I smell your penis, sir?'

'Of course you can't smell my fucking penis.'

'Ah well, then it's probably your socks.'

I didn't dare look behind me – the key to the routine was the customer's passivity and reasonableness at the hands of this raging lunatic. But I knew from the build-up of laughter out there in the darkness that Reg's walk was doing its stuff. It was a preposterous stiff-backed prance, head locked sideways and teak-faced, with all the movement below the knee. A solemn stork; a tango dancer with haemorrhoids. The blades of the scissors snicker-snacked past my nose.

'Tiny nick to the cheekbone there, sir, but nothing to worry about. Touch of the styptic pencil.' He gravely studied the sheep's eyeball I had palmed him from beneath the sheet, then, after a moment's indecision, flipped it into the darkness. There was blood all down the front of the sheet by now, and the audience was howling. You could do a lot with the demon barber routine: sport, politics, holidays, but the core of it was non-communication, mutual in-comprehension, and we'd got them, got them, got them. The heat in my chest and flush in my face was the flame of successful seduction. Seven seconds between the laughs and you can do anything, anything at all.

'So, you going on holiday anywhere nice this year?' Reg was saying.

'We'd thought of Ventnor, or perhaps Shanklin. Do you like Shanklin?'

'Don't think I've ever been shankled, sir, though I had a brother-in-law once who liked to piss on the electric fire. Only short bursts of course. We're broadminded in my family, but my wife she prefers the old-fashioned British seaside holiday: Torremolinos, Lanzarote, St Tropez –'

'St Tropez is in France.'

'*France.* Don't give me France,' said Reg. 'Those French

— 67 —

loaves – useless – you can't put them in the toaster, and where were they at Dunkirk? France, that's where. You can't tear the toilet paper and the money comes to pieces in your hands. And however much you have in your pocket is always just the right amount to pay the cab fare. And why did they want us to join the Common Market?'

'They didn't want us to join –'

'They were after our false teeth,' said Reg firmly. 'See, we've got the NHS. They don't want us for ourselves – no, they just want us for our teeth. They're all gums the French, from crunching up all those snails. You've got your own teeth, sir?'

'Yes I have, thank you.'

'Well that should make up for your hand.' He tossed the blood-smeared rubber glove into the audience, and from the corner of my eye I saw Diana scrabble for it. 'You're not left-handed are you, sir? Well, it must be your lucky day. Used to know a Saudi Arabian shoplifter once that was left-handed. Fingers we used to call him; then Lefty; then Hoppy; then Stumpy . . .'

The American patter-merchant Milton Berle had an old gag about his suit being made from virgin wool – it came from the sheep that could run the fastest. And Berle used to challenge other comics to stick the most boring tag line they could think of on the joke to see if it would still work. They'd give him nonsense tag lines like 'fried egg' or 'Sheffield Wednesday' and Berle would go into his routine, cracking his usual series of one-liners, ten or twelve of them, getting faster and faster, until the audience was laughing in pulse, in a completely neurotic state of laughter. And then he'd say 'How about this suit? That's virgin wool. Came from the sheep with the fried egg!' And they'd roar.

We turned over the garden on Sunday, Diana and I. She had been accepted at University College hospital in Gower Street to do her two years' internship. Reg and I had six weeks of Saturday-night bookings at the club in Camden Town. We were citizens of substance now, with jobs and incomes. We had unpacked my cases and cleared the top landing of debris; Diana had blitzed the kitchen again, and cancelled the book-club subscriptions. We were straightening paths, putting down roots.

'You think we can move those rose bushes?' I asked her.

'Oh, I suppose so. Mum forgot about roses ages ago.'

My mother-in-law had abandoned her Vita Sackville-West role ten years before, though she still liked sometimes to wander about the garden in a straw hat, with a trug over her arm, poking vaguely at the weeds, and holding forth about hellebores and hostas. The beds now were mostly full of fat hen and nettles, with here and there the withered skeleton of a Woolworth's rose bush. As I dug I kept coming across dark rags of greasy fur and splintered wishbones – the remains of a dozen cat funerals.

Diana and I were always best when we did things like this together. We were short on emotional interchange, but we had decided this was really a strength. I grew up in a family that was suspicious of such things, and when I left home for university I turned my handicap to an advantage. Every other undergraduate was drunk on E. M. Forster and D. H. Lawrence, spouting about relationships and wallowing in factitious emotional crisis. I let it be known, dourly, taciturnly, that I had already been through these things, sorted myself out. There was no problem, I liked to say, that could not be solved through strong drink and stubborn silence, and Diana, reared in a Turkish bath of public row, communal confession and strategic breakdown – Diana responded. The truth was I had had no practice in my emotions, while Diana had had too much, and so we liked projects and practical tasks, the mute comradeship of common purpose.

'I thought it went very well last night.'

I knew it, but I wanted to hear it again. 'You really think so?'

'Mmmn. But you ought to do more of the lines yourself. Everyone was saying how good Reg was afterwards, and I kept having to say it was you that wrote it all.'

'I didn't. And anyway Reg has got the knack. I look like I'm on castors when I start to move about the stage.' I levered out the root ball of an old shrub rose and tested a shoot near the base. It snapped like biscuit, and I tossed the whole thing on to the compost heap near the gate. 'I'm perfectly happy to play comedian's labourer. It was always Muir and Norden and Galton and Simpson who made the real money.'

'But you aren't just doing it for the money.'

'In any case the comics all became alcoholics and went off their heads.'

'I wouldn't want you to do that, Philip,' she said seriously. I loved her in her grubby T-shirt and kneed Levis, with the smudge of soil on her forehead. I put my dusty hands up her shirt from behind to cup her neat, rubbery teats, and she let me do it for a while.

'Someone coming,' she said after a bit, and for once there was. The Hangover Hag in candlewick dressing-gown and toerags, squinting fiercely over a fuming cigarette.

'Waffles' grave,' she croaked, waving feebly at the fresh-turned earth of the side bed.

'Oh, *Mum*.'

'My only Wafwaf. My firstest pussy I haddum when I was twelvum. Oh my Wafflaffle, what have dey done to 'oo?'

It was different from the teacup tantrum. Perhaps she didn't throw those in front of Diana. But it was much weirder, this hunched creature shuffling through the loose soil in her Dr Scholls, keening over the greasy rags and wish-bones.

'Who's Wafwaf?' I whispered.

'Fafnir. Old black cat we had when I was small. We didn't even bury him there. It was over by the cherry tree.'

'Ooo the coo-ell Didi. Where the Didi put my 'ickle Wafflesnaffle?'

'Look, Mum, there's dozens of bloody cat graves –'

'*And where's my Peace rose?* The one your father planted in that bed the week before we were married.'

'Those roses were all dead,' I said. 'Really, Adrienne, we were very careful.'

'*Don't you try to tell me about gardening.* I have *studied* roses for *years.*'

'Look, you can see for yourself –'

'*Shut up. Shut up.*' And after a wave from Diana I shut. She got her back inside again, with threats, promises, bribes, drugs, alcohol, cigarettes, and half an hour later we were standing again, looking drearily at the garden. Nestbuilding over.

'We should move out,' I told her. 'It's always going to be hopeless here with your mother.'

'She'd hate that. And we'd never be able to afford it.'

'Just let's get our own bloody flat, and worry about the money later,' I said.

'Oh, *could* we?' said Diana.

I was planting the new Peace rose from the Parkhill nursery, while Diana re-interred the doubtful Wafwaf, when the next visitors arrived. We must have missed the doorbell because it was Saul, coming down the side passage, with a chunky little mastiff of a man in a buff-coloured quilted waistcoat trotting behind him. His body was a packed keg, and his head an outcrop of scar tissue and bristle, with odd, random knobs of cartilage that might once have been ears and a nose. He sniffed the air of the garden alertly, circled the lawn once, and then came to rest, panting slightly, his bright little eyes fixed on Saul.

'Mr Cork,' said Saul. 'Like you to meet sister Diana, friend Philip First. Mr Cork is the erm private, aah . . .'

'You're the detective,' I said to him.

'Scurityconsullen,' said Mr Cork. 'Detective is a bit

PC Plod these days, isn't it? We do domestic, matrimonial, fiscal, missing persons, missing sums. Sortsafings.'

'What does this um, business, come under?' I asked him, and Mr Cork pondered.

'Genruleddin of conciliation and counselling, I should say.'

'He's been counselling our friend Cahill,' said Saul.

'Philip, did you *know* about this?' said Diana.

'Tell her,' said Saul, and Mr Cork told us.

There was the deportation order from Spain I already knew about, and another from Canada. There were three British convictions, one for trading illegally while undischarged under the Bankruptcy Act, one for drawing cheques against a defunct bank account, one for failing to make accurate returns under the something-or-other regulation.

'Spretty minor stuff on the whole,' said Mr Cork. 'Arfur-local Rotary Club have done worse than that.'

'Then I don't really see . . .' said Diana.

'Just a minute,' said Saul.

'Smattera minor offences. Swotisaid to Mr Schondler here,' said Mr Cork. 'Fitwasn't for a few personal matters that have a more direct bearing on your family affairs.' He paused to scrabble at his ear, and hesitated, as if contemplating a swift cock of the leg against the rosebush. 'Fakamatter is,' he continued, 'that Mr Cahill appears to have been married before.'

'We know that,' said Diana. 'He mentioned a Susannah somebody. Years ago.'

Cork consulted a scrap of paper from his waistcoat pocket. 'Samiss Susannah Peary of Ottawa, 1956,' he read. 'Samiss Inez Deja of Barcelona, 1967. Samiss Claire Sachs of Crickle-wood, 1974.'

'Didn't mention those, did he?' said Saul triumphantly.

'I'd have thought that was his own business,' said Diana, more cautiously. 'He may have told Mummy. There's no law against marrying three wives.'

'Smattera *sequencing*, Miss Schondler,' said Mr Cork. 'Snissue of one at a *time*. Lorsez you divorce one before marrying the next.' He gave a little whimper of pleasure.

'So you're saying he's a bigamist,' I said.

Mr Cork was enjoying his moment. 'Snotinna dictionary I don't suppose, sir, but the word I think might be trigamist.'

We didn't see much of my mother-in-law for the next few days. Her domestic routines, which already ran five or six hours later than everyone else's, became completely inverted: sleeping all day until seven or eight in the evening, and then reading all night. There were glimpses of her candlewick dressing-gown, whisking through bedroom or bathroom door, and the glow of her reading lamp under the drawing-room door, when I stumbled to the lavatory in the hour before dawn. In the mornings I found traces of her nocturnal passage through the house: smeared sherry glasses and the crusts of peanut-butter sandwiches, a revolving record turntable, or a telephone receiver off the hook.

'I can't find the Garrard candlesticks anywhere,' said Diana.

'You probably put them somewhere when you were cleaning the kitchen.'

'They're *always* in the salad drawer of the old fridge. Those things are worth *thousands*. I *know* I put them there after polishing them.'

'You didn't hide them somewhere else, did you?' I said, and as I said it I remembered with a pang someone telling me that the best thing for polishing candlesticks was the human hide.

There seemed to be other things missing too, Diana said, though it was hard to be certain in the century and a half of accumulated chaos that was Aberdare House. A set of silver asparagus tongs; a tiny Thomas Tompion clock; a Coalport tea service. Diana ransacked her mother's sitting room while she slept, and turned out the bedroom and bathroom while she read through the evenings. There was shelf after shelf of pill bottles, blister packs, tinctures, lotions, linctuses, suppositories and salves. And Diana dumped the lot, knotting them into clanking, rattling carrier bags, and burying them in the bottom of the next-door dustbin, 'Because she's not above going through our own bins.'

'But she might *need* some of those things,' I protested.

'I know her prescriptions backwards, Phil. She has warfarin for the angina, a steroid for the bronchitis, temazepam for sleeping, and that's the lot.'

'So where did she get all this stuff?'

'Hoarding and lying. Half of these tranquillizers aren't even legal any more, but she'll run around five doctors in an afternoon telling them she's down in London on holiday and lost all her pills. Most of them are too stupid or too lazy to tell her to go away.'

After a week or so, alarming messages, ground out in pencil on yellow legal notes, began to appear on the kitchen table and from beneath my mother-in-law's bedroom door.

'To the Tenants: As the registered owner of this property I wish to remind all tenants that interference with the fabric, internal or external, and particularly telephone and electrical services, will NOT be tolerated. A. Wallis.'

'Diana: Someone has clearly been speaking to my doctor behind my back, and fabricating rumours about my state of health. The doctor–patient relationship is private and personal, and I wish it to be clearly understood that this interference is NOT acceptable.'

'Philip: As a guest in my house I think you will agree that you have been treated with the greatest kindness and generosity. Do not think I am unaware that you have chosen to repay this hospitality by attempting to poison my relationship with my daughter. Do not meddle with the tuning of the Roberts radio set in the second bathroom. As an "expert" on roses you may be interested to know they are pruned only in March and November.'

'Dearest darling Didi: Saul is saying terrible wicked things about you and Philip. I pay no attention of course, but you know how rumours can spread. I love you both for ever and always. I will forget all about the business with my doctor if you promise, promise to forget this silly idea of a flat of your own. Your ever-loving Mummy.'

'TO ALL TENANTS: If there is any further interference with my private correspondence I shall not hesitate to have recourse to my solicitors. A. Wallis.

'PS. Will somebody please stop those bloody cars from racing up and down the street.'

Diana had told her about Cahill, but she had hardly seemed to notice, and there was nothing about him in the notes. Cahill had disappeared somewhere, to his wine bar, or the flat he kept in Kentish Town – nobody knew. Diana and Hon and Reg and I went out a lot, to The Jar, and to The Washington in England's Lane. In the house we found ourselves creeping about and talking in whispers. My mother-in-law had become a neutron star of gloom, crushing the second-floor space of her bedroom and sitting room, warping the nearby air with patterns of nauseous anticipation.

'She doesn't want us to go,' Diana explained.

'So she's trying to charm us into staying put,' I said.

I wondered if this was what nervous breakdowns were like. I had imagined soap-eating frenzies and excrement up the walls; canvas straps and cold-eyed men with shining syringes. I hadn't imagined boredom and repetition, puny subterfuges and childish threats. For my mother-in-law, evidently, going mad simply meant being herself, only more so.

Cork rang after a fortnight and Reg took the call.

'He wanted me to tell you that it was all sorted out about Cahill,' he told me.

'Why should he want to tell me?'

'Search me,' said Reg, and shifted into Cork's accent.

'Smessage from Mr Schondler for Mr First. Snegotiation's complete and Mr Cahill has agreed to go for the five hundred.'

'I wonder what on earth Saul is up to.'

'Smattera few drinks,' said Reg. 'Squestiona few words. Hardly had to hit him at all.'

'Cork hit Cahill?'

'Apparently so,' said Reg, in his own voice now. 'I told him that Mr Cahill was a very nice man who may well have behaved badly, but that we were all still very fond of him, but he didn't seem very interested.'

'But you can't just go threatening people . . .'

'Tried argument, Mr First,' said Reg, becoming Cork again. 'But he woodenave it. Tried hanging him out the window by his feet, but he still woodenlisten.'

'You're making that up,' I said.

'Sgospeltrufe, Mr First. Wordofalie.'

'But does he know that Cahill's got a bad heart?'

'Snunna my concern, sir. But we'd have gone to the funeral,' said Reg.

An era is a short thing when you are twenty-two, and this one was coming to an end already. This marvellous house which had been my escape route from the prison of Cardiff squats and student beer-swills was becoming a prison of its own, with its subtle tyrannies of tradition and possession; its mad demarcations and its drugged, insomniac ruler, brooding in her fastness on the second floor.

Hon had got herself a job, to my disgust, on the BBC trainee scheme, and was looking for a room in Shepherd's Bush. Reg was talking about a short-let council flat in Gospel Oak, and I was hopelessly scouring the property ads in the *Ham and High*. At home in Wales the property ads still said things like 'Lg dtchd hse: 3 bed, 2 recep, K&B, CH. Fhold £22,000.' I'd learned to understand that language, just about, but the *Ham and High* ads were something else:

'Viva Victoriana! Proudly perched on the end of an

exquisite 1880s terrace this lavishly detailed period home provides ample inspiration for the restoration enthusiast! Intricately wrought ceiling mouldings and cornices; original illuminated door glass; cast-iron and marble fireplaces throughout. £65,000 for the discerning collector of historical gems.'

'You realize this sort of flowery garbage costs the estate agents about ten pounds a column inch?' I told Reg.

'You mean it costs *you* ten pounds a column inch,' said Reg. 'At three per cent commission these pinstripe-suited nobodys are making £3,000 a sale, so what's twenty quid for a newspaper ad? Haven't you noticed all the estate agents opening up around here? There's about eight in England's Lane. There's more boards than trees along East Heath Road. We are witnessing a new version of one of the great mass delusions of history: the medieval dancing sickness; the Dutch tulip craze; and now, government sanctioned and officially systematized, the lust for owner-occupation.'

We found a place to rent in the end, near the Royal Free, and backing on to the council's heavy-plant depot. Miss Piggy wrote a faked-up employer's reference and Diana took £200 out of the Post Office for a deposit. The flat stank sweetly of rusty dustbin and the kitchen was a slot where you stood sideways to do the washing-up, but the postcode on the tin sign at the end of the street was still NW3.

The last time I saw Cahill was late one lunchtime, just before The Jar shut, and I was draping soggy bar towels over the pump handles. He was very drunk and much thinner, and he gave me an envelope for Diana.

'She's a lovely girl. You be careful to look after her.'

'What are you going to do?'

'I'm sailing for the Dominions,' he told me grandly, 'to clear my name.'

There was a second envelope inside the first, addressed to

my mother-in-law, and I showed it to Reg, together with the bundle of pawn tickets.

'Well at least he didn't just sell the candlesticks down the pub,' said Reg. 'At least Adrienne can get all the stuff back if she wants to.'

'Saul says that Cork had to give Cahill five hundred quid.'

'There was a man from the Mercedes dealer in St John's Wood came around this afternoon,' said Reg. 'Wanted to know what had happened to the hire purchase payments.'

'Cahill told me he'd bought the Mercedes in Frankfurt.'

'Don't think they do many right-hand drives in Frankfurt,' said Reg. It was our last night in Aberdare House and there was evacuation in the air. Suitcases were standing in the hall; there were bin-liners stuffed with sheets and jumpers around the bed, and the fridge was down to a Greek yoghurt and a greenish rind of mousetrap. Leavings are always panicky, untidy affairs. You remember the stupid things and forget the important ones: packing the toothbrush and leaving behind the passport. We poked the Cahill note under my mother-in-law's door, and went out to the Punjab for a gloomy, farewell curry.

It was about three when I woke up, with a bladder full of beer, and I was shuffling downstairs in the dark when I trod on her hand. She had got half-way up the stairs to Diana's room. So perhaps she had changed her mind. Perhaps it wasn't meant to be a serious attempt, but it was serious enough.

In the darkness I tried pulling her upright, but she was too heavy for me and her torso slumped sideways so she was lying in a hairpin shape, facing downhill. I turned the hall light on, and her face was white, shining, lardy. It retained the print of my fingers where I pinched and prodded her. 'Adrienne. Adrienne. Wake up.' There was a smell from her dressing-gown and a smear of loose turd on the stair-carpet between her legs. I pulled some tissue from the roll in the bathroom, started dabbing stupidly at it and then stopped. There was no reason for me to be doing this. Nobody else in the house was awake. I could turn the light off again, urinate, go back to bed. She was already unconscious, so there would be nothing more for her to go through. I looked again at the greasy white face pressed into the stair-carpet, and examined myself for stirrings of affection or sympathy, or even just regret. There were none.

Things would change quickly if she died. The house and money would be split between Diana and Saul. There would probably be no need to move at all. In a few seconds standing there on the stair I replaced the kitchen lino with terracotta tiles; I installed limed-oak Smallbone units; I converted Diana's bedroom into a donnish study for myself; and I turned the clobber room into a sunshine-yellow nursery with mobiles of biplanes and flying pigs. I held drinks parties in the newly built Edwardian conservatory; and I invited Melvyn Bragg to dinner.

There was a note in her hand, 'Diana you bitch I hate Diana you fucking cow hate Diana I hate you never . . .' I crumpled it in my hand without reading any more, but there was another one in the pocket of her dressing-gown. There was a note on the hall table, and another on the bathroom chest. I followed the trail into the foxy trench of her bedroom and there was a note on the bedside table, another on the counterpane. I crumpled them all and stuffed them under a pillow. There was another note under the pillow. How many fucking notes could the woman write?

I was still crumpling paper when I heard Diana on the stairs.

'Phil? Oh God. *Phil!*'

We dragged her downstairs and shoved her into what Di said was the coma position. Lovely Doctor Di, so tautly calm in my big T-shirt and unlaced baseball boots. She pulled her mother's tongue clear of her throat and poked around for obstructions in the airway; pulled back her eyelids and shouted hard in her ear. Reg was up now and on the phone, and Hon was crying on the stairs and Diana was kneeling, busy and heedless, in her mother's stool.

Two grumpy ambulancemen with a folding chair arrived very fast and said almost nothing. Hampstead ladies with overdoses did not rate highly, I supposed, when you had spent all night hosing people out of car crashes. They drove off without light or bells, Diana sitting beside her mother in the back, while we watched from the pavement, in the Monday-morning dawn.

'Many pills?' said Saul, when I telephoned him.

'About thirty. Not enough to kill her, Diana says.'

'Never is. Many notes?'

'Fuck, I dunno. About fourteen or something.'

'New record,' said Saul. 'Tell Di I'll see her at the Royal Free when I can get away from the office.'

Diana stayed with her all day, and when I went to the Royal Free in the afternoon to relieve her, my mother-in-law was awake. The drips and drains and ducts were real enough this time, and she could hardly speak from the bruising around her mouth. Her hand stirred on the coverlet when I went in.

'Philip.'

I didn't have much experience of talking to failed suicides. What do you say to someone who has just chucked the whole world away, yourself included?

'We're very sorry.'

'Give you.' She flickered the hand again, in benediction. I hadn't wanted or asked for her forgiveness, but it seemed churlish to clarify the point.

'Diana and I. We've decided to stay on for a few days. Until you come out of hospital.'

Her face hardened. 'Not go.'

'You know we have to have a place of our own sometime, Adrienne. We'll be seeing lots and lots of you.'

'I'll tell her,' she said, and her voice was perfectly distinct now, and I remembered why I had wanted to find all the notes.

'I don't know what you mean,' I said, but I did.

'About you and me.'

'You wouldn't dare,' I said, but I knew she would.

—— PART TWO ——

My wife said to me last night, 'Can my mother come down for a few days?' and I said, 'Why?' and she said, 'Well, she's getting a bit tired of sitting up on the roof.' . . . When she knocked on the door I had to get there fast before she blistered the paint . . . I could tell she was upset, her eyepatch was damp and her duelling scars were livid . . . She had a facelift a few years ago, but they arrested the surgeon for disturbing the peace . . . But no, seriously, her mouth was open so much that first winter she stayed with us that we had to lag her tonsils . . . But no, I'm very fond of her really. I often spend all weekend buttering her up — but she still won't fit in the oven . . . I even bought her a Mother's Day present, but it slithered down one of the airholes before I could give it her . . . I took this photo of her that I put right in the middle of the mantelpiece — keeps the kids away from the fire . . .

CHAPTER SIX

'Would you say you were happy?' he asked me.

'What about "Do you believe in God?" or "When did you last cry?" Aren't they on the list?'

Rutherford's eyes flickered uneasily to the notebook on his lap and I suppressed a smirk. A palpable hit.

'I suppose by that you're really asking am I the traditional angst-ridden comic? Tears of a clown and all that? The comedian who burns while Rome fiddles?'

He smiled a little stiffly. 'If you like.'

His biro scuttled across his notepad, while I framed another quotable quote. Malcolm Rutherford was his name: seven or eight years older than me, with a bald, suntanned head, and one of those enormous Japanese suits in fashionable eighties black. He dropped enough 'yeahs' and 'rights' to let me know that he was young once too, and he had remarked approvingly on the Marx and Gramsci in my bookshelves. The revolutionary turned realist. The old hippy turned hack.

I'd read some of his stuff in one of the smarter tabloids: a paper which diluted its neo-fascist politics with spasms of environmentalist anguish over baby seals, and feeble breast-beating about 'the plight of the homeless'. Rutherford specialized in a waspish, alliterative invective: a bit of literary name-dropping to let you know he'd been to university; a dash of vernacular matiness to let you know he'd been around. And he had the popular columnist's knack for counter-intuitive thought – for turning an issue on its head. How feminism oppressed females. Why living in cardboard boxes was a sign of economic vitality. How a media monopoly was the best guarantor of free speech.

'You don't have to talk to him, you know,' Reg told me.

'Ah, you're just jealous because he didn't ask to see you too. And anyway, press interviews are in the BBC contract.'

'He'll stitch you up.'

'And if I don't see him he'll stitch me up anyway, by digging all the stuff out of cuttings files, and interviewing all the people who hate us. At least this way I get a chance to have my say.'

But I wasn't as confident as I tried to sound. I'd only done a few patsy interviews for the London listings mags before, and none of them in my own home. Diana's old bedroom was my office these days, done out in a professorial dark-green, with mahogany-stained bookshelves, a brass desk lamp, and a word processor in front of the window. The books covered three walls, with a place of honour for the videos of the Amnesty concerts, an inconspicuous place of shame for the unfinished dissertation.

I spent the morning emptying ashtrays and bins, and wiping down the desk and window with J-cloths. There was a pair of Dewi's tiny, sweat-stiff socks behind the armchair cushion, and a trail of Lego bricks that led out of the door and half-way down the stairs. I fanned out some magazines on the table – *Marxism Today*, *London Review of Books*, the *Spectator* – and I built a casual stack of hardbacks on the desk: Amis, McEwan, Burgess, Barnes, Theroux. Then to give it a bit of weight, Bernard Crick's *Orwell*, John Charvet's *Feminism*, and E. P. Thompson's *Poverty of Theory*.

I stood back to study the effect, and to rehearse tabloid paragraphs: 'In the serene academic order of his Hampstead home I talked this week to Britain's craziest comic talent . . .' Or what about 'Phil First, TV's new king of comic chaos, lives in a state of surgical hygiene and rigid repression . . .' I added copies of *The Face* and *Private Eye* to the magazines and subtracted the non-fiction from the hardback pile. I was creeping down the stairs on my hands and knees, replacing the Lego bricks in a careful disarray, when my mother-in-law let herself in through the hall door.

'Building a little brrm-brrrm car are we, Philip?'

'I was tidying up.'

'Those bricks weren't there half an hour ago, Philip, and Dewi is at his play group.'

For someone who barely knew what year it was, much less what time of day, my mother-in-law had a terrifying eye for trivial detail. Grandly indifferent to hygiene, order, chronology, law and convention, she could home in like a heat-seeking missile on the repaired toothmug, the missing teaspoon and the white lie. It made life with her a constant anxiety, a permanently needling sense of guilt, for in my mother-in-law's anarchic universe how could you ever know what would matter and what would not? It was a Caucus Race with blindfolds, arbitrary obstacles and no prizes for anybody.

'Perhaps it was the pixies put them there.'

'Don't worry. I won't let Diana in on your little secret,' she told me. 'All talented people have their oddities.' And that was another thing, the way she could dwell on a word like 'secret' to give it an ominous ring in the most ordinary circumstances.

'I thought we'd agreed that you'd ring the bell before coming here.'

'Just delivering your mail for you, Philip.'

'I'm quite capable of collecting my mail from the hall.'

'*And* I thought I'd see if there was anything for my grandson's lunch in the fridge. Diana has a practice conference, and she won't be home from house-calls until tea-time.'

The old slit-trench hallway of Aberdare House had become echoing and empty now, a common entranceway with two doors: one to the granny flat on the ground floor and the other to the upper storeys that were Diana's and mine. The doors were cumbersome, fireproofed sandwiches of teak and rockwool, brass-fitted, rimlocked and hinge-bolted, but they were gauze and breeze to my mother-in-law. I collected up the Lego bricks again, stuffed them under the armchair cushion in the study, and waited for Malcolm Rutherford.

Catch Altcom–Tape transcript Philip First: side two

'In fact I think comics tend to be remarkably resilient people.'

'But what about Hancock, Lenny Bruce, Spike Milligan . . .?'

'There are exceptions, but from what I've read and seen the suicide rate is rather low. There are very few comics who have had nervous breakdowns or gone into mental hospitals. So the tormented soul bit just doesn't wash, I'm afraid. Loneliness, unhappy childhoods, feelings of inferiority – they might contribute to anybody's drive, but they don't account for talent.'

'You consider yourself to be talented?'

(*Pause*) 'I think I have a writing talent. Performing I'm not so sure. I think I've developed a technique which works for me – a sort of machine-gun delivery (*laughter*) – but I certainly don't have the acting talent of someone like Victoria Wood or John Cleese. I can't do mimicry like this man John Sessions – you've seen him? And I can't use my body as effectively on stage as people like Alexei Sayle, or Reg.'

'First and Last, you've not appeared together as regularly as you used to. This one-man show . . .'

'Reg and I have been performing together nine or ten years now, including university. There were things both of us wanted to do on our own. Reg wanted to do more acting – he's in this thing at the Lyric at the moment. I was interested in something that would stretch me a bit more than stand-up comedy. I sometimes . . . (*inaudible*) . . .'

'But there's no split?'

'Reg and I were best mates at nineteen, and still are. He's godfather to my son. We see each other at least once a week, and talk almost every day on the phone.'

'You just have the one child do you?'

'Dewi, yes, but my wife's expecting another in three months. She works as a GP at the local health centre.'

'You ever do medical jokes?'

'Not me. Dewi brings some home from school.'

'Such as?'

'Um, lemme think . . . Oh, I know. Patient comes into doctor's surgery and says, "Doctor, doctor, I feel like a cricket ball." The doctor says, "How's that?" and the patient says, "Now don't *you* start." (*laughter*) . . . It's better the way Dewi tells it.'

'I read somewhere that you live with your wife's mother.'

'Not *with* her exactly. She has the ground-floor flat of the house. It used to be her place, but her health's not good, and it all got a bit much for her. Best thing seemed to be to split the house up.'

'You get on with her?'

'I don't really see that's particularly . . . (*inaudible*)'

'Sorry, I didn't mean to pry. It's just the old thing about the mother-in-law joke, you know. Seemed interesting: the alternative comic who lives with his mother-in-law.'

'We get on fine. I like it when she comes round. All the mice throw themselves in the traps (*laughter*) . . . She had a burglar broke in her bedroom the other day but all he took was one look (*laughter*) . . .'

'Those are all the kinds of jokes you'd never do on stage.'

'I hardly do jokes at all. Never liked them very much. In fact they very rarely make me laugh. There's something too mechanical about deliberate joke-telling. Like pressing a switch and the laughter track comes on.'

'You mean they rely on stereotypes?'

'Yes.'

'But it's been said that there are stereotypes in your own comedy. The Muslim newsagent you used to do, with the porn magazines on the top shelf . . .'

'Mr Patel.'

'Yes. Isn't he just a comic stereotype like the old-style Irish joke or nig-nog joke, or mother-in-law joke? Isn't he a bit racist?'

'I don't actually believe that comedy can operate without stereotypes. Stage and TV sketches have to work very fast or you go to sleep. And to find a character immediately funny he must be of a recognizable type – the embodiment of a set of ideas, or the manifestation of a cliché.'

'So you can do Irish jokes or gay jokes or mother-in-law jokes then?'

'Yes and no. There's a joke you may know about the Irishman who goes for a job on a building site and the foreman decides to set him an intelligence test. Asks him can he tell the difference between a joist and a girder. And the Irishman scratches his head and says, "Wasn't it Joist dat wrote *Ulysses* and Girder dat wrote *Faust*?" (*laughter*).'

'It's an anti-Irish joke.'

'Exactly. It relies on stereotypes, but it also subverts them. It's what Jonathan Miller calls a "leakage" joke, which surprises you because of the way it confuses different categories. You expect a joke about building materials and you hear a joke about writers. You think you are listening to a joke at the expense of Irishmen, but it is really at the expense of yourself and your prejudices.'

'So is there any real difference between yourself and people like Bernard Manning or Jim Davidson?'

'Of course there is. Those sorts of comics are the fag-end of the music-hall, end-of-pier tradition. It's a type of comedy which grew out of traditional working-class life: slums, rent collectors, cramped housing, seaside landladies, domineering mothers-in-law, shotgun weddings. It's a world that hardly exists any more, apart from in the collective memory, and people like Tarby and Davidson, with their Rollers and houses in Marbella, have hardly experienced it. So it's not honest, which means it's not funny – or not to me at any rate.'

'Why has alternative comedy become so big in the 1980s?'

'Partly the baby boomers growing older. Fewer people want to spend an evening going deaf at a disco, or sitting on wet grass at a rock concert. And there's politics.'

'People want to hear you bash Thatcher?'

'Crudely, yeah. But also because there is so little in the way of effective political opposition. A loss of faith in seventies radicalism; the lack of any new agenda for the left. So people express their distaste for the government by laughing at it.'

'Rather negative?'

'Completely. Now, I hope you don't mind, but I've got stuff to do this afternoon . . .'

'No, that's plenty. It's been nice to meet you, and I hope you enjoy the interview when it comes out.'

'When's this appearing by the way?'

'A week Sunday.'

'So you'll be able to let me have a look at it before it's published.'

'I'd love to, no problem for me at all, but it's not the paper's policy . . .'

'I didn't really think it would be . . .'

(*Long pause, shuffling of papers.*)

'You know what Simone de Beauvoir used to say to journalists after they had interviewed her?'

'What was that?'

'Don't betray me too much.'

But I know he will. You have to trust them, even when the trust is always betrayed, just as you have to trust me, although I've told a few fibs along the way. You know already there are details here and there I may have altered or left out. But this is first person, so what do you expect? It's a skewed telescope, but if you compensate for the skew you can still watch the world through it. It's like a stage act: you edit, shuffle, delete details, embroider others. It's not historical truth, but it is performance truth. Comedy is honesty, and if they laugh then there is truth in that.

The girlfriend with the stubbly bottom and the brother from Sandhurst, for instance: you remember them? Well, they never existed, and there was no builder's daughter in Wales. I invented them for Diana, and then for you. And I seem to have left out a few other things, about my mother-in-law and me, but they didn't quite fit at the time. I wasn't all that sure if they were true or not, to tell you the truth. So I left them out, but I'm being honest now. Trust me.

Did I sleep with my mother-in-law? It would be useful in terms of narrative and life if it were true. Domestic blackmail and near-incest make for better plot, and better motivation than inertia or timidity, I think. Let's come clean and say I did it once, under pressure, but didn't enjoy it, and suppressed the memory so well that I hardly know if it's true any more. Such things happen.

My Christian name is Philip, for instance, but when I was a child I used to pretend it was Sion, as more dark and Celtic and interesting. A tiny, pointless lie compared to the grand fantasy my sister wove about being a twin, or the butcher's son at junior school who said his father was an astronaut. I, at any rate, was Sion. I said that was the name on my birth certificate, but my mother had changed her mind. I might reclaim it one day when I was older. It was repeated by me and by others until I hardly knew if it was true or not.

Do you know, I am not a hundred per cent sure even now. As I sit here, writing at my desk, dressed in black canvas slippers and faded denim shirt, there is a filing cabinet at my knee, and in it a copy of my birth certificate. I keep it folded and only glance obliquely at it now and then when I need to take a photocopy. Sion or Phil? I could take it out now and read it properly, but some superstition, some counter-compulsion prevents me.

This story is true; let me tell you about it. It is my first month in Aberdare House, and I am at a party with Reg and Hon, one of the last great seventies parties. It is at Hon's parents' house in Keats Grove, Reg being a friend of Hon's and I a friend of Reg.

The Oswalds are a rich, middle-aged couple. She with old money and he with new. Liz Oswald has a Lambton and a Mitford on her Christmas card list, and an earl for her first husband. The second husband, and Hon's step-father, is Dave Oswald, a Turkish Jew who started his career selling carpets in Brick Lane, and ended it importing handicrafts from Russia. He fought with the Palmach militia in the Negev desert, and then with the anti-fascist 43 Group in the pubs of Kilburn High Road. The matchbox sociology is benefit of Hon, but I've met Dave already, selling the *Morning Star* in Gucci loafers, at The Jar on a Saturday morning, and it was he who took pleasure in underlining the incongruities.

'You didn't tell me you were Welsh,' he roars at me when we arrive this evening.

'The land of my fathers. But my fathers are welcome to it.'

'Welshmen and Jews have a lot in common,' says Dave, with the ponderous solemnity of the seriously drunk.

'Is that right?'

'We have both been made stateless by the Romans and devious by our mothers.'

'And legless by Young's brewery,' says Hon, sweeping past her stepfather and into the house.

It is a tiny Georgian jewel box which has burgeoned at the back into a conservatory and snooker room and sauna, and has even burrowed underground to form a brick-lined gallery for his collection of Orthodox icons. The Oswalds argue, separate and divorce from time to time, but are together for Hon's half-sister's twenty-first birthday party (she studies pottery, makes jewellery – forget about her). There is a friend of Malcolm McLaren's looking after the music; a *sous-chef* from Green's who is opening oysters from a frosty, smoking barrel. I hate oysters and I've already eaten about two dozen, partly because I know they cost a pound each, and partly because I'm very drunk.

'You're very drunk,' says Hon, removing my drifting forefinger from her belly button.

'I'm very miserable,' say I, meaning very horny.

I fancy Hon, and I know she fancies me, in the way you know when a woman is superfluously rude to you – though it is always possible to be wrong about this. It is always possible that she simply dislikes me, so at home we keep a wary distance from each other. She is curiously defensive of Aberdare House, suspecting invasion when I already want to evacuate. I am carefully taciturn when she is around, always fearing another torpedo attack. In accidental encounters, in corridors or at the bathroom door, we circle each other like apprehensive boxers.

The thing is, I don't know about girls like Hon. I only really know about Welsh girls, who are prettily pliable and sweetly submissive. They marry bristly, dangerous, firecracker men, and are so pliant and deferential, that in twenty years or so they run the whole show, while the dangerous man sits in the corner in his cardy, fat as a neutered tomcat, lifting his feet while she runs the Hoover under them. Terrible heresy in the emancipated 1970s of course, and I'd never risk it on stage, but it's always seemed a reasonable trade-off to me.

Diana is a Welsh girl in every respect apart from being Swiss–Jewish and it is the me-and-Diana thing that Hon doesn't like. They shared pushchairs and dummies, then, almost immediately, mascara. They saw the Stones together in Hyde Park when they were eleven. Hon slept with Diana's brother and Diana slept with Hon's. They might have slept with each other if that wasn't too symmetrical. And now Hon dislikes me because Diana does, but is it because she likes Diana or because she's getting to like me and she doesn't like it?

She is wearing a tight silver top tonight, all clever darts and flushed seams, which fits her like a film of water and stops an inch short of the waistband of her black Spandex tights. And there is absolutely nothing underneath those sheeny tights, I'm certain, not even the compressed cross-hatching of pubic hair.

We are wedged in a noisy passageway between conservatory and kitchen. Waiters push past us with trays of drinks; but the roar of the party seems remote as a sea shell. There is that curious clarity of speech and gesture, a fleeting perfection of understanding, in which truths are spoken and everything seems possible. We're totally smashed in fact.

'I don't really love her, you know. Diana.'

'Of course you don't,' says Hon, plucking a bottle of Löwenbrau from a passing tray.

'I suppose I just think that I ought to.'

'So you ought to stop. Pain deferred is pain increased.'

'Stitch in time saves nine.'

'Oh shut up,' says Hon, but she says it affectionately, and I run my forefinger again along the firm band of her belly between tights and top. But the finger is softly crooked this time, and non-invasive, and she doesn't stop me.

'How are you so sure anyway? About me and Diana?'

'Because I know her better than you do. Because I really do love her.'

My finger has uncurled itself and is running along the rim of the waistband, with a millimetre of penetration. And Hon follows its progress in my eyes, never looking downward at the six inches of space between us.

'And do you love her in *that* way,' my finger, greatly

daring, traces up the moulded curve of her silver top to graze her left nipple, 'or *that* way?' and it dives slowly but boldly beneath the waistband, its inner curve following the soft convexity of her stomach. She doesn't flinch at all though there are people all around us in the passageway – Liz Oswald carrying a tray of canapés, Reg's voice beyond, raised in argument – but in the general press of bodies nobody can see.

'It's too hot here. Let's go outside,' says Hon, and I suppose I've asked for it. All very well a bit of steamy talk, and simulated finger fucking, but the ante is up now and the bluff is called. Whole lives can turn on these moments; great architectures of families, jobs, friends and houses teeter on the turn of such cards, so one should really try to be rational here. I fancy her a bit but don't like her all that much. Might even be too pissed to perform. Reg will know for sure, and half Diana's friends, who are gargling molluscs around the oyster barrel. Thoroughly stupid thing to do, in fact, so of course I'm going to do it. It was never in doubt.

The garden is long and narrow, with the dark shapes of big trees stirring at the end. Beyond the sprawl of light from the conservatory, stone flags lead past a rectangular fishpond and a patch of lawn to a semicircular summerhouse with a brick-built bench. We sit, and drink the Löwenbrau, then kiss. Her mouth and gums are syrupy dark like malt extract. The fork of her legs in the sheeny tights is excitingly smooth and featureless to my exploring hand, a silky junction of seamless tubes.

'Still too hot,' says Hon, standing up, and in a dream I watch her wriggle out of the silver top, her heavy breasts tolling gently at the release. So full and white and close together. She shucks down the tights over her shoes and becomes a pale flicker against the sandstone flags; a star-cast shadow dancing away over the grass and into the shadows beneath the trees. I was right about the pubic hair too, because there isn't any: a casual wickedness which makes me suddenly faint with lust.

The dare is implicit, but I can hardly turn it down. I unbuckle my belt, and fumble for the cross-fly fastener inside my trousers. My tie is an Eddie Shoestring number, with an impossible knot, so I have to yank the whole thing off over my head.

'Philip? Where are you?'

I am here, you daft cow, fiddling frantically with my eight shirt buttons and four cuff buttons, and glancing anxiously backwards at the lighted windows of the house, where heads pass to and fro. Trouser cuffs are too narrow to pass over shoes, and I'm shuffling around the flags in my underpants like a one-man sack race. So slow, so slow. Shoelace knots are slippery as cherry stones to sweating, excited fingers. Hop about in frustration, abandon shoes inside trouser legs, kick off socks. Where is she?

'Philip?'

I pick my way painfully over a gravel path, then tread in something soft and wet. You don't want to do this. Be sensible. Get dressed. Go home. A hybrid tea rose attacks my scrotum and I spend tense, tearful seconds detaching it from my pubic hair. No trace of erection now, but we can always work on that again. 'Hon? Where are you?'

A whisper: 'Over here.'

But I have lost my sense of direction now. The lighted windows of the house are to my left, and the summerhouse to my right, which means that Hon should be ahead of me, not behind. Then her voice again, sharp and clear now, with no hint of a whisper.

'Over here, Phil.'

She is standing, silhouetted in the light of the conservatory door, fully dressed, and with one hand theatrically raised.

'What the f –'

And then with a click the lights go on, flooding the garden with pools of green and blue and yellow, highlighting a hunched, naked figure on the lawn, as, in the lighted windows of the house, interested heads turn to watch the next entertainment.

And it's all true.

There really was a party at the Oswalds', though now I think of it, it might have been another year. I did make a pass at Hon one time and she did brush me off, but the Spandex tights belonged to quite another girl, called Jenny, at a BBC party. A girl did once take her clothes off and dance naked for me in a garden, but that was much, much later. A true story then, except that it didn't all happen in that order, it didn't all happen at the same time, and it didn't all happen to me. Phil or Sion? Bill or Ben? It's a silly, po-mo writers' game. It's Phil, of course, and it's on the cover of the book if you want to check.

Dewi always hit the bed like a bomb on a Sunday morning, wet pyjama trousers bagging round his knees, and a full list of non-negotiable demands. Orange juice in the beaker with two handles, an oatmeal biscuit broken in four precise quadrants, the *Sword in the Stone* video and the Osh Kosh dungarees. Diana, beside me, was technically awake but tactically deaf, this being her privilege for clearing up after last night's dinner party.

'It's only fucking seven o'clock, Dewi. Go back to bed.'

'Don't swear in front of him, Phil,' said Diana from beneath her pile of pillows. 'He told the nursery nurse to bugger off last week.'

'You swear in front of him.'

'I don't say fuck.'

'Mummy said "fuck",' said Dewi. 'Fuck Mummy, fuck Mummy.'

'I should be so lucky,' I told his beautiful, innocent, four-year-old eyes, but Diana had returned to tactical deafness.

'Oh, could you check his pee this morning, Phil? And I'd love a cup of tea. I did do it yesterday.'

So I led Dewi into the bathroom, and steered the stream from his tiny penis into the jam jar that we kept there. And it was as clear as it always was.

'Is it all right, Dad?'

'It looks great. I'm going to have some on my cornflakes.' And he giggled.

There'd been some kidney problems when he was born. He was two months premature and the tubes weren't all developed or something. There'd been kidney infections and months of antibiotics, but he was fine now. He'd been fine for years, but Diana still insisted on this rigmarole of checking his urine every day for cloudiness, which was as much to do with oppressing me as protecting Dewi, but why bother to argue.

I poured Dewi some juice, and broke up a biscuit, and plugged in the video. 'Do the bit where Merlin and Wart are goldfish, Dad.' And I fast-forwarded to the fish dance and left him to it. There were four heavies and one tabloid on the mat, most of which would hit the bin unread on Monday. I squinted sideways at the tabloid masthead, hoping the article wouldn't be there, but it was. 'Malcolm Rutherford talks to Phil "Phworr" First about MONEY, MENTAL BREAKDOWN AND MOTHERS-IN-LAW!' Oh Christ.

Diana made the tea on Saturday, so I knew I owed her this one. When affection runs low in a household you start to monitor it carefully like shipwrecked sailors with their last slice of Spam. Before we married there was lots of affection, gallons of the stuff, just sloshing around. You'd make tea, massage feet, buy flowers, give in first in the argument – all that stuff, and nobody would be counting. There was no double-entry book-keeping to say who'd been kinder to whom that month.

But something has depleted the stock. There's been a run on the currency of kindness and we're both counting now. I did breakfast in bed for the last three Sundays, but Diana says that she took the children out two Saturdays running so I could work. But the last Saturday when I was working I had to fix her mother's lavatory cistern so the favour doesn't count, does it? And what about me taking Dewi to school every morning last week so Diana could get to her homeopathy class? Cancelled out apparently, because on Wednesday I forgot Dewi's PE kit and he had to wear his knickers in gym, which made him cry.

'You checked his pee, didn't you?' she said when I got back upstairs.

'Yes, I checked his pee.'

'And gave him a drink?'

'And gave him a drink.'

Diana halted, momentarily baffled, and I dumped my cargo on the bed.

'Tea, toast, papers.'

'Oh no, you didn't leave the toast flat, did you? It goes like an old flannel.'

'Yes, I left the toast flat because the toast rack has disappeared into Dewi's Lego box. And I didn't bring the fruit sugar because I forgot to go to the health food store yesterday. And I didn't iron the newspaper because I'm not the fucking butler, okay?'

'There's no need to be so stroppy.'

'And you could say thank you.'

'*Thank* you.'

It's amazing, isn't it? Two grown-up people with university degrees, wide reading and a fairly well-developed sense of irony. We snigger at these conversations when Alan Ayckbourn or Mike Leigh does them, and yet we do them anyway. A futile, tireless, playground bickering that even Dewi would get bored with in five minutes, and yet this is marriage. And it is everyone's marriage, because I have heard it in friends' houses when they don't know you are listening, or they have switched you off.

'What have you done with my tape-recorder batteries?'

'I never *touch* your tape-recorder batteries.'

'Well someone has moved them.'

'If your study wasn't such a bloody mess . . .'

'It's *my* study and I know where things are so long as people don't keep messing with it.'

'*Your* study. *Your* study. I wish I had a room I could shut myself off from the rest of the world and please my bloody self.'

'Well of course you don't *need* a room to shut people out . . .'

'And what's *that* supposed to mean?'

'For a start the total lack of *sex* in this house for the last three months.'

And so we leap nimbly from batteries to sex to laundry to privacy to child-minding to tea-making to tidiness to breakages to overwork, to sex, and on and on and on. When you meet and fall in love there is nothing you aren't eager to agree on. I pretended to like Joni Mitchell and Tolkien. Diana feigned attentiveness to my theories of comedy, and tried hard to find George Orwell interesting. We celebrated our mutual tastes for liver and bacon, fish pie and Woody Allen as astounding coincidences, full of promising portent for future compatibility.

Then suddenly you don't agree on anything any more. I could argue with Diana now about whether it's better to put rice or peas in the salt-cellar (it's peas, because rice gets in the little hole). We can have a shouting match over whether to knot the bin bag or use a tie (knots are stronger). We've had set-tos over what you can put in the dishwasher (bone-handled knives are fine in my opinion); how to get to Muswell Hill (much quicker via Cranley Gardens); the carcinogenic properties of sugar (bullshit); and the dangers of swallowing Lego bricks (non-existent). We could probably have a pretty good row over whether it's three forty-five or a quarter to four. She says tom*ah*to and I say tom*ay*to, but it's too late to call the whole thing off.

They'd used one of my least favourite pictures for the article, taken from floor level at one of the Amnesty concerts, and making me look sweaty, hunchbacked and hysterical – a pocket Mussolini with a masturbatory stick-mike jammed up my nose. *Former socialist Phil First has dumped equal relations with erstwhile partner Reg 'Last' Goldberg. 'We were best mates,' says First, whose one-man show opens on BBC 2 this week, 'but I'm on my own now.'*

Friends of Goldberg say he is hurt by the split in the best-known duo in new-wave comedy, but the wild-haired comic with the funny walk is too upset to make any public comment.

'Fucking bastard.'

'What's that?' said Diana, through a mouthful of Butter Osborne.

'This cunt Rutherford is making out I've split with Reg.'

She studied the opening paragraphs over my shoulder.

'Did you say you were on your own?'

'I might have said those words, but he's taken it totally out of context.'

'Who do you think these friends of Reg are?'

'Figments of this little shit's imagination. Reg probably refused to talk to him, or more likely he didn't bother to ring him up in the first place, but just decided to invent something that seemed plausible and legally fireproof.' I read on.

First, who likes to make much of his Welsh, working-class origins, drives a plush Mercedes, and lives in an elegant Hampstead house, the home of his mother-in-law, actress Adrienne Wallis, whose father was John Gascoigne, the noted art collector and criminal barrister. 'You don't have any of the traditional mother-in-law problems?' I asked him.

'Oh, she lives in the basement,' said First with a laugh. 'We think she's a lot better off down there.'

'I've never claimed I was working class in my life.'

'You do go on about being Welsh,' Diana said. 'And I

told you people would say the Mercedes was swanking. I wonder how he got the stuff about my grandfather?'

First and Last were among the stars of the early seventies alternative cabaret scene based on London's Comedy Store, but came to wider fame with the late night Radio Two series Wired For Sound, with their celebrated sketches of a pair of police phone tappers, eavesdropping on the conversations of government ministers and opposition alike . . .

'Well, that's quite accurate,' Diana said.

'Except that it was late, not early seventies; we never played at the Comedy Store; *Wired For Sound* was on Radio Four, not Radio Two, and they were MI5 not policemen. Four salient facts and he's got all four wrong. I'm surprised the stupid sod can spell his own name.'

'You don't think you're just nit-picking do you?' said Diana. 'You're always saying it's the publicity that matters. And the general drift seems fairly true.'

'That I've split with Reg?'

'Well, you have *talked* about it sometimes.'

'*With* Reg. And what about this crap about exiling my poor old mother-in-law to the rat-infested basement?'

'He doesn't say *anything* about rats. And anyway she does live in the basement.'

'It's a ground-floor semi-basement; with a garden; full of cat shit. And I only agreed to live here in the first place under pressure, and on condition we had quite separate accommodation.'

'Well I think you're just cross that it's not some piece of PR puff like that *Time Out* profile,' she told me. 'He's actually quite observant about the way you sit, with your hands stuffed under your backside. And the way you smack your lips at the end of your sentences. And you are getting bald on top.'

'Look, this thing is a straight hatchet job. Lies and distortions from beginning to end.'

'You tell stories on stage – about yourself, about your family, about me – which aren't true.'

'But that's a fucking performance. This is supposed to be a newspaper, which has some kind of obligation to objective reality.'

'People don't always see things from the same point of view,' said Diana.

'Well I'm going to get the bastard,' I told her, though of course I never did.

CHAPTER SEVEN

What is it about the BBC that always gets up my nose? Thank you, no, this is a rhetorical question, because I can start listing it as soon as I drive up to the gate. The grinning security men for a start, who refuse to let you in when there are dozens of free parking spaces. 'Sorry, *sir* (a glance at the leather jacket), but you'll have to try the White City car park.' And the White City car park is a mile away, with a walk back down narrow sidewalks of packed dirt and railway sleepers, flinching in the blast and backwash of eighteen-wheeler trucks.

And when you get back to the gates they are grinning even harder, these Toytown soldiers with their grog-blossom noses and campaign ribbons. Like the coppers and commissionaires and school porters, they are all pumped up with the reflected glory of the Falklands that has put the uniformed mob back on the map again. They may still have to defer to all these scruffy subversive softies who sidle past on the way to make their clever-dick programmes, but there's no doubting who's on top these days. Ho-no.

And there is this self-conscious squalor about the Beeb which gets under my fingernails as well. The sickly yellow reception, and the threadbare carpets, and the fag-scorched Festival of Britain furniture. All those claustrophobically curving corridors, with their grimy parallel tracks at hip and elbow height; the oily, sulphurous tea in the heat-warped plastic beakers; the elbowed jackets with that crease between the bum-vents like the hinge of a tweedy cat flap; the anxious air of public-service piety on every face.

What they are telling you, of course, is that they are *saving money*. The reason they go without the pot plants and the leggy secretaries and the Alessi cafetières normally necessary to the creative spirit is *artistic integrity*, but you shouldn't believe a word of it. Downstairs, on the ground floor, where the Outside Broadcast trucks are banked two deep on the access road, there are a dozen studios, each one a Darryl Zanuck wet dream. Mobile cameras the size of plesiosaurs, control consoles like the fighting bridge of a Dreadnought, and overhead cranes that would do for a Clydeside shipyard. Saving money? The place is a money *furnace*.

Reg and I could have made the first series for half the price, with a Wapping warehouse, a four-man crew, and a freelance video-edit suite, but oh no, where would our artistic integrity be then? We had to have a fleet of OB trucks the size of furniture vans, fifteen layabouts with keyrings clipped to their belts, a catering wagon to manufacture their sausage sarnies, and three sulky debs to buy their snout for them. And what happened when we needed a couple of dancers for the launderette crucifixion sketch? 'Terribly sorry, Philip, but we do have to keep an eye on the budget.'

The hassle we had with that sketch was unbelievable, right across the board from 'Would it offend the Christians?' to 'Did it exclude the Muslims?' Never mind was it *funny* or not. But that was nothing to the earache we got over *Wired For Sound*. If our two secret policemen were going to wiretap Labour then they would have to bug the Tories too. The SDP had to have a mention for the sake of balance, and weren't the Greens becoming quite a significant force? Perhaps it would be better to avoid politics altogether, since this did come under Light Entertainment after all.

The Beeb, it gradually dawned on me, had carried the concept of 'balance' to its logical conclusion of complete paralysis. Fairness had become impotence; reasonableness had mutated into bland unreason. By ostensibly eschewing politics it had ruled out all political positions but its own: which was the self-serving C-politics of caution, consensus and corporatism. Diana says I sound like the Duchess of Gridlock when I start to go on like this, but when it comes to the Beeb I'm with Mrs T. The old Establishment doesn't live in the Oxbridge common rooms or Church House, or the sidestreets of Whitehall. The government-in-exile is living in a shabby Festival of Britain office block at Shepherd's Bush, with a keyring clipped to its belt and a cat-flap jacket – and roll on the day when it's all squashed under a big fat satellite footprint.

I'd never have done another series for them at all if Hon hadn't twisted my arm. She was riding high there now: her title was Acting Deputy Assistant Controller of Kiddiecrap or something, but her real job was trawling the club scene for talent with teen-appeal. The cat-flap men all assumed an air of genial bafflement when the phrase 'young people' came up in conference, and handed the potato to Hon, who at thirty was still in nappies so far as Auntie was concerned.

'Frankly they're all shitting themselves over satellite,' she told me, 'and half their best directors have pissed off to independent production companies. It's different from two years ago, Phil. You can write your own production schedule now. Hire who the hell you want. Shoot it in a railway arch in Camden Town. Dictate your own percentage of foreign sales and video royalties.'

'So why haven't you pissed off to an independent?' I asked her suspiciously.

'Because when I've got the right people and the right contacts and the right money I'm going to start my own fucking company.'

I thought she probably would as well, because while Diana had rather dwindled in the last decade, Hon had got bigger. Not physically bigger, of course, though she looked it in her three-inch spikes and sticky bouffant, but psychologically larger. She swore all the time now, for instance, while Diana had got squeamish about fucks and buggers. She battled her way through the greedy new world while Diana just moaned about it, and quoted me doomsday paragraphs from the *Guardian*. Diana had faded into magnolia emulsion and putty-coloured T-shirts, but Hon had grown brighter, in jumpers like TV test patterns, fluorescent spectacle frames and Day-Glo cycling shorts.

And we seemed to have buried the past somewhere along the way. The Oswald party disaster, for instance; that was all written off years ago in one throwaway line: 'Remember we got so pissed and I dared you to strip off, Phil? He did look funny, Di, when I turned the lights on him.' And thus a mountain of shame and loathing is dissolved.

'How's Diana?'

'She's fine. Doing a homeopathy course.' Hon led me across the sick-yellow reception to the wheezing lift bank (half out of order – *saving money*) and punched buttons.

'What about, um, Alec?'

'Ancient history,' said Hon.

She had avoided marriage and children so far, and opted instead for a succession of incrementally more interesting, and wealthy, lovers, invariably married. There was the bass guitarist from that heavy metal band – Manifold Coupling or something. Then the last *New Statesman* editor-but-one; then that Tory MP who just got out from the Telecom shares scam; and then Alec Smith the publishing tycoon I'd met in the Groucho one time – but I was clearly out of date. 'I really think Hon has lost her way, you know,' Diana told me, while I wondered enviously how we could start losing ours.

'That was a good interview they ran in the filth last Sunday.'

'I thought it was incredibly snide,' I told her.

'Christ, they used a big picture, they mentioned the series and there weren't more than half a dozen serious libels. What more do you want?'

'Oh, I dunno. A flattering profile in the *London Review of Books*, gums that don't bleed when I brush my teeth, a Mercedes SEL coupé, an advancing hairline, a receding paunch, more sex . . .'

'Well, you'll just have to wait until after lunch,' said Hon, as the lift whimpered to a halt, six inches short of the floor (*saving money*). 'Pillock wanted us to eat in the Bridge Restaurant, but I said you had an appointment. We can go to Julie's.'

Pillock was Jeremy Bullock, the series producer: a cat-flap man with a flowered Liberty's tie and Buddy Holly horn-rims that were so fantastically and asymmetrically out of date they were on the brink of being fashionable again, though he was certainly unaware of their impending trendiness, and would be equally certain to change them the instant that the cusp occurred. As a contraindicator of fashion, designers would do well to follow Pillock around with notebook and camera, for when he stopped wearing flares or stack heels or cheesecloth, they'd be sure to be on the way back. There might even be the germ of a sketch there, but it wasn't the moment. We found him in a hot beige room on the seventh floor, a room with yellow cellophane taped over the windows like a struggling suburban draper's.

'Wonderful scripts, Philip. Everyone's very excited about them.'

'You hate them.'

'They're *perfect*, Phil. Wouldn't change a word.'

'You only want a complete rewrite?'

'Ha ha ha,' said Bullock, and he did say it rather than laugh it. 'It's really just a few tiny things. Hardly worth bothering ourselves about at this stage. You might even want to leave it to the script editors.'

'No.'

'Ha ha ha.' He removed his glasses to polish them on his tie, and his face, which looked youthful behind its plastic scaffolding, collapsed abruptly into old age. 'Well, why don't we go through them one by one, since you happen to be here.'

'It is strange I should be strolling down the hard shoulder of the Westway just at the very moment you thought of having a script conference.' Hon giggled and Bullock blinked, his unglazed eyes as blind as boiled eggs.

'I'm sorry?'

'Oh, never mind, Jeremy.'

I wish I went to meetings all the time, like Hon and Pillock and Saul and half the other people I know. When you spend most of your life flogging a word processor, meetings feel like nothing. They feel like mucking about, having a chat – but meetings are *work* to these people. Whenever you hear them swanking about how hard they work you have to remember they're not really working, they're just going to meetings. When someone like Saul is crashed out on his office sofa he's not just asleep like an ordinary mortal; he is preparing for a meeting. When he goes out to Sweetings afterwards, he's not getting pissed with his mates; they're having a post-meeting debriefing. He chats to someone by the coffee machine and he's in a meeting. He chats to two people and he's in conference. Three people and it's a brainstorming session. He reads the *FT* sports page and he's researching the financial markets; doodles on a Post-it note and he's writing a report.

It's the same with these politicians who are always talking about how little sleep they get, how many hours they work, how many miles they travel. It's all crap. They lie in bed all morning eating pop and chocolates. And when they're not doing that they have meetings, and when they're not having meetings they're having a 'working breakfast' or 'working lunch' – which is just a meeting with your mouth full.

What happens in this meeting? Pillock says he wants the cannibal sketch and the Westland sketch abandoned – 'just a tweak here and there'. He wants programmes three and seven completely rewritten – 'just run them through your typewriter'. He wants six weeks' work, in fact, and he wants them in the two weeks between now and production. I throw a strategic tantrum and start talking about Channel Four. Hon suggests another meeting, which is brilliant of course, because Pillock can't resist them, and by the time we have it there will be no time to change anything.

Another meeting, the same day. I am sitting in, on, around a sag bag, on the floor of a Highgate sitting room. Evening sunshine, filtered through the leaves of a giant fig tree, sprawls over the polished parquet floor. In the centre of the room, her tasty brown legs arranged in an effortless lotus position, is Serena Arum, the leader of our natural child-birth class. Around the walls in attitudes that range from discomfort to rapt enthusiasm are another dozen people, all in couples. We have all taken our shoes off and they are lined up beside the door: Reeboks, Timberlands, desert boots, Korean canvas sandals, Natural Shoe Store clonkies, and a still-archaic pair of Kickers (no longer, thank God, Diana's). Not a polished toecap to be seen.

We are going through the process of introducing ourselves, an inevitable ritual now of every large meeting, from corporate boardroom to Kilburn squat. Officially it is to set everyone at their ease, to draw them into the circle. Unofficially, I suspect, it has the same purpose as calling the register at school – a disciplinary routine which establishes the ascendancy of the leader, and stops everyone nattering.

Robert is a healer, Jasmine runs a stall at Camden Lock, Damien is a gardener, Chloe makes jewellery, Edward runs a schools' theatre project, Amanda is a community liaison officer, Joe is looking for himself, and helping out meanwhile at an after-school play centre . . . They're joke jobs, all of them ('What's *your* job then?' – Diana), but they must make money at them somehow or other, because it's fifty guineas a head for just three of Serena's feelgood sessions. I contemplate being a South African mercenary, a pork butcher, a whale processor, a tester of shampoos on bunny rabbits. But when the turn comes around to introduce myself, I decide on a more modestly vicious career.

'I'm a management accountant for Price Waterhouse.'

'*Phil!*' This is a fierce whisper from Diana, at my side, and a ripple of gentle bafflement spreads around the room. 'I thought you said he was Phil Thingummy . . . Could have sworn he was the one that used to be on TV . . .' But Serena handles it deftly. 'Of course we all know Philip better as one half of First and Last. Welcome to prospective fatherhood, Phil.'

'I'm a father already.'

'Then we'll all be able to benefit from your experience,' says Serena smoothly.

She is dressed in a purple leotard with a broad black sash. Long, black, glossy hair, a handsome hooked nose, and a brown, bendy body that holds my attention a lot more closely than anything she says. For this is all to do with recapturing childbirth from the male hegemony of doctors, and throwing off the tyranny of drugs and anaesthesia, and learning to understand the rhythms of your body, and all that crap.

Diana is more and more into all this stuff: homeopathy and reflexology and aromatherapy and astrology and acupuncture and meditation and yoga and Rolfing and Alexander Technique and shamanism. And that's the most stupid thing about it – that you can be into *all* of them, at the same time.

'It's like Chesterton said,' I tell her. 'When people stop believing in God they don't start believing in nothing, they believe in *everything*.'

'But you don't believe in God,' says Diana, 'and you don't believe in everything.' So she's not stupid you see, or if she is stupid, it's in quite a clever sort of way.

'That's not the point.'

'And you always used to say Chesterton was a reactionary old fart.'

'Old *fuck*. And that's not the point either. The point is how can you go around believing in all these contradictory things? How can you believe one day that sticking needles in yourself makes you better and the next day that you have to swallow squashed buttercups in brandy?'

'Bach flower remedies.'

'Whatever they're called. They're mutually exclusive systems.'

'They're not. They're complementary.'

'Only because all these profiteering quacks who peddle them are unwilling to push their theories to any logical or coherent conclusions. They won't even *test* them properly.'

'It's because double-blind testing isn't appropriate,' she says. 'It's a hostile, technocratic approach which upsets the fragile, symbiotic environment in which alternative medicine can work.'

'Well I call it moving the fucking goalposts,' I tell her, 'and the day I'll believe in it all is the day I see someone crawling out of a car crash with his leg hanging off and asking for a Bach flower remedy. There's no atheists in foxholes, and I bet there's not many homeopaths in labour wards when a baby's coming out back to front and sideways.'

And she flinches, because there are nasty memories here, of Dewi being born, eight weeks early and just about everything wrong with him. But I carry on anyway, because this is becoming one of my favourite set pieces.

'I mean, either we're meat machines who need to be fixed when we break down, with scalpels and antibiotics, or we are blobs of ectoplasm or orgones or whatever, who make ourselves better by sniffing daisies. You can't have it both ways. It's like believing in a flat earth and a round one at the same time. Aristotle for breakfast and Galileo for lunch.'

'Or Newton for lunch and Einstein for tea.'

'What?'

'We believe in Newtonian and Einsteinian physics at the same time,' says Diana smugly. 'A cause and effect universe on the one hand and a random one on the other. Two mutually exclusive systems which coexist quite happily.'

She might be right as well, because I know practically nothing about science though I have almost total respect for it. It works; it fixes my broken arm; makes my car run; cures my ear infection; stops my house falling down. But Diana, who knows lots about science, seems to have no respect for it at all. She has a first-class BSc from Cardiff University and an MD from University College. She not only understands how levers and light-bulbs and car engines work (I haven't got a clue), but she can also describe the structure of ribonucleic acid, solve third-order equations and carry out an emergency appendectomy in a snowstorm with a blunt breadknife if she had to. Diana knows everything about science so far as somebody like me is concerned, and yet she believes in fairies at the bottom of the garden.

My mother used to believe that a cut between thumb and forefinger gave you lockjaw, that a blow from a goose's wing could break your leg, that potato water gave you warts and that every plant in the garden apart from the apple tree was poisonous. What has changed? Diana believes that bracken gives you cancer, and mutton, and coke, and white sliced bread. She thinks aluminium saucepans make you mad, and beef, and lead pipes. She thinks that salt gives you heart attacks, aspirins give you stomach ulcers, eggs give you salmonella, cheese gives you listeria and practically everything gives you migraine.

God knows, she may be right, some of them might give you some of those things, but I haven't got the time to worry about it. I'm careful when I cross roads, try not to smoke, control the booze habit, but I haven't got the time for all the other stuff. You need a joke job as a part-time gardener or jewellery-maker just to keep up to date with it all. And life's too short to spend it worrying about new things to shorten your life.

So why am I here, wrestling with a creaking bag of polystyrene granules in a Highgate sitting room, listening to some planet person in a purple leotard spouting gibberish? Serena has told us we can have successful births if we listen to soothing music, and if we take favourite cushions with us to hospital. Smooth deliveries are guaranteed by the squatting position, and the birthing stool, and the Michel Odent submarine technique. Dim lighting is effective, and so are breathing techniques. Use scented oils; take a favourite night-dress; walk about between contractions.

'Yes, Phil?'

I've got my hand in the air, and although we've been told this is a *participatory* group where everyone's contribution is welcome I can tell that mine isn't. Believe me. I've stood on too many stages not to recognize the wary, combative glint in Serena's eye. It's probably my half-hearted contribution to the breathing exercise, or the attack of the giggles I got when we were practising squatting, or the impatient squeaks that keep coming from my sag bag, but Serena has me down as a troublemaker.

'I was just wondering which was the most important.'

'I'm sorry?'

'Which of these techniques will be most important to use in the delivery room? I mean, if Diana's having a contraction when she's squatting and the Paul Simon tape runs out should I turn it over for "Mother and Child Reunion", for instance?'

'*Phil!*' It is Diana again, tugging nervously at a fold of my jeans.

'Or if the third stage of labour begins while I'm still applying the scented oil, d'you think I should finish the bottle or ring for the midwife?'

'I think Phil is just having a little tease,' says Serena.

'No really, I'm serious. There's such a lot to take in at once. So many different options. I was just wondering if perhaps you could give us a list of priorities. You know: cushions at the bottom; then scented oil; then squats; then music; then birthing stool; then if all else fails, when exactly do we call the consultant for a shot of pethidine up the arse.'

'Oh do stop it, Phil,' says Diana loudly and clearly. There are a dozen pairs of eyes inspecting me with wonder and pity. Mercenary, pork butcher, accountant. And so I stop, But I've got Serena tabbed; I've got her number now, this rising executive in the new anxiety industry. A Sloane Street new-lifer, with a failed Cert. Ed., a correspondence course in psychobabble and a head for figures. The fresh-faced natural look is cheek gloss, Champneys and Clinique exfoliating scrub at fifteen pounds a bottle. The husband (name of Boru if you can believe it) only appears briefly at the door in saffron harem pants, and as co-author on the cover of Serena's books. But he's probably too busy in the back room, burning up the keys on his calculator, because twelve people at fifty guineas a head, times five or six classes a day, with no visible overheads, is healthy stuff. The Bach flower remedies and natural childbirth bullshit are paying for a house in Highgate that I couldn't bloody afford, and the matched pair of hot hatchbacks in the driveway, and I wouldn't mind betting a string of Harley Street consultants.

'You're very *anxious* about your role as a partner, Philip,' says Serena, silkily, and there we have it. The shot across the bows which says if you don't shut your lower-class lip we're going to drag your sweaty little inadequacies right out on the parquet floor for public inspection. And all in the word 'anxious', which is one of those wonderful cosh words like 'defensive' or 'unprofessional' or 'inappropriate' which smack you right down with no possibility of reply. How can you defend yourself without being defensive? Please Dr Freud how do I avoid seeming anxious about my anxiety?

'I'm more *anxious* we don't end up in the delivery room with a lot of golden expectations about natural childbirth, followed by a lot of guilt if things go wrong and we can't measure up to them.'

'The techniques on this course . . .' says Serena.

'And I'm very *anxious* we should get something for our money other than a string of platitudes.'

'If money is the problem you are welcome to a refund in full at any stage in the course,' says Serena, icily now.

'Look,' says Damien the gardener, from his sag bag, 'this really is getting . . .'

'I think you are upsetting some of our group, Philip.'

'And I think you should shut up,' says Diana, who chooses this moment to burst into tears.

But I'm right about Serena, even though I'll never be able to prove it. I know I'm right because when I am getting our coats from the hallway at the end, and I'm all alone, she comes up to me and asks if we are coming again, hoping that we won't. So of course I say I wouldn't miss it for the world, and she smiles the silky smile and we look at each other with mutual knowledge and mutual loathing, and Serena says, 'Well if you do, I hope you can manage to make a *big effort* to take your nasty little eyes off my tits.'

CHAPTER EIGHT

And I was looking at Serena's tits. Guilty as charged. But what do these women expect when they flaunt it all over the place in their leotards and bustiers and little Lycra miniskirts? Boys, you may not have noticed this, because it's been happening quite gradually, but there are girls walking around out there in outfits that would have had them locked up at the fever point of the Swinging Sixties. I saw this kid the other day, about seventeen years old, outside Waitrose in the Finchley Road, and she's wearing a kind of red satin waspie, half laced up the front, a ragged denim jacket on top and *nothing else*. I'm not kidding – there's a pair of denim knickers with a suspender belt over the top holding up some black stockings, but that's it. No skirt, no trousers, and nobody passing by turns a hair. *I* hardly turn a hair, and only then when I hear her asking a policeman the way to West End Lane, and he calls her madam. *Madam!*

Now don't get me wrong. I'm not one of these deserve-what-they-get characters. I'm not standing at the bar of the local with a *Sun* stuck down my arse pocket telling my mates as how half these birds gets raped are really begging for it. No. What gets me is the *discrepancy* that's lurking here: the total severance of sexual signals and sexual behaviour. For if I'd gone up to the Waitrose waspie and patted her on her perfect little bum, or even just asked her up to Farquharson's for a friendly coffee, the best I could expect would be a crisp fuck off, and the worst a piercing scream for the departing plod.

Put it the other way around and imagine me walking

down the Finchley Road in PVC waders, a silver Lurex jockstrap and a broderie anglaise blouse sawn off just below the pecs. All very nice, but what are the results? One, all the blokes think I'm a prat. Two, all the girls think I'm a pervert. Three, I don't walk fifty yards without the plod feeling my broderie anglaise collar for me.

So there's a special kind of licence been granted here, a licence to the girls only, which allows them to dress like whores but expect to be treated like nuns, with real sex squeezed out of existence in the middle. We're living in liberated times is what you read in the papers. Children of the promiscuous sixties, wallowing in a tide of random sex and hard porn, but it's all crap. The eighties are the most puritanical decade since the First World War. Have a riffle through the top shelf at Smith's if you don't believe me; rent yourself an Electric Blue video for some sociological research. Girls on horseback, girls in bubble baths, girls in the innocent athletic sweat-sheen of the squash court. And even when they are all togged up in the tart's gear of stockings and suspenders and basques it's all so stunningly innocent: such anodyne, anaphrodisiac *fun*.

Ah, but it turns you on, you say, and so it might, but this is a third- or fourth-level conditioned reflex you are feeling. Remember Pavlov and his dogs, who learned to drool to the sound of the bell rather than the dinner? Well, when your groin twitches over the centre spread in the soft porn mag it's that old electric bell you are rising to and not the smell of meat, because there's no real sex there, not a sniff of it. Like the pork in the deep-frozen sausage roll it's just a marketing memory now.

My groin was like that for years, slumbering away in the permafrost at the back of the freezer. You take it out now and again when you're doing a blitz of the fridge, then put it back because it's not really worth the trouble of defrosting. What's this thing dangling between my legs? Oh I remember, it was for sex, but then they called the whole thing off as a bad idea. They've got porn mags and smut videos and tarts' outfits to make up for it. How did Dewi get conceived? Total fluke, because even then Diana and I were only doing it about four times a year. How come Diana is seven months pregnant now? I deny all responsibility. She must either have been watching the calendar like a hawk and sprang the annual lay on me at the height of ovulation, or maybe it was just one of Reg's immaculate conceptions. We promiscuously used the same flannel one morning, or shared a toothbrush in an abandoned moment. I dunno, I really don't.

Probably the only reason my miserable member had been taking an interest in Serena Arum's purple leotard was because of Hon. You can go without sex for years, hardly noticing it apart from a certain irritable congestion in the sinuses – but once you actually get close to some sex again you start responding to it all over the place, and I'd been getting more than close. Because we've skipped an episode in this day of meetings, haven't we? There's a bit of a gap here between my BBC meeting with Hon and Pillock in the morning, and my Highgate antenatal class with Diana in the evening.

It even crossed Diana's unsuspicious mind as we set off for the evening class: she waddling cautiously around to the passenger door of the Mercedes, and me keeping a responsible, paternal eye out up the mews outside Aberdare House, for mad mechanics trying out their customers' supercars.

'So what were you up to this afternoon, Phil?' she asked me brightly as I popped the central locking and tossed some videos on to the back seat. The interested wife; involved in her husband's work; adding still more sturdy cement to the relationship that is already eight years and nearly two children old.

'Oh, just meetings,' I told her innocently, and stepped straight out into the path of an Aston Martin DBS, which stopped three smoking, shuddering centimetres from my shin. But I did not tell a lie.

The meeting started at Julie's restaurant in Holland Park where we had thin asparagus and fat Bayonne oysters, and played footsie under the table, invisible behind the potted ferns. Hon was smoking one cigarette per oyster while I drank a glass of Chablis to each spear of asparagus. There had been certain preliminaries to all this, of course. A number of rather unnecessary postcards and over-extended phone calls. We had even kissed once in the back of a taxi; apologized to each other for being foolish; and then kissed again. I had never betrayed Diana before ('cheated' is American and evasive I think), but there seemed to be a pattern to follow: some invisible machinery was operating in the background and I surrendered to it gladly enough. Perhaps Hon was operating it, because she had certainly had more practice.

'What would you *really* like to do this afternoon?' she asked me, for instance, and there is only one possible answer when a woman asks you that, in full face flush across a lunch table, when your knee is already locked between her thighs. You'd like to watch *Match of the Day*? Replace the big-end shells on the motor? Finish reading *The Devil's Alternative* for the third time? No.

'I'd like to go to bed with you,' I told her, with a casual chuckle, and there was no going back.

'Can't go to my place, I'm afraid,' she said. 'Someone might be coming round.'

'Someone with a key?'

'Someone with a key.'

'Um. There's a lot of bed and breakfast places in Shepherd's Bush Road,' I said. 'We could drive around and . . .' Perhaps with any luck they would all be full.

'You must be fucking joking,' said Hon. 'We'll go to the Savoy.'

'That's about two hundred quid a night.'

'What's the matter? Don't you think I'm worth it, Philip?'

'I didn't mean . . . I'm sorry, I just . . .'

'It's all right. You just ring them up and ask if they've got a day let. It's usually a little room they rent out for the afternoon. All the posh hotels do it. They pretend it's for people from out of town to change for Royal garden parties and so on, but they're just up-market knocking-shops really.' And she eased down her last oyster, drained the dregs of her Chablis and prepared herself to be led astray.

While she went to the cloakroom I phoned the hotel and asked the waiter for the bill and a taxi. Every divorce I'd ever heard about seemed to centre on Access receipts, so I paid cash, shredded up the bill and left the restaurant matchbook on the table.

'I've seen you on stage, haven't I?'

The waiter was about nineteen, with a carbuncular neck, a blond flat-top and one earring. I imagined him shouting 'Heeyar' at the back of some club crowd, swigging Pils by the neck, and it was a plausible picture.

'No, you must be thinking of somebody else.'

'Garn, you're that Phil First. Seen you on that late night thing on BBC2.'

'As a matter of fact I'm a management accountant with Price Waterhouse.'

'Give us your autograph, will you, Phil?' So I scribbled my name illegibly on the menu, hoping he would do what every other autograph nuisance did, which was lose it immediately.

Hon was wearing a black Lycra dress from Swanky Modes with sculpted breast cups and a ruched waist that bit deep into the curve of her coke-bottle body. A silver leather jacket from Katharine Hamnett was slung over one shoulder. 'They're never going to let us in the Savoy looking like this,' I told her.

'The only accessory they're interested in is your Amex card,' she said, and the certainty of what we were going to do suddenly turned my knees to water. On the pavement outside the restaurant she kissed me hard on the mouth, and grabbed me by the hand. Something small and soft and hot as a bird passed from her palm into mine.

'What's this?' I said, not daring to look, but knowing anyway.

'My knickers,' said Hon. 'You're not getting out of this now, Phil First.'

I didn't want to get out of it, not really, but I was worrying about my performance. I mean, Hon had probably been to bed with hundreds of people, while I'd only ever screwed four, or was it three? I'll have to go back and check my story on that. All I'd had for the last half-dozen years was my quarterly bunk-up with Diana, an encounter which had increasingly acquired all the enthusiasm and inventiveness of a minor surgical procedure.

'You don't mind if I close the window?' she told the driver, and slid the dividing glass shut before he could grunt his reply. She arranged her jacket and shoulder-bag on the seat. 'Now I think I'd like you to kneel on the floor.'

'What for?'

'Oh, don't be so bloody dense.'

Sound thickened in my ears, and sweat cooled my spine. 'We're sitting in a Wednesday-afternoon traffic jam on the Bayswater Road, Hon.'

'Then there's fuck-all better to do is there?'

'Do you know how Pinocchio and Snow White make love?' I asked her, playing for time.

'How?'

'She sits on his face and makes him tell her lies.'

'Get on with it, Phil.'

And so, with the odd, anxious glance over my shoulder, at the driver's hogged, impassive neck, I knelt on the floor and did as I was told.

'Is this all right?' I asked her, somewhere around Marble Arch.

'Lovely. But I think the trick is to keep your tongue still and let the taxi do the vibrating.'

'Oh, right.'

I laboured on in the dark tunnel of Lycra and lily of the valley, half listening to the muffled squawk of the driver's radio; sensing his route through the lurching of the slatted floor beneath my aching knees. Right down Park Lane, left into Piccadilly, a squealing stop at the lights outside the Royal Academy, which made me wince with pain and Hon gasp with pleasure.

'Would you mind driving us around St James's Park a few times?' I heard her call, and the driver grunted assent. For fuck's sake. Some mania for locomotion had possessed the woman, which was almost a quote from somewhere, but I couldn't think where. There was grit and toffee papers under my hands and a dagger blade in each kneecap. I had seldom felt less aroused.

I decided to become a lorry driver for a while, glancing down from my cab into the submarine light of the taxi beside me at the traffic lights. I noted the pale spread thighs of the woman in the back seat, and the urgent, burrowing back of the kneeling supplicant, his jacket rucked under his arms. Phworr. Take a butcher's at the back seat of this taxi, John. Thank you for not smoking, eh? Have to give the old woman a proper going over tonight.

I'd lost track of our route by now, but at a guess we were somewhere near the Victoria Memorial in front of Buckingham Palace, and for some reason seemed to be going round and round it. Snatches of conversation found their way past the clenching and unclenching of thigh muscles.

'Did you want to go round the park again, ma'am?'

'Oooh yes.'

'Beg pardon?'

'Mmmmmnnnn, yes. Like that.'

'One more time round the park it is.'

I heard the flight of geese taking off from the lake in St James's Park at just about the same time as Hon.

'You mind if I take a breather now?' I asked her in Trafalgar Square.

'No, that was very nice. I always enjoy coming by taxi.'

I straightened my jacket and took my seat beside her, very hot and out of breath. With her skirt adjusted and jacket folded across her lap, she looked perfectly composed.

'You've done this *before*?'

'Oh, I do it on my own sometimes. It's the diesel engine I think.' The pain disappeared from my knees and the numbness from my tongue – to be replaced by that unmistakable, lustful thickening at the base of the throat. All men think that women are better than they are: more sensible, more grown up, more hygienic. Women change their underwear, remember birthdays, clean lavatories, remember children's music lessons, and face up bravely to illness and death. It is we men who are the nose-pickers and spot-squeezers and masturbators. We are the ones who are furtive, lazy, unreliable and reckless, pushed to and fro by secret lusts and suppressed fantasies that are merely comic in the breezy air of feminine common sense. And so it was that half the notions I had ever had about female virtue – all the guilty impedimenta about the basic niceness of the other sex, which all men carry with them, was blown away on a simple phrase. *She did it on her own sometimes.* And she did it in *taxis*. Phworrrr!

I paid off the driver in the Strand, but he called us back before we had walked three yards.

'You haven't forgotten anything have you, guv?'

'Oh, sorry about that.'

I scrabbled shamefully on the back seat, for the tiny scrap of black silk.

'No problem, guv.' I turned to go.

'But you might like to know you've got a toffee paper stuck to your knee.'

'Then you ought to clean your bloody cab more often,' said Hon.

A flunkey in tails showed us to the room, which was small but very elegant, with wonderful, curvy, ocean-liner furniture, chunky chrome fittings, circular mirrors and a marble bathroom with a shower head like a car wash. The flunkey insisted on showing us how the taps worked in case we had never seen taps before, and on demonstrating the mysteries of the telephone and light switches. He then hung around for ages, shifting from foot to foot, clearing his throat in Bootsie and Snudge style, and asking if that would be all, until Hon told him to piss off.

'You don't think we should have given him a tip?'

'Why give someone a pound just because he's shown you how a fucking bath works?'

She turned the taps on again, and the great tub surged full and green in seconds, from powerful, concealed faucets.

'There's plenty of room for two in these things,' said Hon, and then she took all her clothes off.

I undressed more slowly, in the bedroom, hanging my clothes in the wardrobe. I tested the door lock, counted the miniatures of spirits in the refrigerator, and checked my teeth for fragments of asparagus in the circular mirror. I tried to imagine the reflection of two pale bodies in rut upon the bed below.

'Oh, *come on.*'

The bathroom was too steamy to see much more than a pinkish blur. I clambered heavily into the empty end of the tub and slid gingerly down into the suds. My coarse, hairy legs spliced with her pale, slippery ones and I felt the damp mound of her pubis beneath the sole of my foot. 'Oh, sorry.'

'This way round.' And she slithered about to lie alongside me, her breasts bobbing pink and slippery in the suds. The bath was so deep that we were both almost floating, our bodies weightless and sliding gently against each other in the warm water like basking seals. We kissed a soapy kiss, and my hands embarked on the routines of arousal, squeezing her nipples and gliding softly over her belly, but she stopped me. 'Not like that.'

'You're very bossy.'

'I want it like *this*.' And she seized my erection hard in her hand and pulled herself over me. It was so deft and easy, and I must have looked shocked, because she giggled, sending oily ripples down through her body and the water to where I bobbed and nuzzled in her, a nibbling, silken fish. And I tried to push, but she held back, teasing and nibbling at me in the blood-warm water. And as our bodies warmed and the water cooled I lost the sense of my skin boundaries, until I was floating in a dreamy vacuum, where all I could feel was the gliding heat of the lower belly and the silken lap of tongues in mouths half-filled with water.

'It's nice, isn't it?'

'You've done it before, I suppose.'

'Of course.'

'I'm glad,' I said, and I was.

We got out of the bath when the water became chilly and our fingertips were turning into grey Christmas trees, and we sawed each other dry on enormous white towels, and went to bed properly, and did it properly. But that is all repetition, unless you are there of course.

And then we dressed and said that was nice, and made vague arrangements, and walked out of the hotel into a different world. I was going to an antenatal class with my wife. Hon was meeting somebody at the Groucho for drinks. The man with the key to her flat, perhaps. The Strand looked the same with its gridlocked traffic and sick pigeons and smut drizzle. Lawyers and clerks and journalists were stamping home, eyes front, down the patched pavements towards Charing Cross. A tough-looking gypsy woman with a pinch-eyed child was begging outside McDonald's and I saw the child pick a chip from the litter bin and gobble it.

It was the same as three hours ago, but different, as if the colours had shifted subtly up the chromatic scale, or the sounds were transposed to be a different, brighter key. I remembered the moment in the Oswalds' garden, all that time ago, when I felt my life was pivoting, and I knew as my feet led me towards Leicester Square tube that it was the same change, but eight years late in arriving.

CHAPTER NINE

The set was one that we'd used a lot over the years. A sketchily drawn MI5 listening post, with a table; a few bits of electronic junk; and Reg and myself in Bakelite, Bomber Command headphones. 'Wired For Sound' was the script title, but Reg and I had always called it 'The Buggers'.

'What you listening to, then?' Reg was saying.

'Prince Charles on the phone to his grandma.'

'Wonderful old lady the Queen Mum,' said Reg. 'Eighty-six years old and she isn't even dead yet.'

'Wonderful.'

'I had that Ronald Reagan tapped last week. Seventy-four and he's still got his finger on the nuclear button. Zap the lot of us he could. My dad's younger than that and we won't even give him the controls to the telly.'

'So what you got on yours now?'

'*The Archers*,' Reg told me. 'Had that Cecil Parkinson on the job for a bit, but it was so boring I had to turn over. Where are the men of vision on the modern political stage?'

There was a snatch of the *Archers* theme tune, overlaid with orgasmic grunts, and a surge of giggles from the in-visible audience. I punched the fast-forward on the video, watching our faces become twitchy and mechanical on the screen. I'd wanted to run through the tapes of the last BBC series, to see what we'd been doing a year ago, but it made depressing viewing. 'The Buggers' was a good set-up: almost infinitely flexible, it could switch topics as fast as Reg and I could switch our phone taps. But I was getting bored with the relentlessly agitprop flavour of the gags, the routine slagging of Tories and royals and policemen.

I was getting right wing, Reg told me, and I told him to stuff his smug little categories up his self-righteous arse, which was surely big and baggy enough these days. The Tories had won two elections and were going to win a third, while all the left had to offer was an Unpopular Front of ill-assorted 'isms'. Reg and I were getting rich on a Tory-engineered consumer boom, and to pretend otherwise was the self-indulgent posturing of a superannuated student Trot – so I wasn't fucking right wing, just realistic, okay?

While the tape whimpered I stared out of my study window, down into the green well of the garden, where my mother-in-law was pottering about in a patch of sunshine, a trug across her forearm. From the mews beyond I could hear the phlegmy gurgle of an outsize engine running too slow: a Maserati maniac waiting to hoover one of us up as we stepped out of the gate. I'd written to the council about them three times; threatened legal action; organized a residents' action group. But Camden Council was more of a Spartist crèche than ever that year and said that workshops preserved the 'mixed character of the neighbourhood' – this is a Maserati garage we're talking about, remember. And the residents wimped out altogether and decided we must protect traditional skills and working-class jobs, and I just despair sometimes I really do.

So I went back to staring at the old ratbag as she waddled about the garden down below, much fatter than she had been before the last great suicide attempt. She was wearing a kind of striped marquee, from Laura Ashley of course, and I really don't know how I could ever have fucked her, even in fantasy. She was three feet across the hips at least these days, and with a belly like a bargee.

But once I'd told her we would stay on at Aberdare House for a while, she never mentioned *that* directly again. When she came out of hospital she sat in the darkened drawing room for months, stuffing herself on Black Magic and Harvey's Bristol Cream, and reading mad religious books that she shoplifted from Smith's. *I Am The Light! You Know It Makes Sense! Why Darwin Was Wrong!* She never ate the Brazils or the hazelnut clusters, but she puffed up to fifteen or sixteen stone in three months, and then just as abruptly crashed down to seven or eight, on Lean Cuisines and gallons of Diet Pepsi.

She grew thunderously flatulent and marmoreally constipated, but though Diana fed her health-centre pamphlets on exercise and sensible eating habits, my mother-in-law seemed to prefer to ride her tremendous tides of adipose tissue. Powerful oceans of flab ebbed and surged across her body in oleaginous waves, until the skin hung from it in withered fronds, like exhausted bladderwrack.

'I think it's because of Cahill,' Diana said. 'She's frightened of having another boyfriend. So she's making sure that no man will ever look at her again.'

I popped the fast-forward button on the VCR and on screen 'The Buggers' ground down to normal speed, half-way through a ramble about the meaning of life.

'You lie awake at night sometimes wondering what it's all about, don't you?' I was saying.

'Oh, I worry all the time,' said Reg. 'Why do people write to *Points of View*, for instance? And why are all the big Branflakes always at the top of the packet? Why do policemen call their cars "vehicles"? I was worrying just the other night about how the bloke who drives the snowplough gets to work in the morning.'

'That's right. What's it all about? Why are we all here?'

'Because my dad forgot to use a condom, I suppose.'

'And why not, pray?'

'Because God doesn't exist.'

'No, no, no. I meant why not . . . pray?'

'Because God doesn't . . . exist,' said Reg. 'I went out in

the garden the other night to look at the sky. You ever do that?'

'Oh, I do that all the time.'

'And you look up, a small speck of consciousness, in this vast universe, and you can't help thinking to yourself, "How come all these bloody stars are named after chocolate bars, eh?"'

The audience howled; I yawned, and squirted them into fast-forward again.

Perhaps the old bat really was still in mourning for Cahill, but it felt too pat for me, the idea of the poor wounded creature in retreat from the world. If she simply wanted to be hideous, for instance, why did she still spend such vast amounts of money on clothes? She pinched a lot it was true, but she was also bringing home a receipted carrier-bagful practically every week. It was all viscose and polyester from British Home Stores, naturally, for my mother-in-law always combined extravagance with parsimony to the least pleasing possible result: candelabra from Woolworth's and light-bulbs from Harrods would sum up her shopping style. But even so she was spending a lot of time and money on her appearance.

She developed exotic new diseases as well, like a faulty pyloric valve which allegedly swelled her stomach with gas: 'It's not *fat*, Didi, it's this wretched valve.' Ingrowing toenails returned whenever there was a threat of exertion: 'I'd love to go for a walk on the Heath, but these dreadful toes of mine are just blood puddings, darling.' Angina encroached when there were tedious letters to be opened or bills to be paid or decisions to be made: '*Could* you deal with this bank business, Didi? My ticker is just . . .' And though Diana said the diseases were imaginary or exaggerated or self-inflicted through ferocious smoking and drinking and a catastrophic diet, my mother-in-law had hand-picked teams of expensive consultants who were always willing to testify otherwise.

I used to look at her sometimes, gobbling Silk Cut on the sofa, swigging Lucozade from the bottle and scowling piously over *Honest To God*. And I'd wonder how she had got away with it, this great 58-year-old woman, who had contributed nothing more to the world than a couple of lightweight stage roles, two moderately fucked-up children and then thirty years of feeling sorry for herself.

'You don't have to be so horrible about her, Phil,' Diana told me.

'*I'm* horrible? Look, hang on. You come to me and moan about your mother. I sympathize with your complaints, and then I'm being horrible. Is that right?'

'I just tell you what she's like.'

'You tell me she smokes too much and eats too much; she's bone idle, a nag, a liar and you can't stand her, and this is an objective, daughterly character sketch of her mother. I agree with you and I'm getting at her.'

Diana's face began to fold itself into stubborn lines of self-pity. 'Perhaps I'd just like a bit of sympathy and under-standing for a change.'

'Look, you *know* I sympathize . . .'

'Oh that's right, I forgot. You were sympathetic a week last Tuesday, and that fulfilled your quota for the month. Next instalment of compassion due on the 21st.'

And she was right. I *did* think I'd done my bit for the month. I'd heard all about my mother-in-law's quarrel with the curate. I'd listened to the story of her battle with the wicked Dr Turnbull who wanted her to give up smoking. I'd taken Squimbleshanks or Wum-Bum to the vet to be wormed or voided or trepanned or whatever disgusting and costly treatment had been due. I'd hacked back the laurel hedge that was blocking the light from my mother-in-law's window. I'd returned her library books with my own and paid her six-month fine. I'd endured an hour-long lecture on the superiority of my mother-in-law's techniques of child-raising – which were based on *listening*, that means really *listening*, to the *inner voice* of the child, Philip – and frankly that was quite enough. I'd paid my dues, and I wanted to get on with my work. I had the TV series to finish, a whole new script to write for an Amnesty show with Reg, and I just wanted to *get on with it*. But you can't, apparently. So far as Diana was concerned you couldn't just make a healthy deposit in the emotional bank of marriage and then bugger off for a while, living off the credit balance. You just paid in all the time, and somehow – the mechanisms were never spelled out, the geometric nature of the APR was never made explicit – but somehow or other you were always, always, overdrawn.

'Right. I'm sympathetic, I'm understanding. I'm sorry for you and I'm sorry for her. Now is there anything else?'

'She really does have a bit of a heart problem, you know? Turnbull at the Royal Free has been talking about bypass surgery.'

And that was true too, for like all the most professional hypochondriacs my mother-in-law had always been sure to have a touch of real disease. Her heart condition was elusive, and never severe enough to prevent her doing anything she really wanted to, but I never doubted that when circumstances required she would produce a major coronary out of sheer bloody-mindedness.

'Okay, her health isn't great. But there are sicker women than your mother scrubbing floors all day at the Royal Free, and standing twelve hours behind paper-shop counters.'

'You're suggesting my mother should work in a sweet shop?'

'I wasn't, but why the hell not? She could retrain, go into teaching, run a little business. If a sweet shop isn't posh enough she could go and help out at the local Oxfam shop, for God's sake.'

'There's the old people she looks after.'

'Eating cakes with them in Louis' Patisserie all afternoon,

you mean? Most of the old ladies she "looks after" are under the impression that *they're* looking after *her*, and d'you know I think they're probably right.'

And there wasn't really an answer to that, because The Trust had always been there for insulation, and the children of course – those ultimate alibis for timidity and failure and self-indulgence. After The Divorce and the departure of the Wicked Father, who as years passed I found myself viewing with ever greater sympathy, my mother-in-law was left to bring up the children *on her own* – meaning with the help of grandparents and nurses and squads of Norland nannies. Truth was, it had been Diana who'd brought up her mother: coming back from school to mop cat pee and make dinners and foil insincere attempts at suicide.

'Just because you're so competitive doesn't mean everyone has to be,' Diana told me, in faint defence.

'*Me* competitive? Your mother is the most competitive person I've ever met. She won't even let Dewi win at Snap, and when it's her turn at Botticelli in the car she'll only ever choose seventeenth-century Flemish clockmakers. The one reason she's never played grown-up games like having a job or getting married again is that she cares too much about bloody *losing*.'

No, it wasn't competitiveness, but the Welsh Nonconformist in me did demand purpose, and it was the shapelessness of my mother-in-law's life which appalled me. All the evasions and delays and excuses for inaction. The mornings in bed and the afternoons at the cake shop, and the evenings in front of the video: that terrible, volitionless drift towards death. Maybe life *was* all pointless in the end, but you still had a duty to make pretty patterns from your travel through time. Teacher, priest, writer, artist: those were the noble roles in the Protestant pantheon. You had to serve or create to keep futility at bay, but my mother-in-law had made herself into an anti-artist: the Picasso of pointlessness, a Flaubert of futility.

She should have been looking after Dewi at that moment, for instance, while Diana was out on her rounds and I worked, but instead she was shuffling round the garden, with the particoloured quilting of cats boiling around her bandaged feet. My son was downstairs in her filthy flat – probably pouring paraffin over himself while he smoked one of her Silk Cut, or drinking Domestos while he watched *Driller Killer* on her video machine.

On my own screen 'The Buggers' had given way to the cost-effective crucifixion sketch, where Reg, as a time-and-motion expert, was arguing with me, a jobsworth centurion, at the foot of the Cross.

'Look, there's clearly no need for four nails.'

'We've always done four nails,' I told him. 'Regulations says four nails. You can read for yourself. Two hands, two feet, four nails. It stands to reason.'

'Reason? You might call it reason, I call it restrictive practices.' Reg glared at me and whacked the cross with his scroll. 'You're going to have to sharpen up your ideas around here, you know. This is the first century AD we're living in here.' He glanced up at the figure on the cross behind him. 'Well, it will be in a minute. This is the Roman Empire PLC, and in the ancient world we all have to pay our way.' He sucked his teeth irritably and scribbled on his scroll. 'We all have to make sacrifices these days. Nails aren't cheap, and crosses don't grow on trees, you know. On a strict cost–benefit basis these crucifixions are becoming a thing of the past.'

'So what are you going to do with all these false Messiahs? What about all these here prophets without honour in their own land?'

'For a start you can make them cross their legs. We all have to do our bit for productivity.'

I'd written the dialogue as usual, but it was Reg's idea this sketch and the audience wasn't sure of it. The laughter wavered here and there, and there was almost a silence after the line about crossing legs. Reg's delivery was too rushed, too urgent and too angry. The mad, wall-eyed detachment which could make him so funny as a performer was all missing. He kept pushing these very engaged sketches about religion and politics and Aids, but they embarrassed the audience nowadays. You had to coax issues out of comedy, not shove them down people's throats. I was going to have to talk to him.

Dewi wouldn't really be doing any of those dangerous things downstairs, of course. Diana worried about him all the time: I think she believed the waves of anxiety she projected actually wrenched Dewi back from cliffs, buoyed him up in swimming pools and shielded him from speeding cars. A relic of his birth, I suppose, though you'd think she'd be over it by now.

I was up at The Jar with Reg when Diana's waters broke, and I was at home five minutes after Miss Piggy took the phone call, but I don't think she ever forgave me. Never mind the fact that Dewi was premature, and that I could hardly spend the eight weeks before the delivery date hovering around Diana like a slip fielder. The fact was that I hadn't been there but *down the pub*, that ultimate haven for the faithless male. Dewi had been premature; Dewi had been ill. Ergo I had made Dewi ill. And ever since, Diana seemed to believe the Angel of Death hovered constantly over Dewi, and if the concentration of her anxiety ever wavered for an instant he would descend.

But he was all right old Dewi. He was fine. He would be quietly cutting out scraps, or drawing, or dressing up among the mountains of civet-scented clothes in the dark flat downstairs that I hardly visited any more. I might have done any of those dangerous, destructive things as a child, but Dewi did not take after me. He was tall for his age, where I'd been short, and plump where I'd been skinny, with myopic brown eyes and flat, silky hair. He was growing up a diplomat and negotiator, a skilled quattrocento courier between the tripartite world of mother, father and grandmother.

He had a horrible orange plastic pony toy called Horsey Horsey, which he cherished, and for which he collected saddles and bridles, clothes, companions, stables, and even, I kid you not, a miniature Horsey Horsey smithy and anvil. 'When will they produce a Horsey Horsey knacker's yard and glue-pot?' I asked him once, and he laughed, though Diana told me not to be so horrible. And Dewi had secret places he went to in the garden shrubbery, where treasures were buried in a biscuit tin beneath the leaves. He had large collections of tiny objects – stones, buttons, a hatpin, a mouse's skull, a withered conker – which looked inchoate and unrelated to me, but which, if any became lost or disordered, would make him tearful and frantic. He had frequent nightmares; he was frightened of the dark, and each night there were elaborate rituals of sympathetic magic to be gone through before he would sleep.

When I went into his room late one night I found him athwart the tangled sheets, dressed in his mother's bra and knickers. I undressed his sleeping body and put on his pyjamas without him waking, and for some reason I never mentioned it to Diana. He was a quiet boy mostly, and without close friends, though he would sometimes become wildly excited and exhibitionist: performing some fractured mime he had devised, before the fixedly tolerant grins of dinner-party guests.

In the garden below me The Zombie had appeared, a ghastly, stricken, tottering figure, frail as the column of ash on an overlooked cigarette. His name was Harold Ledbeater, one of my mother-in-law's gaga groupies, and he lived in a basement bedsit in Eton Avenue and hung about the church crypt, between spells at Colney Hatch. Apart from his supplementary benefit, which he spent immediately at the betting shop ('gambling is a disease, Philip, a *terrible* disease') he was penniless, and relied on my mother-in-law for soup and cigarettes. He had never had a job so far as I could tell, though he did have a vaguely military air: his tweed jacket decorated with epaulettes of dried egg, and the side-seams of his cavalry twills braided with crystallized snot.

'Phil-ip!' My mother-in-law was waving to my window from the lawn, and I ducked back from line of sight several seconds too late. 'Phil-ip!'

It was bound to be some tedious crisis involving The Zombie, and I had no wish to get involved. The few times I had spoken to him directly he flinched as if I had hit him, which of course made me want to, and he started talking to the ceiling about swastikas floating down from the trees and CIA microphones in his bedsit. This seemed to me such standardized schizobabble that I suspected him of fakery, though it was hard to imagine why anyone would want a life as physically uncomfortable as The Zombie's was, just for the sake of skiving.

'Phil-ip!'

My mother-in-law knew dozens of nutters like Ledbeater ('they're *mentally challenged*, Philip') – a whole deranged and semi-derelict subculture. Inadequates and inebriates; potty old women and dotty old men; incompetent gamblers, untalented spongers, unconvincing imposters. They haunted GPs' surgeries, library reading rooms, church crypts, off-licences and social services offices. They lived off meals-on-wheels and clothing grants and special payments, and in their rare moments of lucidity they all embraced the most rabid right-wing politics. Nursed, transported and served by kindly and tolerant West Indians they espoused a savage racism. Blotto on British sherry and permanently dazed on diazepam they demanded the severest penalties for drug abuse. Seldom upright they believed loudly in the need for everyone to stand on their own two feet.

'Phil-ip!' Her voice was outside now on the stairwell. I

switched off the VCR and went to open the door. 'Oh Philip, I'm so glad you're in.' She swept past me into the room while The Zombie hovered, grey and apologetic, on the landing. My mother-in-law had a talent for occupying rooms more completely than anyone else I've known. In seconds she would be sitting in the most comfortable chair, and have filled any others with knitting, pill bottles, magazines and cats. She'd have scanned the book you were reading, taken in the prose on the screen of the word processor and passed judgement upon it. She'd have adjusted the lighting, television, ventilation and music levels to her satisfaction, scattered ash on the carpet, and lost several items of jewellery, about which she would subsequently harass you for days. Like some large, clumsy, unhousetrained beast she needed to leave her spoor in every new corner.

It was all some complicated rigmarole about The Zombie's rent book which should have been sent to social provision but instead had gone to housing services who had forwarded it on to provisional housing. When Diana and I decided to stay on at Aberdare House I suppose I had hoped for an expansion of the life I scented when I first arrived, but instead there had been a contraction of it. Where I had hoped there might be eccentrics and poets and millionaires there was Harold Ledbeater and his stupid rent book. She was trying to borrow my car, an event which occurred two or three times a week now she had sold her own Fiat. A car was far too extravagant for a mere paper millionairess, particularly when she could scrounge her son-in-law's. To save argument I gave her the keys and shooed her out. With any luck one of the Maserati maniacs would get her and Ledbeater in one sweep, and I could always walk up to Hampstead to see Reg.

I found him at his usual table in the back room of The Jar, drinking bourbon and lemonade and eating a plate of Miss Piggy's sausage and chips, in a puddle of HP.

'That looks disgusting.'

'Miss Piggy wins *awards* for these, I'll have you know. Hand-hewn from Maris Piper potatoes, seethed in beef dripping and seasoned with choicest non-brewed condiment.' He dipped the end of a sausage in the brown sauce and licked it clean with a long, furry tongue. 'She's the Elizabeth fucking David of the deep-fryer. The face that launched a thousand chips.'

His own face was pale and oily in the amber gloom of the pub, with a scattering of amyl nitrite pimples around the mouth. He too was growing gently pear-shaped, on pub grub and sweet whisky, and even the flowing shirts and baggy conjuror's trousers did not disguise the porkiness of his neck and thighs. He rented a studio flat near the railway line in Chalk Farm, but he ate there never, and slept there only seldom.

'Why don't you buy somewhere decent in Hampstead?' I used to ask him.

'And you were the one who always despised postcode snobbery, *Philippe*.'

'At least you're buying something instead of tipping it into some greedy landlord's pocket.'

'Must regard investment *opportunity*,' he said, in flawless imitation of Saul.

When I needed him in a hurry I phoned Saul, then Miss Piggy, and then his mother in Mill Hill. He owned an elderly Porsche but never drove it. And his income was almost as big as mine, so I didn't know what he was spending it all on. 'Coke and cock,' was all he said when I asked him.

'So then, my pretty *Philippe*. What will you have to drink?'

'Orange juice and soda.'

'Two large Jim Beams please, Clive,' he called to Miss Piggy.

'You're face is all spotty,' I told him, and he wiped his mouth with the back of his hand.

'Well, we can't all be Dorian Gray. You should have seen it when I was seventeen. The acne pits were so deep my mother used to grate the Parmesan on my cheeks and then make me spit it out on the pasta.'

'D'you know I think I might have heard that line on stage once or twice?'

'Oh that's right,' said Reg, smiting his forehead in mock amazement. 'Phil First. We used to be in a double act to-gether.'

Miss Piggy slammed down the drinks on our table and stumped off back to his deep-fryer. It was four o'clock now and The Jar was shut, but Reg, who ran a terrifying tab behind the bar, was exempt from official opening hours. 'Miss Piggy just wants to be sure that when I drop dead she'll be the first to go through my pockets.'

'I've been trying to put together some stuff for this new series . . .'

'Do you know why dogs lick their balls?'

I raised my eyes to the ceiling. 'No. Why do dogs lick their balls?'

'Because they can.'

'Very good. These programmes . . .'

'How's Diana?' he asked me abruptly. 'She must be due in about four weeks now?'

'She's fine, fine. Yeah, it must be about four weeks, I dunno, look, if we're going to do this series, we're going to need a lot of new ideas, and a lot of them from you . . .'

'I don't suppose you've heard from Saul?'

He was always like this: maddeningly evasive, always changing the subject, never turning up for meetings and rehearsals, never learning his lines. I'd been so impressed by Reg when I first knew him that I hardly noticed how few of his projects ever came to fruition. The script he was writing that never got finished, and the novel that never got started. The slab-chested, deep-honking jocks he was always about to deflower, and the snotty, limp-wristed layabouts he always seemed to end up with. Reg was going to unseam Saul the day after he first met him, and all he'd done in the eight years since, so far as I could see, was to nurse him through his girlfriend crises, and shyly try to hold his hand, which made Saul hoot and splutter and punch him manfully in the arm.

'Saul? I think Diana saw him last week for lunch. Flat Wapping was burgled again. Fourth time this year. But he never comes round to see the old ratbag – not that I blame him.'

'She's all right, Adrienne.'

I ignored this patent idiocy.

'Why? Haven't you seen him?'

'He's got his Y-fronts in a twist about being queer again, I think. Hides in shop doorways when he sees me coming.'

'You don't *know* he's queer, Reg.'

'Of course he's fucking queer. He's been to bed with me enough times. I think I should know.'

I didn't believe they'd been to bed at all, but I let it go.

'Well perhaps he's decided he doesn't want to be queer any more.'

Reg sighed deeply. 'It's not something you *decide*, *Philippe*, I thought I'd explained this to you. People don't *decide* to be regarded as weirdos at school and by their parents and by their friends. They don't sit down and think, "I know, I'll be different from nine tenths of the human race. I'll miss out on marriage and children and ordinary friendships. I'll get beaten up by psychopaths and locked up by pretty policemen. I'll spend my life being patronized by women and pitied by men. That'll be fun."' He drained the glass of Jim Beam and burped noisily.

'But I thought you were a good liberal, Reg.'

'So what?'

'Well aren't we supposed to pretend there's no such thing as inherited traits? You wouldn't agree that IQ was inherent, for instance?'

'I think in the case of some people it's actively fucking *rejected*.'

'Meaning what?'

He dipped a long, flabby chip in the sauce puddle and sucked it, wriggling, into his mouth. ''Eenina rickle 'icky ... Sorry. Meaning a little dicky bird tells me you've been playing hide the sausage with your executive producer while your wife sits at home knitting matinée jackets.'

'Well you can tell Jeremy dicky-bird Pillock to stuff his gossip up his arse.'

'You know how many psychiatrists it takes to change a light-bulb?'

'I couldn't give a fuck.'

'Only one, but the light-bulb must really want to change.'

He drained his glass, and Miss Piggy brought two more, though I hadn't touched my first. I noticed as he stamped back towards the bar how meagre his buttocks had become beneath his Levis, and how sparse the grey hair on the back of his head. Reg followed my eyes.

'I know. Clive had the test six months ago.'

'Was it positive?'

'He isn't saying.'

'Why not?'

'Perhaps he thinks the brewery might not be too keen on the idea of a pub that serves up HIV with its sausage and chips.'

I looked at Reg's congealing plate, and he laughed. 'Just one of our little jokes. Though in fact I did have this great idea for a sketch about safe sex with a royal corgi.'

'Forget it.'

'Why?'

'Because people are fed up with carping stuff about Aids and Thatcher and Reagan and royalty and the *Sun*. The audience is growing up.'

'You mean they're growing richer and greedier and more frightened. They want to hear jokes about food-mixers and Ladas and Red Mountain coffee adverts.'

'I've been thinking that perhaps it might be an idea to do this series on my own.'

'Like the one-man show last year, you mean?'

'You could have been in on that if you'd been bothered to get out of bed in the morning. Write a few sketches. Come to bloody rehearsals.' Reg drank off the new glass of bourbon and then giggled, as if he had just remembered something.

'Do you know what Postman Pat's called when he gets made redundant?'

'No idea.'

'Pat.'

'Terrific. I'll build the whole series around it.' I was getting up to leave. He grinned at me raggedly, and turned on his Bela Lugosi accent.

'I haff created a monster.'

'And he lives on chips and whisky,' I told him.

I got back at six, and Diana was waiting for me at the door. I could read the story on her face before she opened her mouth. Fear, triumph and righteous rage, but how did the story begin?

'You've been out.'

'Ten out of ten. I've been out.'

'Where've you been?'

'What d'you mean where've I been? I'm thirty years old, not fucking three. I don't have to tell you where I've been. Your mother was getting on my tit. I had to see Reg, and so I went out. Okay?'

'My mother went out.'

'That's right,' I said very patiently. 'She went out. The Zombie had left his head behind on the tube or something. I loaned her my car.'

I added this detail for a modest brownie point. Showing tolerance to the mentally challenged. Helping out my mother-in-law with her problems. But there were dried tear-streaks on Diana's face and hard lines at the corners of her eyes. I'd never seen her look so angry, and there was a cold trickle of fear in my stomach.

'You're just not getting this are you, Phil? The penny hasn't fucking dropped, has it?' She never swore. My face was heating up with anger and panic: I didn't know which to feel. 'You went out. My mother went out. *You don't think you might have fucking overlooked something, do you? Some small fucking detail in your plans for the afternoon?*' She was screaming at me now.

Oh Christ. I was craning my neck to look behind her, through the kitchen doorway, up the stairs, through the open door of the living room. 'Dewi.'

'That's right, Dewi. Your son. A four-year-old child that you walked out on and left alone in this fucking house for two hours. Wandering about downstairs on his own. Trying to break a window. Crying himself sick until Molly Jacobsen next door hears him and rings the police.'

'Is he all right?'

'Oh yes, he's fine. Just completely hysterical, with his fingers cut on the window glass and his trousers full of shit, because his daddy and his granny have forgotten all about him and left him on his own to play with the paraffin stoves and the kitchen knives and a bathroom full of dangerous drugs . . .' And she started crying again then, and hitting me on the chest and face, quite hard, and quite painfully, and I just stood there with my head down and let her do it, because there really wasn't anything else I could do.

CHAPTER TEN

The house was one of the oldest in the village, its walls rendered in buckled folds of grey mortar like elephant's hide, its splintery floorboards so dry they creaked with the smallest movement.

'I don't much like the look of that wiring,' Diana said, pointing to the cables that straggled along the walls, looping between economically spaced staples. She was only casting about for uncontroversial topics. We hadn't spoken much on the three-hour drive across the empty mountains of the island. When we did it was only to remark on the fraying edges of the tarmac road, and the pitiful Third World engineering that took a dozen hairpin bends to climb the smallest gradient.

Dewi had grumbled and dozed in the back of the rented Fiat. Diana sat with her hands folded across the eight-month bulge of her pregnancy: almost too far gone for the airlines. We watched the shadows of the mountains lengthen in the valleys, and the sky stain with bands of earth-colour as the bloating sun picked out the strata of dust and moisture and insect swarms in the evening air. In the valley it was dark already, and oil lamps were flickering among the graves of the village cemetery. It was late in the year for a Greek holiday; the temperature barely in the seventies, the sea ruffled white with northerly breezes. Dewi had been back at nursery school for a month already, and Diana was worried there might be nobody on the beach for him to play with.

But I had been busy through the summer. The BBC series to write and then record; the voice-overs we'd done for that building society advert; the trip to New York; the Aids benefit I'd agreed to do for Reg . . .

'Are you all right, Phil?'

'Yeah, yeah, fine.'

But I must have flinched, I think, at the memory of the Aids concert six weeks ago. A bloody silly little twenty-minute spot for a one-night concert at the Hackney Empire, but it still made me wake up sweating. And God knows why I did it, except to shut Reg up, and make me feel not too bad about breaking up the act.

'But you haven't even been on stage for two years, Phil,' Diana said. 'And I can't even remember when you last did a show on your own.'

'Might as well have been on my own for all the work Reg has done lately,' I told her. 'Don't worry. It's okay. It's a charity do. They just want my name on the bill and a gentle little shuffle through some right-on jokes.'

But it was actually more like three years since I'd done a live show, and the audience seemed to have changed subtly. There were fewer men with pony-tails, and more with boxy suits and flat-top haircuts. There were fewer women with crewcuts and dongly earrings, and more with Big Hair and black rubber frocks. They looked a bit glossier, a bit younger, a bit less woolly: an audience that expected its money's worth.

'So what have you written for us then, Phil?' said Reg, his head around the dressing-room door.

'*Written* for you? New material requires dosh up front. I was thinking of a stroll around some old favourites.'

Reg pursed his lips for a reverse-thrust whistle. '*Mon brave.* You know that last year's series is now on its second repeat. They'll know your jokes better than you do.'

'So what do you expect for puffing a poofter's charity?'

'Well, it's your liver, squire.'

'I thought they were all vegetarians in Hackney,' I told him. But they bloody well weren't.

I came on after the first interval, when people were still finding their way to their seats, and there wasn't much applause, so I decided to go on the offensive.

'Did I hear a handclap there? You, sir, did you clap? Don't you realize this is a place of entertainment? Show some respect please, sir.'

But the acoustics were wrong, or the mike wasn't working properly, or there was just too much movement going on. Someone shouted out from the back, 'Can't hear you!' I could see Reg in the wings, miming something, and I tried again, more loudly.

'I was just saying I do appreciate a warm hand on my entrance. Wouldn't you like a warm hand on your entrance?'

It's not a bad line, but it's for small clubs, not vast amphitheatres like Hackney. My words were floating away into the shadows, getting lost among the plaster cupids and swags of dusty grapes. Someone shouted something else from the back of the theatre.

'I beg your pardon?'

And even as I said it I was thinking, if you can't hear the heckle then make one up, but it was too late.

'Your arse is too tight,' the heckler shouted, and there was a big laugh this time. The story of Reg and me splitting up had been in the tabloids off and on through the summer. Tightwad Phil First had wanted more of the take, that was the story. And Reg had come out as gay very openly in a few recent interviews, so there'd be a lot of sympathy washing about an Aids benefit. I decided to take him on.

'Stand up that punter,' I shouted, but nothing happened, just a stirring and turning of heads: I couldn't locate him.

'Have you ever noticed . . .?' I began, and he came in fast.

'No!' and there was more laughter, and confused shouting, and I was beginning to sweat. Basic comedy rule number three I think it was. Never ask an open question.

'Gerrooooff!' came a shout from another direction. And

I'd never heard that before, in my whole career, that arrow flying out of the darkness and into my guts. And suddenly the distance from microphone-stand to wings was a very long way indeed. Because there is no way off a stage when things start to go wrong. No way at all.

'I think we're there, Phil,' Diana said, and I nosed the car into the patch of dirt beside the back door. It was shabby, but it was our own big house on the beach. Two weeks in Greece, with swimming, lobsters, retsina – and no bloody mother-in-law. But of course Diana had to start worrying straight off about something, and the electricity would do as well as anything else.

'They don't need our kind of wiring in this climate,' I told her. 'Look at all the flat roofs. No guttering; downspouts; damp courses. They probably only get five inches of rain a year.'

'What about all those leaves in the drains on the street?' said Diana. 'And those big bolts on the shutters? And they've pulled all the boats right up the beach.' Diana always had to find something to be anxious about. Worry about the small things and the big things can go wrong on their own.

'It's the southern Mediterranean,' I said. 'They'll be swimming here for another month.'

That night it began to rain.

We ate in an empty taverna, which was decorated in the Greek light-industrial style, with posters of forest glades sellotaped to the walls. The steel-framed windows were hazy with salt spray. The blue fluorescent tube of an insect killer buzzed overhead. Naked light-bulbs on furry chains flickered in phase with a distant generator. A curtain of threaded peach stones and bamboo knuckles shielded a footprint lavatory, with brown streaks around the black hole in the porcelain.

There was no fish on the menu. 'Fishing all finish,' said the proprietor. 'Meatballs and sauce. Stuffed tomato. *Potates*.'

'The boats will be out again tomorrow,' I told Diana. 'Once the storm is over.'

'Fishing all finish,' said the proprietor again, and made a sign for waves with his hands.

'Nobody comes to Greece for the cooking,' I said.

In the morning the beach was innocent of footprints and the shore fringed with the flotsam of the storm: empty bottles of suntan oil; a dead jellyfish; a disposable nappy; cigarette filters; the little brown marbles of sheep droppings. I decided to be energetic and positive. 'Look at that, Dewi, a whole beach to ourselves.' I tidied the area around the beach mats, scooping litter into a carrier bag with a shrimping net while some locals looked on, uncomprehending. I began building a Thomas the Tank locomotive from damp brown sand, the texture of demerara sugar. 'Perfect for sandcastles,' I told Diana.

'What's that little plastic scoop thing that Dewi's using to dig with?' she said.

'I dunno, they're all over the beach.' I picked one up and turned it over. It was a blue plastic dish with petalled perforations, and a hooked plastic handle.

'Oh God,' said Diana, 'it's one of those blue loo things that you hang on the side of the toilet.'

But Dewi was becoming absorbed in the sandcastle; the sun came out from behind a ridge of cloud, and I took off my sweater and jeans.

I had to swim briskly, because the sea was cool as a British August. Beyond the shelter of the headland waves slapped my cheeks and stung my eyes. Turning my back to the breeze I trod water and watched the sandcastle taking shape a hundred yards away. Diana was patting down a bucket of sand to form a smokestack. Dewi was collecting shells and stones along the water's edge.

'Daddeeee!'

I waved back and started swimming, more slowly, to the shore. Another family, with two small children, had appeared. Introductions were being made. The sun filled the beach with light, making the wavetops spark and warming the nape of my neck above the chilly water. It was going to be fine.

We ate lunch with the other family at the beach taverna. They were called Robinson, and they came from Northampton. This was a lovely place, they told us, but very quiet. They were leaving on the Wednesday plane. 'You've left it a bit late, haven't you?' said the man.

'We've had a super fortnight,' said the woman quickly. 'There are meant to be lots of walks. A monastery, and a beach with terrapins for the children. There's a guide book in the shop.'

'I'll have a look,' I said. 'I need to buy some postcards.'

'*He'd* never buy the cards,' said Mrs Robinson. She wasn't bad looking in a streaked, suburban way, with hard little breasts under one of those roll-down swimming costumes. Her husband was bald and blubbery.

'I got some quite nice ones this morning,' she said. 'Views of the beach and the monastery.'

'No, I've decided I'm going to be very New Man on this holiday,' I said. 'I'm going to buy my own.'

'I could do with a new man,' said Mrs Robinson, and Robinson pinched her on the thigh, making her giggle.

'So when are you due?' she asked Diana.

'End of next month.'

'You're very brave. I wouldn't move more than five miles from Whipps Cross when Oliver and Samantha were on the way.'

'Diana's a doctor,' I said. 'If she goes into labour on the plane she's going to shout out instructions to me on how to deliver it.'

I stayed down the beach on my own after lunch, and when I got back to the house I found Diana talking to an old woman. She was sweeping sand from the oilcloth floors with a bunch of hemp fibre and a dustpan cut from a petrol tin. She had a stern, martial face, like a carved Indian, and a matted grey cardigan over her black dress. 'She's called Aphrodite,' Diana said. 'This is her house.'

She spoke to the old woman again in her not-bad Inlingua Greek. 'She says that in summer she lives in a room in the basement.'

The old woman was following the conversation intently, looking from Diana to me and back.

'I thought we had the whole house.'

'She only comes in to clean. She has her own entrance, at the back.'

'It's not the same as having the house to ourselves.'

Diana shrugged. 'I'm sure we'll hardly see anything of her. She's only here now because she thought we were on the beach.'

We ate with the Robinsons that evening while the children played with a video game in the bar next door. He was a salesman with a pet-food firm, and she had just given up work as a receptionist. They talked about other places they had been on holiday, and her husband ordered a small bottle of ouzo.

'You speak Greek?' said Robinson.

'Only a few words,' I told him. 'Diana is much better, she did a course once.'

Diana explained: 'We started coming to Greece when we were still at university. Sleeping on beaches; living on bread and olives.'

'Hippies,' said Robinson.

'Not quite that old,' I said.

'Philip's on the telly, aren't you?' said Mrs Robinson, and I allowed myself to preen a little. It is rather gratifying to be recognized on one of the quietest Greek islands in the Aegean. 'I told him last night, but he wouldn't take any notice,' Mrs Robinson said. 'Watches nothing but sport, don't you?' She poked him in his tallowy thigh. 'Philip did that advert for lager with the corgi.'

★

I did too, because when you get down to it one TV series every eighteen months doesn't support a family, not on BBC rates, and there hadn't been many new offers since I'd split with Reg. So I'd taken the five grand, and spent two days in a St John's Wood studio smooching with a bottle of low alcohol lager, and getting pissed in the pub in the lunch-hours with the rather tasty PA.

That terrible night at the Hackney Empire they had this little smart-arse on a few acts before me, who kept taking the mick out of all the old right-on comics and pop stars from the seventies, who were doing the ads for American Express and lager and condoms.

'How can you tell an alternative comic?' he demanded. 'Dunno? They're the ones who do the building society adverts.' And it wasn't a bad line I had to admit. Got a better laugh than anything I did that night anyway.

Not that I was actually crucified or anything; it was more a gentle expiry, with the audience getting more restless and distracted, and my voice getting shriller and my hands on the mike more slippery. I did locate the heckler in the end: a big beery bastard with one of those dopey hooded sweat-shirts, half-way up the gangway, with a gang of mates around him. I tried some standard put-down or other: 'Is that your face or has your neck thrown up?' But he was in fast again, with a loud 'Heeaarrd it!' and he was getting more response than I was.

I knew by then that all the material I'd slung together was far too small-scale and intimate for this great space. I'd got used to cuddling with the camera, and now I was having to project frantically with big gestures and a straining squawk that bounced all around the ceilings and balconies of the theatre.

I wanted to run away half-way through, when the queues were lengthening outside the ladies' lavatory, and a paper dart landed on the stage beside me, and I could see Diana looking at her feet in the front row. I could see Reg making wrap-up gestures with his arms in the wing. But you have to go on, and I slogged away through some dreary stuff about dullness: about people so dull they read those books on the SAS you see at station bookstalls, and whose idea of a rave-up is a Cadbury's Creme Egg, and who believe Felicity Kendal is an actress and David Attenborough is a great communicator . . .

'You're dull,' the fat bastard shouted at one point.

'You're right,' I shouted back, and it was the only good laugh I got. I slunk off to the tiniest ripple of applause, and a pat on the back from Reg.

'Ever see Tommy Trinder in *The Bells Go Down*?' I asked him.

'It happens,' he told me.

It rained again that night, and when I woke some time before dawn to go to the lavatory I found the electricity was off and none of the lights would work. The sea rushed in the distance and rain pattered on the broad fig leaves outside the lavatory window.

The morning was cool and grey and we ate breakfast of bread and thin apricot jam around a card table in the hall of the house, looking out at the puddled street and dripping fig trees. As we were drinking coffee Aphrodite appeared at the door to the cellar steps and spoke to Diana.

'A bad noise – no, a storm – last night. She says a yacht was broken – wrecked, I suppose.' The old woman circled the breakfast table and patted Dewi on the head. She picked up the Horsey Horsey doll from beside his plate and clucked over it, but he snatched it back.

'Dewi, that's not polite.'

'Who's that ugly old woman?'

'Sshh. She might understand.'

Dewi did not look up from his plate again, though the old woman continued to hover, uncomfortably close to the break-fast table. She was wearing two cardigans today, and football socks over her stockings. She spoke directly to me once, pointing at Dewi, and I tried to smile politely. Another bloody mother-in-law.

'Can't you ask her not to come in like that?' I said, when the woman had gone.

'It's her house.'

'We're renting it.'

'She seems a nice enough old thing. You were always keen on meeting the locals. The real Greece.'

'Doesn't mean I want them sitting on my lap while I eat breakfast.'

A German yacht had dragged its anchor in the bay and run aground on the beach. A group of fishermen in oilskins and caps examined the canted hull, planning their day around it. Two more were burning paint from the bottom of an upturned dinghy. I felt foolish walking past them with my shorts and T-shirt, the striped bag and bright towels. The everyday, working village was coming out of its summer hibernation, and we were overstaying the tourist welcome.

Robinson had shaved off his holiday beard and he bought bottles of wine for our lunch together. 'Our last day,' he said. 'Have to celebrate.'

'A shame for your little boy,' said Mrs Robinson. 'They really have made friends, haven't they?'

'Sent your cards yet?' said Robinson. 'Some hot ones at the village shop. Knockers and everything.'

'I must go and look after lunch,' I said.

But I went for a swim instead, and Mrs Robinson decided to come too, her top rolled down. 'I'm determined to come back with brown boobs this holiday.' She had told me her first name, but I'd forgotten it, and it seemed stupid to ask, after three days, and when they were leaving in the morning.

'You're nice and thin. Jim's put on so much weight since we were married. They'll never believe we met someone on the telly when we get home.'

She was slightly drunk, and in deep water she decided I should take off my trunks, and started making playful grabs for my groin. I laughed and dodged about a bit, but I wasn't in the mood for tipsy gambollings. I glanced at Diana and Robinson on the taverna terrace two hundred yards away, and thought what the hell, I'll call her bluff. Under the waves I let Mrs Robinson do whatever she wanted, and her hands became more tentative, her expression thoughtful.

'A pity we're going back so soon,' she said.

When we got back to the house that night the noise of a television and laughter was coming from the cellar door. 'Dewi will never sleep through that,' I said. 'Can't you do something?'

'Why don't you?'

'You speak the bloody language.'

Diana knocked on the door and a square of bluish light appeared. Several faces upturned at the bottom of the stairs. Diana went down, closing the door behind her. I lay on the bed until she returned, an hour later. 'She's got her granddaughter and great-grandson staying. And the boyfriend from Kavala.'

'Did you ask them to turn the noise down?'

'They're all in one room down there, while we've got their whole house.'

'They get money for it. Quite a lot.'

'And they gave me some grapes for Dewi.'

'He doesn't like grapes.'

I watched her undress in the moonlight that filtered through the shutters and made a silver crescent from the globe of her swollen belly. Her breasts were ponderous and pointed with milk, and I reached out a hand from my bed, and trailed it down the incurve of her back.

'Ooh don't. That gives me goose-pimples.'

'We haven't made love for a long time.'

'So you want a premature baby on a Greek island with no proper hospital and two flights a week, do you?'

And I didn't know enough, or perhaps care enough to argue with her, but she climbed in anyway, into the narrow single bed, with her back towards me. And after a while I slipped inside her from behind, and brought myself quickly to an end, my hands clasping the hard round belly where her baby stirred.

'Better now?' said Dr Di, her medicine dispensed, and I said it was, although it wasn't. This was a kindly woman: all the facts pointed to it. She was tender with Dewi, tolerant with her mother and considerate with her patients. She fretted over famines in Ethiopia and cardboard-box houses on the Embankment. She grew white with anger over health-service cuts and she hated the prime minister with a fully orthodox hatred. She was helpful in practical matters and compassionate over abstract ones. So why did I have this belief deep down, embarrassed and unspoken, that my wife was insensitive as a breezeblock? But it didn't matter. I wasn't going to see Hon again – I'd decided all that before we left for Greece. There was too much to lose.

'It's nice being on our own, isn't it?'

Diana mumbled sleepily.

'Just the three of us without your mother.'

No reply.

The old bat had wanted to come, of course, but I had ruled it out. She would babysit Dewi while we went out to the taverna. It was a big house, wasn't it? If the air fare was a problem she'd be happy to chip in. I pretended there were no seats left on the plane, and in one of her rare but terrifying bursts of efficiency she discovered that there were. I just told her we didn't want her in the end, and she sulked the whole week before we left.

We didn't need to live at Aberdare House any more. It was a cheap option eight years ago. I wouldn't have been able to afford such nice cars, or such erratic earnings without it, but we didn't need it any more. 'We should think about moving again when we get back to London,' I said. 'We could even think about the country. Somewhere with our own garden.'

But tactically or factually, Diana was fast asleep.

Aphrodite appeared again at breakfast the next day, and settled down on the staircase to watch us eat, chattering away to Diana, while she buttered bread for Dewi and poured juice into his beaker. What was it, this enthusiasm for old bags?

'I want you to tell her we'd like to eat breakfast on our own.'

'She's very interesting, you know. Used to look after the old woman who owned this house. Her husband was killed in the war by the Italians.'

'Daddy wants her to go away,' said Dewi. 'I hate that old lady. I'm going to stick my tongue out at her.'

'You've been teaching him bad manners.'

'Doesn't need any lessons from me,' I said, scowling at the old cow, who was still squatting on the bottom stair.

I hid the postcards inside my paperback copy of *Money*. There were three of them, the modern, semi-abstract kind produced by some Athens photographer. A blinding white wall, with a pot of herbs; a blue wooden shutter; the curve of a wet brown buttock against the sky. Diana always bought the kinds with a proper view so people could see where you had been. I went up to the village after lunch, and bought my own stamps, and Diana seemed pleased with me.

In the afternoon I took Dewi out fishing on a pedalo. I had two hand lines from the village shop and a lump of raw squid a fisherman gave me. 'You cut this up into little bits and stick it on the hook.'

'Is it alive? It's all squidgy.'

'I'll put it on. Look. Then you dangle it in the water under the boat, and catch a fish.'

'If I catch a fish can I have an ice cream?'

'This isn't supposed to be an *ordeal*, Dewi. We're supposed to be enjoying ourselves. Having fun.'

'I want to make sandcastles.'

'Look, you've got a bite. It's pulling.'

We caught a dozen fish, smaller than sardines, and Dewi became wildly excited, and forgot about the horrors of the slippery squid and flapping fish. He even took charge of knocking them on the head with my Opinel. 'Look, this one's eyes have popped out.'

We took them up to the beach taverna afterwards, where I asked the proprietor to cook them for our dinner. 'Why did he wink at you, Dad?' said Dewi.

'Because he thought they were such good fish.'

'Can I have an ice cream now?'

'All right.'

'An ice cream with a handle on.'

'Yes.'

It rained a few more times, but we went on expeditions to the monastery and a castle and the terrapin beach. We built many more sandcastles. Diana went to drink coffee with Aphrodite for an hour each morning, and she stopped appearing on the stairs at breakfast. Dewi and I went fishing three more times, and his plump body grew brown and smooth like a seal pup. The water did not get too cold to swim. The holiday was announced a success. 'It is a lovely place,' Diana said to me. 'We should come here earlier another year.'

When she was packing the shells and presents we had bought into the suitcase she remembered the postcards. 'You did send them, didn't you?'

'Yes, of course. One for mum and dad. One for Reg.'

'But you bought three. They were in that copy of *Money*, weren't they?' I felt terribly tired all of a sudden. So it wasn't to be Access slips or restaurant matchbooks after all.

'No, you're wrong,' I said, hopelessly, on that late holiday of our marriage. 'It was only two.'

── PART THREE ──

She just stood there looking at me, running the Black and Decker over her moustache ... Oh yes, she's a powerful woman my mother-in-law. She'll break a swan's wing with one blow of her nose ... got drummed out of the Gestapo for cruelty ... I took her to the zoo once and the lion picked up a chair and a whip ... the Museum of Natural History took one of her shoes and from the footprint they reconstructed a dinosaur ... When she was kidnapped once, the kidnappers took one look at her, blindfolded themselves and gave her an address where to take them ... they sent us a ransom note for ten thousand pounds and we settled up three years later for an all-in price of fifteen quid – they couldn't afford any more ... No, really, when she walks through the supermarket the fish fingers go for her throat ... I'd say my wife and I had a perfect union until my mother-in-law became shop steward ...

──── CHAPTER ELEVEN ────

I'd started running every morning, partly to try and stop myself from crying all the time. It blew away the hot, panicky dreams of the night before and lowered the reservoir of moisture in my body, which seemed always ready to bloat the tissues of my face into silly, involuntary weeping. I came back sore, and light and dried out from these runs, the ache still there but manageable for the day, until I went to sleep again.

I hadn't cried properly since I was fifteen or so. I thought I was over that kind of thing, long gone with school bullies and swampy teenage lusts, but it kept jumping on me from behind, when I was quite contented; not unhappy at all. I would drive the Mercedes out of the carport on a sunny morning, and look behind to see that the child belts were buckled, and suddenly I'd be crying. I'd scan the menu in a restaurant, instinctively checking for children's portions, and in a moment my face would be foolishly wet.

And so I started to run, first for a mile or so, with flailing arms and heaving smoker's chest. I had to turn my face away from other people running, and when I got home I would be speechless and drowning. But gradually the mile became two and then three, and my feet began to stitch a tight seam, and my elbows to tuck neatly into my sides. I began steadily to climb from four strides to the breath, to six, and eight and ten. After a month I could run head up, and smile into the faces of other runners.

I could speak when I got back home, but there was still no one to speak to, and I was scared the magic was wearing off. I ran five miles one day, and still cried at lunchtime over Dewi's drawing of a clown on the kitchen pinboard. I was frightened that the crying might be tougher than the running. The crying had legs of iron and lungs of leather, and I was afraid that it was catching me up.

The island where I'd come to was built upon the leavings of London: all the refuse of three centuries and more, carted down river and dumped into the marshes of Poplar and Millwall. I went running in the mornings along the old river levee, where the piling machines made the tarmac tremble, and puckered the stiff mud of the foreshore. And there were deep cuts everywhere, for the next office block and apartment building and shopping mall. Great slices out of the layer cake of history.

There were pounded oyster shells at the bottom, pearly strata twenty feet down, interleaved with the sweet black layers of night soil. Oysters and shit, oysters and shit: an alimentary diary of eighteenth-century London. And then higher up, nearer the surface, there was the city's Cambrian explosion into consumerism, with pottery flasks and coarse glass stoppers; mummified shoes and sodden wharf timber that crumbled in the fingers like chocolate cake. There were treasures here as well: belt buckles and watch cases; clouded marbles from Victorian toy-boxes; a fragment of a phrenological head. Some of them, cleaned and mounted and spot-lit, were on Dewi's special shelf in my James Bond flat.

But the newer strata of garbage were broader and coarser, with buckled prams and burst bin bags; dead dogs, cheese sandwiches, slimy potatoes, TV tubes and reeking takeaway cartons. It was still alive this stuff, still simplifying its organic compounds into methane and sulphur dioxide and ammonia. It exhaled bubbles into the stagnant ponds of building sites, tough blue bubbles that grew to enormous size on windless days, wobbling fatly and bursting with a phosphorescent pong.

The block where my James Bond flat was built stood on

stilts above the gas bubbles. There were ventilation shafts driven deep into the poisoned cake; powerful extractor fans and concrete pontoons; but the antique garbage still broke wind above the ground sometimes, with a fearsome, prewar-London fart. And there was a pond outside the flat, a 'water feature' in the developer's prospectus. It was lined with tough plastic sheet and weighed down with boulders and nurserymen's baskets of lilies and water iris. But the gas had built up beneath so the plastic bulged above the water like a blue-black boil. And we fretted over the boil in our tenants' association meetings, but no one volunteered to lance it.

I found the flat with Hon, after a month of searching that began at the Tower of London, and threatened to end in Tilbury. She was excited by flat-hunting – she liked spending money – and we both knew what I needed. A place like Saul's, with a river view and wide floorboards, and a whiff of spice in the stairwell. It had to be near the tube for casual visitors, and with three bedrooms minimum: one for me, one for the children and one for Hon when she came to stay, because Hon never spent a whole night in anyone's bed.

I was rich enough, and I deserved it after eight years of cats and mother-in-law. But all the Sauls seemed to have got there already, and it seemed that I wasn't that rich after all. Who were these Jamies and Pippas, with their Shoguns and Porsches and weekend cottages, and what the fuck must they earn? St Katharine's Dock was all sewn up, and Wapping High Street was pretty tight. And so we drove eastwards, with Hon navigating through unthumbed pages of the *A–Z*, with me steadily shedding my compunctions about river views and floorboards, and Hon growing steadily less excited.

I lost a contract race on a three-bed maisonette in Limehouse, and I was gazumped on a two-bed flat in Narrow Street. Prices were going up ten per cent a month, fortunes were being made overnight, and I was spending two hundred pounds a week on a damp hotel room in Highgate. I found the flat on my own in the end: a one-bedroom hutch in a neo-vernacular block on the unfashionable eastern shore of the Isle of Dogs. The floors were chipboard, the stairwell smelled of marsh gas, the neighbours were all divorced and my view was of a pustular water feature. But lusty demand had finally kissed shrinking supply, and my new postal code was London E18.

The flats were being sold part-furnished, with taps in the kitchen that you could control with one elbow. 'Very nice if you're a double amputee,' said Hon. Every switch was a dimmer switch and the developers threw in a microwave with every flat, which was just as well because the oven recess was too small for anything but my pedal bin. The ceilings were covered in drippy Artex instead of being plastered properly, and I could touch them with my arm bent. There were no cupboards, of course, but I wouldn't be bringing much stuff with me anyway.

'It's a bit far from the tube,' said Hon.

'They're building a new line soon.'

'In five years. And what about the bedrooms? You wanted one for the children and one for visitors.'

'Dewi and Megan can have the bedroom when they stay. There's this clever thing in the living room.' I showed her the spare bed that let down from a recess in the wall.

'Very James Bond,' said Hon, and she got back in her Golf, and she drove back to her little white house in Shepherd's Bush, and she never did spend the night with me there.

I used to sit there, counting it up at the kitchen table, and it couldn't have been more than six or seven times, since that terrible afternoon in Aberdare House. Twice at Hon's house, twice at the damp room in Highgate, which she hated and refused to come to again. And then one more time at the Savoy, when the crying caught up with me, leather-lunged and iron-legged, and I could only sit on the edge of the hotel bed, rocking myself in my arms. 'What is it, Phil? You can tell me.' But I couldn't tell her, could I? In the comfortable corruption of a day-let hotel room, with its empty half-bottle of champagne, and crusts of smoked-salmon sandwiches, and opulent tumble of towels on the floor, I couldn't tell her it was the babysitting service on the hotel phone card. I could never have said it was something as simple as that. So perhaps it was really only five times since that afternoon in Aberdare House.

Diana was only away for a week, but my mother-in-law didn't waste any time staging her usual strategic heart attack. I had always thought of heart attacks as something ca-lamitous and frequently terminal, but my mother-in-law managed to have them all the time. She seemed, single-handedly, to have redefined the condition, to combine maxi-mum drama with minimum risk to health. Whenever there were lawns to be mowed, or babies to be sat, or any plausible form of employment to be had, her heart went into failure. Diana was out of the door with her suitcase, and half an hour later my mother-in-law was croaking on the bathroom floor and I was on the phone to the Royal Free. Ambulances came and went; doctors scurried; ECGs bleeped; and my mother-in-law was confined to bed for a month of total rest.

'But doesn't a heart attack mean your heart has actually stopped?' I asked her tame specialist – a Harley Street croco-dile with a castle in Totteridge Lane and a Rolls-Royce Corniche that ran on high-octane bullshit. 'Doesn't it mean you're about to *die* or something?'

He looked at me condescendingly over his half-rims. 'There is a distinction between cardiac arrest and heart failure, Mr . . . Um. Your mother, Mrs . . . Ah . . . is in a condition of chronic heart failure.'

'My mother-in-law.'

'As you wish.'

'Or not.'

And the scaly old shit almost smiled.

'But you say her condition is chronic rather than acute?'

He scowled at me then, and fidgeted impatiently with his briefcase catch, and checked his watch, which was Patek Philippe. This was a man who operated on a meter, and it was the kind of meter which only accepted golden guineas.

'I shall be calling in daily to monitor her condition.'

'Of course you will,' I said, and smiled my brightest smile. 'It's just that I'd like to be sure I appreciate the distinction between angina, which I know she has, and I understand is a symptom of heart weakness, and an actual heart attack which might threaten her life.'

'I don't think this is the moment for a medical discussion, Mr . . . Ah. My recommendation as Mrs . . . Um's physician is for a period of complete bed rest. Now I must be going.'

'More lives to be saved,' I called to his departing back, and he slammed the door hard behind him.

Diana had left a list of memos on the pinboard before she went. Feed cat, feed tortoise, feed goldfish, feed stick insects, feed Dewi. And don't ask me where all this livestock had come from. I don't even like pets apart from dogs. And I certainly didn't issue authorization for them all.

The cat was the offspring of one of my mother-in-law's six un-neutered queens and was called Shuffle, a soppy name selected by Dewi; but it was a far from soppy creature, with nasty close-set eyes, and a habit of hiding on the stairs in the dark to claw my ankles. How can anyone like cats when their arseholes are so pink and clean? The tortoise was huge, and inherited from Diana's aunt who christened it Mahatma, after Gandhi, who it did rather resemble. It was otherwise lacking in interest, as Pevsner would say.

The goldfish and stick insects were just goldfish and stick insects. They lived, they died, and were buried beneath lollipop-stick crosses in the garden. These alien, un-authorized creatures were all 'educational' according to Diana, though the only thing I ever learned from them was to wear slippers on the stairs in the dark.

I'm okay at looking after myself, I really am. I don't do anything too aggressively New Mannish like cleaning out the lavatory (the Great Symbolic Lavatory), but I can cook and iron, I know which drawer the bin-liners are in, I can press the right buttons on the dishwasher. But curious buried systems in the running of a house begin to emerge when you are on your own for a while. Previously invisible milkmen and newsagents and window cleaners appeared at the door, roughly demanding to be paid for their services. I found that laundry baskets refused to empty themselves; Dewi's clothes wouldn't fold themselves into drawers; dead light-bulbs and empty toilet rolls stubbornly failed to self-renew; and my socks declined to pick themselves up from the bedroom floor.

And all these things took so much time – time I should have been spending writing and rehearsing and organizing. Take Dewi to school, pay a bill, wipe a bottom, answer a phone, bandage a knee, slam down a plate of food in front of my mother-in-law, and half a day had gone. Pick Dewi up, set out some paints for him, make some tea, fill the washing machine, feed a tortoise, and the rest of the day had followed.

Normally when I was looking after Dewi I just read him the odd story, tossed him the odd Lego brick and shouted at him when he got on my nerves. But with Diana away, life became a frenzy of dressing, undressing, washing, picking up and putting away. And perhaps it was just guilt, or the dread he would say he wanted Mummy to come home, but it somehow became imperative to *entertain* him all the time. At the weekend we built complex elec-trical circuits from nails and fuse wire and torch batteries. We made papier-mâché models. We flew kites. We went to Madame Tussaud's, the museum, the park. And still it always seemed to be eleven o'clock in the morning with unfilled eons of time yawning before bath and bed. I had too much time and I had too little time, and I had them both at the same time.

Hon phoned on the Saturday evening and I tried to cancel our Monday dinner.

'I can't leave Dewi with Adrienne, she's too ill to get out of bed, or at least she says she is.'

'Can't you get a babysitter?'

'Well, you know Diana, she's not that bothered about going out much. We've hardly ever used babysitters, and I think the phone numbers are in Diana's diary, and –'

'You are hopeless. Look, I'll call you back tomorrow,' she said, and hung up.

Dewi woke me at six on Sunday morning and by eight we were both washed, dressed, breakfasted and wondering what to do, while sensible, childless London slumbered around us.

'What about the zoo?'

'Oh, not the zoo *again*.'

But we went anyway, and by nine thirty I was gazing blearily up at a baby giraffe called Jo, named after Jo Durie the tennis player according to Dewi, who knows all about everything from watching *The Wideawake Club*. And I don't know how big baby giraffes are when they are born, but Jo was about the size of a dockyard crane, munching bale-sized mouthfuls of hay, way up in the stratocumulus layer.

'Why do you think giraffes have such long necks?' I asked Dewi, in the approved manner of the Socratic educator.

'So that we can see them better,' he replied promptly, with the relentless homocentrism of childhood.

Why do cows have udders? So that Dewi can have strawberry milkshakes, of course. Why do crocodiles have waterproof skins? So that ladies' shoes don't leak, silly. For Dewi, zoo animals were rated mainly on the prominence of their buttocks and genitals, with bonus points for particularly spectacular acts of excretion. Baboons, with their huge red bottoms, were the favourites, followed by rhinos (tremendous turds) and zebras (enormous bollocks).

But we had done the zoo too many times. The mummy baboon's titties held no charms any more. The donkey's willy had lost its fascination. Even the elephant's most titanic acts of evacuation could hold Dewi's attention no longer than a moment.

'I want to go to the shop now.'

'We've only just got here. And anyway the shop's not open on Sunday.'

'Yes it is, Daddy. It said on the sign.'

'Dewi, have you ever wondered about the remarkable discrepancy between your ability to read any form of commercial advertising, and your complete illiteracy in the face of danger warnings, privacy signs, prohibition notices and any form of improving literature?' I talked to him like this sometimes, as a way of talking to myself.

'What?'

'Never mind, son,' I said, and led him to the zoo shop, where we bought a tiger mask, and a model hippo, and an ice cream. Who eats ice cream at ten o'clock on a freezing Sunday morning in November? Dewi, that's who.

'I want to go home now.'

'And what shall we do then?'

'Go out again.'

Hon rang again at lunchtime, when Dewi and I were making an egg-box robot on the kitchen table.

'I've fixed a babysitter for this afternoon.'

'Really? That's amazing. But I don't know if I should really let someone Dewi doesn't know ... I mean, he's very –'

'It's a friend of mine from the Beeb. Loves children. She's been organizing parties of schoolkids to go to the recording of a Christmas show at Shepherd's Bush. They always bus in lots of kids, but she'll take special care of Dewi.'

'Would you like to go to a special children's theatre this afternoon?' I asked Dewi. 'With a kind lady who's a friend of Aunty Hattie?'

'She's called Hon not Aunty Hattie.'

'All right then, a friend of Hon.'

'Can I take Horsey Horsey?'

'Yes, you can take Horsey Horsey.'

Diana would be appalled of course. The casual parking of Dewi on a friend of a friend would certainly rank as a major crime against parental responsibility. But I conjured up an image of a sisterly *Blue Peter* type in one of those sweaters like a TV test pattern and joky plastic hairgrips. I looked at the debris of shredded cardboard and flaking polystyrene and puddled glue on the table, and I'd already made up my mind.

'The only problem is Adrienne. She was asleep this morning, but I can't really leave her on her own again in the house all afternoon.'

There was a long sigh on the other end of the phone. 'Now the man wants me to fix up a minder for his mother-in-law.'

'You could always come here. I'll make something for tea. I think there's some crumpets and a malt loaf and –'

'Champagne in bed will be fine,' said Hon. 'I'm on my way.'

There was a scuffling sound when I called through the door of my mother-in-law's flat, but she was in bed with the greasy quilt up to her chin by the time I entered her earth.

'Bit out of breath aren't you?' I asked her kindly.

'Dreadful stabbing pains this morning, Philip. I've been on the brink of telephoning for Dr Carew, but I would hate to disturb his Sunday.'

Taking shallow breaths I braved her kitchen, put some

eggs on to boil and heated up some lobster bisque on the crusty rings of her cooker. There was a new and expensive wall-oven which still had the gasket of cardboard packaging around the door from four years ago. As far as I could make out through the smeary glass of the door, it seemed to be full of tins of cat food.

'That's very kind of you, dear.'

'I've got some work to do this afternoon, and I've arranged for someone to look after Dewi, but I'll be upstairs if you need anything.'

I watched her gobbling the scalding soup with one hand and cramming bread into her egg with the other. She'd been in bed for a week, done nothing but smoke and watch videos, but there were Irish road-layers and oil-rig roustabouts who would envy my mother-in-law's appetite.

'I think I might have left a pair of glasses upstairs the other day.'

She was always mislaying the possessions she scattered about her wherever she went. It provided endless excuses for her to come rooting about in our half of the house, and to have Diana constantly running about in search of earring butterflies and spectacle cases and bookmarks and other impedimenta. Mother and daughter both had a passion for sentimental clutter, which meant they were always in a lather of anxiety about losing something, or grief because they already had.

I waved around me at the piles of cheap, soiled clothes on chairs and bed and floor. 'It would be much easier to keep track of things if you could just get rid of some of this stuff.'

'Do you know they are talking about closing down the Oxfam shop on Haverstock Hill, because of the new rates? I was thinking of writing to the *Ham and High*. Unless you could do it on your word processor . . .'

I found it interesting, in a scab-picking sort of way, to try to anticipate the tangents at which my mother-in-law could fly off whenever a topic arose which contained any threat of exertion, or economy, or responsible behaviour. To attempt to keep her to any given subject for more than two consecutive sentences almost had the makings of a game: tedious but mildly challenging, like a crossword puzzle.

'I don't suppose the Oxfam shop would be very interested in this sort of stuff anyway,' I said. 'You could just chuck it in the bin.'

She eyed me narrowly over an egg-smeared soldier, sizing up the challenge.

'Those bin men make such a noise in the mornings. You might have a word with them, Philip. There were chicken bones and tins all down the path the other day.'

'You could just stuff the clothes in a double bin-liner –'

'I was going to ask if you could get me a few things like bin-liners when you next go to Waitrose. We're almost out of cat food . . .'

And so I gave up, as I always did.

Hon arrived at two o'clock with her child-loving friend, who was a taciturn, six-foot German, dressed in black from head to foot, with a blank, powdered face and a bleached crewcut that made her look like a pint of Guinness.

'She's called Lotte,' Hon explained, 'and she's a bit down at the moment because her girlfriend slit her throat.'

'She's *queer*? I thought you said she liked children.'

'Gays are allowed to like kids, you know.'

'Dewi's going to be terrified of her.'

But when we got back to the kitchen Dewi was sitting on Lotte's lap and examining the tattoo on her arm, which was a snake twined around a dagger, with an 'Ein Volk, Ein Deutschland' legend.

'Why is your face all white?'

'Because I am a vampire.'

'Can I be a vampire too?'

'Only if you learn to speak German.'

'What's German for brassière?'

So we escorted them out to Lotte's Karmann Ghia, and we waved them off, and we took the bottle of champagne out of the fridge, and we went upstairs to bed.

I was feeling more queasy than excited: the familiar marital bed, Diana's things on the dressing table, Dewi's photograph on the mantelpiece, the neighbours across the road. I pulled down the blinds and drew the heavy curtains. I was worried about Dewi, tearing across London in a sports car with a Nazi vampire, and my limbs were feeling heavy. I'd been up since six o'clock, and I felt it would be nice just to snuggle down in the big bed and go to sleep. I'd had six days of cleaning and cooking and child-minding. I had dishpan hands, a pocket full of Lego bricks and a severely reduced vocabulary. It was going to take a complete miracle to give me a hard-on.

I sat on the bed, and fiddled with my shoelaces. Hon pushed off her shoes and trousers in one movement and walked across the room towards me, a dark puff of pubic hair winking through the slash of the white silk shirt, which was all she was now wearing.

I had a hard-on.

'Help me move this mirror.'

It was a tall mahogany pier-glass which stood beside Diana's dressing table. Hon plucked off a pair of Diana's greyish J-cloth knickers, which were hanging from one of the swivels, and tossed them on to the floor.

'What do you want that for?'

'I want to watch myself.'

She was always in charge in the bedroom. And always I found my throat thickening, my voice becoming slurred and stupid.

'What do you mean watch *yourself*? Don't I come into it?'

'No.'

I helped her carry the mirror to the end of the bed. 'I'm sure Diana knows about us, you know,' I said. 'She kept going on about those postcards on holiday.'

'Get undressed,' said Hon, and so I did that, while she watched me, standing at the end of the bed, with her back to the mirror, and I could see the beginning of the curve of her buttock in the glass, and I could see my own legs threshing themselves free of their trousers in the vee of mirror between her thighs.

'I've got some things in that bag,' she said, and I brought it over to the bed.

'I want you to wear this,' she told me, and my stomach gave a tiny lurch.

'It's a mask.'

'No, it's a blindfold.'

It was a plain black thing, cut like a Lone Ranger mask but without the eyeholes, and made of kid or some other soft leather, with black silk ribbons to tie behind the head.

'I don't know if I want to wear that.'

'You want me, don't you?'

'Yes.'

And so I put it on.

In the velvet darkness I sensed rather than heard the swish of the silk shirt as she pulled it over her head. And then she took my blind hands in hers, and I felt them fill with a warm, scented liquid.

'Rub that on me.'

And I rubbed it on her, over her chest and belly, and the swollen, bursting rounds of her breasts. Round and round the contours of her waist and hips and belly and breasts, in a slow, hypnotic pattern. Her body grew huge and detailed in the blindness. I could feel the fineness of the skin near the breastbone, and the coarsening of the pores towards the shoulders, and the fine oily hairs near the nipples. And in the dark I could hear the little, slick, sucking sounds that my hands made on her body, and the rise and fall of our breathing, and the roaring in my ears, and I was there and not there, awake and dreaming. Then suddenly awake.

'What's that?'

There was a cool weight on my wrist, a metallic rasp, and a dense, chunky click like a shotgun being cocked.

'Don't be frightened, Philip.'

'What is it? What are you doing? I'm going to take this off.' But her hands were suddenly hard on my other wrist, wrenching it across my body and there was a giggle and another hard click, and my hands were caught tight by something. I was pushing up against her weight. But her voice was cool, amused and reassuring.

'I said don't panic. It's only handcuffs.'

'*Handcuffs?*'

'*Un peu de bondage*. Don't worry. You're going to enjoy yourself.'

I wasn't so sure. I suffer from claustrophobia. I always get a little flutter of fear in those slot-like lifts they have in French *pensions*, and I hate low ceilings above my head when I'm lying on my back. In double beds I have to lie on the side that's nearest the door, and I loathe the feeling of my head being held down on a pillow. My chest begins to tighten up in seconds and I begin to fight for breath. As Hon tied my ankles to the bottom rail of the bed, and then my handcuffed wrists to the top rail, it was beginning to happen now.

'I really don't think I like this very much you know, Hon.'

'Shut up, Philip,' she said, and taped my mouth shut, which was when I really began to panic.

I started pulling hard against the ties at my head and feet, and dashing my head from side to side against the pillow to get the blindfold off. But the ropes, or stockings, or whatever they were just got tighter, and the effort was making my mouth fill with spit, which I had to swallow back or drown. And the effort was making it hard to get enough breath in through nostrils that were already swollen with asthma panic, and I had to recognize then that this was serious, no messing stuff.

In the black velvet cave of blindfold the flicker of craziness was brightening in one corner. A smouldering of real insanity that made me want to scream and thresh and vomit into the wall of plastic tape. And I knew then I was either going to have to give in to this thing of Hon's, and surrender myself up to it, or I was going to have to go mad. And so I gathered myself together to give in, and forced my breathing to slow, and willed my bunched and sweating shoulders to relax into the sheets.

'That's better,' her voice said, sounding far away through the thickness in my ears, and I felt her body slide down beside mine, and her hands reach for my groin. I lay there in my darkness, forcing my breath to come slow and regular, and my chest eased gradually and my nostrils cleared, and there were delightful flickerings around my cock and balls as her hands drifted and teased and warmed. And it was impossible but I was growing and stiffening in her hands; my body slack and useless but my cock growing twangy as she played gently with fingers and lips and wisps of hair.

And then her weight was on my body and I didn't dare to tense because the panic would come back, but just lay there slack and shipwrecked, as she eased herself over me; sliding up and down, deeper and deeper. She was straddling me now, facing the mirror at the foot of the bed, and I imagined what she saw, her pale naked body, riding the trussed and helpless one beneath her, and I didn't have to try to relax any more, because the undertow of pleasure was washing over me, dragging away at the shores of consciousness and –

'Phil-ip!'

'Oh fuck,' said Hon.

A door had slammed two flights below us and there were footsteps on the stairwell.

'Phil-ip!'

'Oh Jesus.'

I was wagging myself frantically from side to side, shaking my head, jerking my hips. And I was out of Hon, and she was tugging at the blindfold, but the steps were pounding towards us, two at a time, three at a time. A giant athlete, bursting doors and hurdling stairs and leaping landings. Joyful, exuberant and full of gleeful anticipation.

'Phil-ip!'

The tape was still on my mouth, and the handcuffs still on my wrists. The black silk stockings still bound my ankles, and my erection was miraculously still wagging, bound at its base with a dainty bow of black satin. But Hon had got the blindfold off, and so it was that the light and these sights burst on my eyes at the same moment as my mother-in-law burst into the room.

She had expected something, certainly. She must have monitored the comings and goings from her flat, perhaps noted the passengers in the Karmann Ghia. Maybe Diana had even told her about the postcards from Greece. It was a fierce knowledge of power and joy and triumph in my disgrace that carried the cardiac case out of bed and up those stairs, three at a time. But I don't think she expected what she got.

'Philip?' said my mother-in-law, a little timidly.

And of course there wasn't really anything else for Hon to say, but I did rather admire her afterwards for it. For her relaxed shoulders and impassive face, and the awesome cool of her reply.

'Philip is rather tied up at the moment,' said Hon.

There is a detail missing here, accidentally or on purpose. A salient fact left out for reasons of shame or narrative climax – you must decide, but I can't delay it longer. I cross my legs now beneath my writing desk as we shift again to the real, the really real.

A shrink would ask why does Mr First contrive these situations of danger, humiliation, exposure. A critic might ask why does Philip's maker create these situations for him, and the two might even be the same question. I ask it now myself, but in asking it I am gone again, receding into the infinite regressions of the first person. In a single bound I am free, while I, Philip, wriggle upon the bed in my silk and chains and satin bow.

The answer might be guilt: the abstract, needling, perpetual guilt of men to women, or in my case the guilt of Phil towards Diana, so harshly treated she is hardly here. There is certainly shame enough in the discovery of me and Hon in my marital bed, my mother-in-law freeze-framed in the doorway, with her face a fresh-minted mask of power and simulated shock. But it is farcical too: the stained sheets and ugly white buttocks, and ludicrously arrested lust. And it wasn't farcical then, only horrible.

Diana is away for a week, remember, but Diana never goes away. She is in hospital to bear Megan our second child. Coarsely stitched across the stomach from Caesarean cuts; still woozy with pethidine; only visited twice. Diana nurses my daughter in a hospital bed, while I fuck her friend in ours.

Very strange phone call this morning. A woman's voice, screamingly pukka, and talking to somebody else. It's this new habit, of people who are *so* fucking busy and important they can't be bothered to stop the conversation they're already having to talk to the person they're bothering with their phone call. She was yattering indistinctly to somebody in the background called Peter, and I was about to bang the phone down when her voice came on clear.

'Philip First? . . . I've got him now, Peter, yes . . . sorry, we've been trying to get hold of you for . . . hang on just a minute . . . right, yah. I've got the leader's office for you now.'

'Sorry, look, who is this?'

'The leader's line is free now, Mr First.'

'The leader of what?'

'I'm just putting you through.'

'Hello? Hello?'

But her voice had faded, and there was a burst of a Brahms piano concerto for about thirty seconds. I was just going to hang up again when another voice came on the line. Loud and cheerful and Welsh, but I don't know anyone in Wales now apart from my parents.

'Phil kiddo! Smashing to talk to you. We've been meaning to get in touch f'rages.'

'Hello? Who is this?' I was running through the uncles and cousins who might conceivably be leaders of anything.

'Turn that bloody music off will you, Pat? I can't hear myself bloody think by here.' But the Brahms kept on playing, and the Welsh voice decided to shout over it.

'Loved the Channel Four series last year, kiddo.'

'You mean the BBC series.'

'That's the one. And Rachel and Steven always listen to you on *Loose Ends* on Saturdays.'

'Sorry, who are Rachel and –?'

'Can't anyone get rid of that bloody music? I'm trying to have a conver . . . Phil kiddo? Are you still there?'

An absurd suspicion began to form. 'Look, just a minute. Am I talking to –?'

'– and the wife says she'd love to have you round one weekend. Loves theatre people. You know Judi and Glenda and Simon already, don't you?'

'No, I don't know who –'

'Doesn't matter. It's very informal. But I'll leave Pat to sort out the details. Meeting I've got to get to now across the river, but it's smashing to –'

'Hello? Hello?'

But the Brahms had come crashing back again, and then the pukka woman's voice talking across the mouthpiece: 'Yah, yah . . . right. I'll arrange a car to pick him up. You know you've only got five minutes before you have to be at Walworth Road . . . Hello, Mr First?'

'Still here.'

'So sorry the leader had to go off like that, but he's very pleased you can come.'

'Where am I –?'

'Just press the left-hand button on the fax, Peter . . . the leader said 8.00 on Saturday . . . no, not that one . . . we've got your address somewhere . . . yah, the red button on the end.'

'But what am I – ?'

'So don't worry about dressing up or anything, and we'll see you then.'

And the Brahms came crashing back, followed by a click and a purr.

I phoned Reg then, to check the possibility of a send-up,

but he had just got out of bed, and sounded convincingly grumpy, with sleep or hangover.

'I don't seem to see very much of you these days.'

'Well you would go and move to the fucking Ukraine, *Philippe*. You know I need three base camps and a team of Sherpas to get me anywhere east of the Barbican.'

'All right. Why don't we have a drink at the Groucho some time this week?'

'Bit difficult at the moment. Moving flat and all that.'

'I didn't know you were moving.'

'Mmmn. Saul found a little mews house in Belsize Village. Clarendon House, just like the Queen Mum. We're going to have ruched blinds and tapestry-work egg cosies, and a tea towel of Tower Bridge.'

'You're going to live with *Saul*?'

'Didn't Diana mention it to you?'

'I hardly ever see Diana now. I don't suppose I've spoken to her for nearly a month.'

'Pity.' There was a silence, during which I suppose Reg was thinking the same as me, which was that we hadn't spoken in a month either.

'Look, you can't seriously be setting up with Saul can you?' The faggy, French drawl disappeared abruptly from Reg's voice.

'Why not?'

'Well, I mean, I know you've always fancied him, but the guy's a fucking thick banker. He spends his days screwing people for interest, and making them bankrupt, and taking their businesses off them.'

There was a long sigh on the other end of the line. 'Saul is a loan broker to the Housing Corporation, Philip. He finds finance for low-cost housing projects. Urban renewal, getting people off the streets and out of nasty little bed and breakfast hotels.' It always made me uneasy when he called me Philip.

'Really? How long's he been doing that?'

'It's what he's always done, Philip, ever since leaving university, where, as you know perfectly well, he got a first in PPE.'

'I didn't know that.'

'Well you are noted for your highly selective memory, Philip. And in any case I don't suppose you ever fucking asked him, did you?'

I had some cold shepherd's pie for breakfast, tidied up the tidy flat and set out some games and toys. At ten I drove over to Hampstead to pick up the children for their Saturday session of paternal access. They had such a prison-like ring, all those words from the divorce settlement: access and custody and care and control. They were supposed to be the instruments of sustaining love, and they sounded like bolts being shot and locks being turned.

My mother-in-law answered the door, looking breezy in a white linen suit and black canvas pumps. A light tan, newly bobbed hair and no jewellery to speak of. Back in the saddle again she had blossomed since my departure. The bladder-wrack under her chin seemed to have tightened up with the keen astringent of triumph. She was even looking after the children while Diana did her rounds.

'Hello, Philip dear. Are you all right? You're not looking very well you know.'

'Aren't I?'

When any middle-aged woman says you look well it means you are two stone overweight, while if they say you look ill it is only one stone. I took no notice of her.

'Are Dewi and Megan ready?'

'I'll just have to get their shoes on. Why don't you come in for a minute and sit down?'

'I'll wait in the car.'

Reg wouldn't believe me when I told him on the phone how my mother-in-law had plotted the disaster with Hon. I gave him all the details about the holiday postcards, and Diana telling her mother about them. Then the faked heart attack, and the lying in wait for us in her flat, but he wouldn't listen.

'Haven't you ever heard of Occam's razor, *Philippe*? Entities are not to be multiplied needlessly. Simple explanations are always the most probable. You were having an illicit legover and your mother-in-law walked in. People are generally far too lazy to be devious.'

'Not when they hate your guts as much as she does.'

'Adrienne is very fond of you. She's been very upset about you leaving.'

'Oh yes. So upset that she's hired half the Inner Temple to make sure I don't leave with anything more than my toothbrush.'

'One old family solicitor to draw up a separation agreement.'

The solicitor had been about sixteen years old, in fact, with a wide Armani suit and a two-dimensional, Jack of Diamonds face. If I wanted to see Dewi and Megan again I would have to sign away any claims to property and money. It took twenty minutes, with a lot of shuffling of matters appertaining and parties aforementioned, but the deal boiled down to money or kids, and I chose kids. Over ten years I'd paid for the building conversion, the furnishing, the rates, the maintenance, the bills, and I walked away from Diamond Jack with five days a month parental access, no home and two pocketfuls of fresh air.

'How the fuck do you know about all this anyway?' I asked Reg. 'I suppose Adrienne and Diana have been pumping out the poison to everyone they can, have they?'

'I've known them almost as long as I've known you, Philip. They're friends.'

'There was never any need to get lawyers involved at all.'

'There wouldn't have been if you hadn't decided you wanted half the value of the house.'

And I began to get angry then, and told Reg a few things I thought about old friends who turned against you when you needed their support. And about people who stuck their long Yid noses into other people's private affairs. And about self-righteous cunts who became sanctimonious over other people's marriages, when they had spent half their own lives buggering little boys under bushes on Hampstead Heath. No cliché was left unturned, no sir.

There was a long silence on the phone after this, and eventually Reg said, 'Have you finished?', and after another silence I said that I had.

Dewi came running out of the house towards the car with Horsey Horsey under his arm, and jumped on to my lap in front of the steering wheel. Megan followed slowly, holding my mother-in-law's hand. Only two years old, she didn't even have the language yet to wrap around these great mysterious patterns. No concepts to encompass these arbitrary comings and goings, and this stranger called Daddy who arrived once a week to take her to a poky flat the other side of London, where toys and games were arranged, neatly as ammunition.

'Hello, my love.'

'Lo.'

'Can I have a kiss?'

'No kiss.' She buried her chin in her chest.

'I want a kiss,' said Dewi the diplomat. I buckled Megan into the child seat in the back and checked Dewi's strap beside me.

'Aren't you getting a bit old for Horsey Horsey now?'

'He's going to retire when I'm nine.'

'Knacker's yard and glue-pot?'

'He's going to an old horsey's home,' said Dewi firmly. 'Do they really put horses in Granny's cat food?'

'Only their toenails and eyelids and bottoms.'

'Yeeaarrch. Granny says it's just fish.'

'Then you should get her to eat some.'

'Will you eat some cat food, Granny?'

'You'll give them nightmares, Philip,' said my mother-in-law. 'What time shall I tell Diana you'll be back?'

I moaned inwardly. There was always a major performance about the precise time I would pick them up and the precise moment I would take them home. They lived with their mother all week without me feeling the need to harass her, but when they were with me I was on the end of an elastic band of maternal paranoia.

'Some time this evening.'

'She did ask me to find out. Can't you be a bit more definite?'

'No.'

I took them to McDonald's for lunch and we ate, half standing in the beige glare, at a table with narrow, sloping bench seats, or rather bum racks. I had to hold Megan in place with my arm, while her feet dangled.

'Why don't they have chairs, Dad?' said Dewi.

'Because they want us to get out as fast as possible.'

'Why's that, Dad?'

'So they can get rid of someone else just as fast.'

'Why do they want people to come in if they really want them to go away?'

'It's all to do with the Labour Theory of Surplus Value.'

'What's that, Dad?'

'Never mind.'

I bought a Filet O'Fish for myself, which the counter-hand said was a *filet* and I told him was a fillet. Dewi asked for a McChicken Sandwich and I got Megan some Chicken McNuggets. A Ronald McDonald clown came around and gave the children McDonald's hats.

'Hello, little boy.'

'I'm not little. I'm the biggest in my class.'

Beneath the synthetic hilarity of the white make-up and its red, painted rictus, was a fat, unsmiling face, with eyes at the side of its head, like a sperm whale.

'Ow, well then! Would the big boy like to hear a joke?'

'All right,' said Dewi, rolling his eyes at me.

'I bet you don't know why the dinosaur crossed the road.'

'Because they didn't have chickens in those days,' said Dewi.

'Ow,' said the sperm whale, floundering already. 'And, um, do you know why elephants have big ears?'

'Because Noddy wouldn't pay the ransom,' said Dewi, patiently.

'That's right,' said the sperm whale, struggling hard now. 'You do know a lot of jokes for a lit . . . big boy.'

'My dad's a comedian,' said Dewi proudly.

The clown turned to me, a spark of recognition on his face. 'Ow, right. I've seen you on *Saturday Night Live*. Ow, right. You're Phil F –'

'That's right.'

To salvage some self-respect he had decided to form an adults only exclusion zone, but I wasn't having any of that.

'Very bright little boy you have.'

'Perhaps they were just crappy old jokes,' I told him.

And he left, looking as dignified as any adult can look, in a giant Day-Glo romper suit and a red nose. And I sat there in my McDonald's hat with my McChildren, and our McFood: a late-twentieth-century McFather in a restaurant full of other McFathers.

'Dewi, you're not eating anything.'

'I'm not very hungry, Dad.'

I wasn't hungry either, and lit a cigar. Dewi was a big eater, a little too heavy for his age, and he loved McDonald's, but probably my mother-in-law would have been stuffing him with biscuits all morning.

'Is it McHorrible or something?'

He giggled and screwed up his face: 'It's really McNasty.'

'McSmelly.'

'McPooey.'

'McSgusting.'

'McFarty.'

Dewi was shouting, and Megan, who didn't understand, was laughing because we were laughing. She started windmilling her arms, and knocked over her Fanta, and then wiped her arm across the mess of sticky orange and ketchup. 'My juice. I want my juice.' She was crying now, as I tried to mop her and the table with a tiny paper napkin. Her flailing arm sent a packet of chips scattering on to the floor. Dewi shouted: 'Those were my chips, Dad.' A family on the next table got up to leave.

'Is there anything wrong, sir?' The clown had reappeared at my elbow. 'Something wrong with the Filet O'Fish?'

'It's fillet.'

'It's McShitty,' said Dewi, still giggling, but the sperm whale did not smile.

'I'm sure your mummy wouldn't like to hear you use bad words like that, little boy.'

'I want my mummy,' shouted Megan, crying even louder, and even in the crashing restaurant other heads were turning to look.

'I'm afraid this is a non-smoking area, sir.'

'Look could you just take your stupid smile somewhere else until I've cleared up this mess and stopped my daughter crying?'

'I'm only doing my job, sir.'

'What? As the silly painted smirk on the face of a grasping corporation that loves kids so much it flogs them factory-farm junk full of salt and fat and sugar.' I was shouting now, over the restaurant din and Megan's snivelling. 'Loves them so much it can't be fucked to give them proper seats or tables or napkins.' I tossed the scrap of soggy tissue on the floor. 'You call that a job?'

'Don't, Dad,' said Dewi.

'I'm going to have to ask you to leave if you disturb the other customers.'

'Da-ad.'

'You'll have to make me.'

'I'm going to fetch the manager.'

'Why don't you just McFuck off?' I shouted to his back.

I drove them back across London to the Isle of Dogs, with Megan still sniffling in the back and Dewi quiet with Horsey Horsey on his knee. There wasn't time now, before I had to take them home, to do anything much. On the one weekend a month they stayed with me overnight we went off to places like Thorpe Park or Chislehurst Caves, but the afternoon now yawned empty. Too much time, too little time.

'Would you like to go to Greenwich market, Dewi?'

'Can I buy something?'

'Yes, you can buy something.'

I parked the Mercedes at the end of the old Thames foot tunnel in Island Gardens, and helped them out of their seat-belts. A half-mile away, on the south bank of the river, Wren's creamy palace sprawled in the sunshine, an elegant heraldic beast, basking at the foot of the green park.

'You remember the name of that old ship over there?'

'The *Cuttle Shark*.'

'Nearly right.'

'Can I go down in the lift on my own and race you down the stairs again?'

'Oh, all right.'

I hoisted Megan on my shoulders and watched Dewi into the lift, which is huge and wood-panelled, like a Cunard stateroom.

'You have to wait until the lift starts, or it's not fair,' said Dewi. 'Do you promise?'

I made the promise, with no intention of keeping it, and started jogging fast down the spiral stairs as soon as the lift gates crashed to, Megan squealing with excitement on my shoulders. 'Faster, Daddy, faster.' London children are imprisoned in homes and cars much longer than I was as a child, but Dewi had begun to want to do things on his own now, like walk to the shop for chewing gum, or post a letter in the box on the corner of the street. Diana talked about child-abusers and kidnappers, and I ate sour bile for the few minutes he was out of my sight, but I thought he should be able to do it if he wanted.

I reached the bottom of the shaft before the lift wheezed to a stop, and there was quite a crowd of people waiting. The foot tunnel under the Thames was a popular place at weekends, and there were often buskers and beggars hanging around the narrow throat where the tunnel entered the lift shaft. There was one now, squatting on the floor with a hat between his knees, an old pink tweed jacket matted to the texture of rotted carpet, a filthy rag that might once have been a cravat around his throat. His hands, fiddling with the money in his hat, were a dark pewter colour; darker than the coins. At the sound of the lift gates crashing open he looked up.

'Cahill!'

He heard his name being shouted, and his eyes wandered unseeingly over my face. He saw a man of thirty-two getting thin on top, dressed in an expensive cream linen jacket, with a child on his shoulders. It was nobody that Brendan Cahill knew, and his eyes fell back again to the money in the hat. He was only fifteen feet away from me. 'Cahill!' But he didn't look up again.

'Daddy!' Megan was tugging at the loose flesh of my cheek with her sticky hand. I dragged my eyes back to the lift door. People were pouring out, blending with the waiting crowd. I tried to stand on tiptoe, which was difficult with the weight of Megan on my shoulders.

'Dewi!'

The crowd inside the lift was thinning out. I shoved hard, not caring, past sharp elbows and cross faces, right up to the door, and there were only three or four left now, with no Dewi. You don't think at moments like this, about the stupidity of a seven-year-old boy vanishing through the wall of a moving lift cage; vaporizing himself out of existence in the forty-five seconds it takes from the top of the shaft to the bottom.

'Where's Dewi, Daddy?'

'Shut up a minute.' I shoved roughly back through the departing crowd, checking fiercely and methodically now for a single man or woman with a child in hand. *Concentrate. Look. Stay calm. They can't have got far.* But there were only single figures and family groups tramping off down the echoing tunnel. I ran back to the lift door and grabbed the operator by the shoulder.

'Here, steady on.'

'A little boy, seven years old, dark hair.'

'Daddy,' he said timidly, and he was there, standing behind me.

'Oh, thank Christ.'

'I was first one out before anyone else. Did I win?' And I picked him up and held him.

'Yes. You won.'

'Everything all right now?' said the lift operator with a lift of the eyebrow. These bloody New Men.

I looked around the base of the lift shaft again and it was empty now. Cahill had disappeared and the foot tunnel, as far along as I could see, was deserted. I listened, but there were no footsteps on the spiral staircase above my head.

'Did you notice that old tramp sitting on the corner?' I asked the lift man.

'Get a lot of dossers down here in the summer,' he told me.

'Come on, Dad, let's go,' said Dewi.

'Just a *minute*.' The lift man was turning away. 'He's in his sixties, old pink jacket, Irish.'

'There's one old Irish bloke they call Dennis.'

'You mean Brendan. He's called Brendan.'

'Nah, definitely Dennis. 'Cause he's a menace, always pissed and scrounging for snout.'

'Come *on*, Dad.'

The lift man was looking at me humorously. 'You want to be careful, losing two people in one day.'

'I lost him ten years ago,' I said.

We bought ice creams on Greenwich Pier and visited the painted figureheads in the hold of the *Cutty Sark*. In the market I bought a pair of tiny sandals for Megan with brilliant motifs of palm trees and pineapples.

'Can I have one of those telephones, Dad?' Dewi was pointing at some old Siemens telephones in black Bakelite.

'You haven't got anywhere to connect it in your bedroom.'

'You could ask Mum to get a plug place.'

'They're very expensive, Dewi.'

'I want a phone so I can ring you up without having to go downstairs.'

Diana would complain about the extravagance. I'd be accused of buying their affections.

'Please, Dad.'

'Oh, all right.'

It was a long walk back through the tunnel to the north bank of the river, and Megan was tired. She began to sniffle and drag her feet.

'Look, it's not very far now.'

'Want a carry.'

'I've got all this shopping to carry.'

'Mummy gives me a carry. I don't want to be with you. I want to see Mummy.'

It always makes me feel hollow and hopeless this kind of thing. All the treats and outings and presents in the world can make no difference to a little girl of two who wants her mummy.

'Don't take any notice of her, Dad,' Dewi said. 'When she can't get her own way with Mum she says she wants to be with you.'

And I loved him for that: for his acuteness and his tact. And it made me feel a bit better for a while, but worse again afterwards, because children of seven shouldn't have to feel responsible for the happiness of their fathers.

There was no Cahill at the end of the tunnel, only an empty bottle of Bushmills rocking minutely in the warm downdraught of the ventilators. I picked it up and stored it in my carrier bag beside the sandals and telephone.

'What's that for, Dad?'

'Oh, just tidying,' I told him vaguely, but the truth was I didn't really know.

Megan fell asleep in her child seat before the car started moving, and Dewi was dozing by the time we got back to Aberdare House.

'You're late,' Diana said when she opened the door.

'No I'm not.'

'And the children are exhausted. I wanted them to be able to stay up tonight.'

'Daddy bought me a telephone. You've got to fix it up.'

'How kind of him,' said Diana. 'Have they had anything to eat?'

'Dewi hasn't been very hungry.'

She ran a hand over his forehead. 'You're very hot, darling. And pale. Too much excitement.' The message of all this, the unwritten *sous-texte*, but clear as a *Sun* headline, was that the responsible, grown-up, financially prudent people were back in charge again.

I followed her upstairs, over the carpet we chose, past the walls I once papered, through the doors I stripped and waxed, towards the sound of voices and the smell of cooking. There were candles, and linen napkins, and the flicker of good silver. Diana had just begun serving from a smoking casserole. My mother-in-law was sitting at the head of the table, with Reg on her right and Saul on her left. Serena Arum and husband Boru were next, followed by a Japanese woman I'd never seen before. And over at the sink, with her back turned, doing something with a strainer was, unbelievably, Hon.

'Don't mind me,' I said into the sudden silence, 'I'm just someone who used to live here.'

'Hello, *Philippe* old mate,' said Reg. 'Come and have a drink.'

'Well, that's uncommonly kind of you, Reg. A drop of my own wine in one of my own glasses at my very own table. You'll be telling me one of my jokes next, or have you started writing your own now?' Which shut him up pretty fast, and I helped myself to a big slug of wine. In the corner of my eye I was conscious of Diana, hustling the children out of the kitchen.

'How are you, Phil?' said Hon, from the other end of the kitchen.

'Why Henrietta! What a surprise. I almost didn't recognize you without your handcuffs. But of course I'd know your voice blindfolded. You seem to have got your feet back under the table remarkably quickly. Whipped and made up, is it?'

'Don't think really quite ...' said Saul, so I turned to him next.

'And my brother-in-law. That's a lovely head of skin you're getting there.' He patted his head gingerly and cleared his throat in embarrassment. 'What's the matter? One of Reg's little curlies stuck down there somewhere? You ought to try sucking a Fisherman's Friend, Saul.'

The Japanese woman was looking bemusedly from face to face, trying to work out what was going on. 'And what's your name, dear?' A blank look. 'Any idea at all?' Still blank. 'Go on, have a guess. You Japs are so clever at names. All those Cherrys and Preludes and Aftermaths. Let's just call you Interlude, shall we, until you fetch your brain out of cold storage?'

'You want me to get rid of this man, Adrienne?' says

Boru; he of the saffron pyjama trousers and turquoise worry beads.

'Oh, I shouldn't ask my mother-in-law to make a decision just like that,' I told him. 'She's liable to develop an acute cardiac condition if you ask her to pass the salt. But by all means try to get rid of me. I've always wanted to know what it was like to be attacked with a mantra, or hit about the head with a haiku ... What was your name? Bingo? Biffo?'

'It's Boru.'

'Well, I knew it was something ludicrous.'

He started moving out of his chair then, but his knees were still crippled by the table, and I pushed him back, hard. Serena Arum gave a little whimper.

'Don't, Boru,' said Hon.

'I think this man should know I have a third dan in karate.'

'And I think *you* should know that if you move from that seat again I'll break this fucking wine bottle across your throat, okay Desperate Dan?'

And Reg decided then that the show was over, and he pushed his chair back from the table and started clapping in the silence, the slow, ironic clap, but I wasn't finished. 'You should never clap on your own you know, Reggie. The size of your gut these days somebody might throw you a fish.'

'Get out, Phil,' said Diana from the doorway.

'I was just going, dearest. But I thought I'd like to take that tablecloth of mine.'

'What tablecloth?' she said, and she does ask for it sometimes, she really does.

'This one of course,' I told her, and yanked it off the table.

I felt pretty good after all this, I must say, and I gave a cheerful wave to Dewi, who was peeping timidly between his bedroom curtains as I got into the car. On the way back to Docklands I picked up another bottle of Bushmills, full this time, though it was half empty by the time I scraped the Mercedes on the pillar of the carport.

There wasn't much food in the fridge, so I had some of Dewi's Frosties for my dinner, which went surprisingly well with the sweet whisky. And then I thought the flat was looking a bit messy, so I decided to give it a good tidy, but somehow I kept dropping things, and managed to break the piece of phrenological head from Dewi's collection, which made me cry for a bit.

I rang up Reg then to say sorry about the fish joke, and he said it was all right, and was I okay? And I said of course I was okay, what the fuck did he mean? And he said he didn't mean anything, but why didn't I get to bed now and sleep it off? And I said what the fuck did he mean sleep it off? He was the one who was always too smashed to turn up for rehearsals and learn his lines and work on the scripts.

And then he sighed a bit and said 'Anyway . . .' which always pisses me off, because when someone sighs and says 'Anyway . . .' on the phone, what they are really saying is why don't you fuck off because I really haven't got anything to say to you, so I just smacked the phone down to teach him a lesson. He depends on me, Reg, because I'm always the one who's got the work in and organized the gigs and negotiated the contracts and written the material, but I have to remind him of it now and again.

I decided to go for a walk then to clear my head, and have a look around the Island Gardens to see if old Cahill might be hanging about there, and I might give him a swig of his favourite Bushmills. But there was nobody there in the little park, apart from a Rottwanker type with a huge dog and he didn't want a swig of the Bushmills. And then one of the police cars that patrol the Prestons Road pulled up and asked if everything was all right, sir, and I said I had noticed a suspicious type in the Island Gardens, and he wished me good night, and watched me all the way up the road to the flat.

Then I remembered what I'd forgotten to tell Reg in all the excitement, so I phoned him again, and said I was sorry about hanging up, and he said that was all right, and I said did he know Cahill was in London again?

'What do you mean?'

'I saw him today, in the Greenwich foot tunnel. But he was down and out and pissed, and he didn't recognize me. We should try and do something to help him.'

There was a pause on the other end of the line and I could hear Saul's voice in the background asking sleepily was it him again.

'Cahill is dead, Phil.'

'Of course he's not dead. I told you. I saw him today, ten feet away from where I was standing.'

'Like you saw him a year ago on the platform at Trafalgar Square station. And three months back on the TV documentary about down and outs?'

'That was just someone like Cahill. This was him.'

'Look, Phil, it's four o'clock in the morning, and this is the third time you've rung tonight.'

'Second.'

'Fourth time,' said Saul in the background.

'Why don't you get some sleep and we can talk about it tomorrow?'

'The man might be starving, wandering drunk. He could drown himself, fall under a train. He needs our help.'

'He's dead, Philip,' said Reg again. 'He went to Canada and died of a heart attack six months later. The private detective you hired told us about it. There was a newspaper cutting.'

'What do you mean the private detective I hired?'

'Oh come on, Phil. Not that again. It was your idea.'

So I began to understand their plot then. I was the only person Saul had told about hiring that little thug Cork to spy on Cahill. He had wanted me involved so he wouldn't have to carry the can, but now he was putting it about as my idea. And he would have told my mother-in-law about it, of course, which would explain her hatred of me, and Reg's disloyalty, and Diana's coldness. Saul had worked the whole thing so as to get me out of my house. I could see it now.

'I had nothing to do with Cork. It was Saul who wanted Cahill out of the way, so he could get the house and money when Adrienne died.'

There was another long pause, and a sigh from Reg, as if this was all very old ground.

'So don't you think it's funny how it was you and Diana that got the house?' said Reg. I could hear Saul's voice in the background, saying 'Look, he never bloody listens. Just come back to *bed*, Reg,' which made me feel sad and lonely somehow.

'All right,' I said. 'So what about Cahill pinching all that stuff and pawning it?'

He couldn't deny that. There'd been the Garrard candlesticks and the Tompion clock and God knows what else. It took the police months to get it all back from the pawnshops. But there was a tinny stain in Reg's voice that I hadn't heard before.

'You stole that stuff, Phil.'

'*What?*'

'You stole it. You know you did.'

'This is unbelievable.'

'Oh, Phil,' he said sadly. 'You told me yourself you were taking stuff to the pawnshops.'

My throat was thick with whisky and my scalp hot and crawling and I was trying to remember the last days after Cahill left and before my mother-in-law tried to top herself. There were bits missing all over the place, though nobody knew what exactly, and the police were checking the pawnshops, and it didn't seem to make much difference if I popped the odd teaspoon for some beer money, but that wasn't the same as –

'And you were the one who turned up with the pawn tickets, and told everyone that Cahill had given them you, and you were the one who . . .'

But it was obviously no use reasoning with Reg now, so I rang off and took the whisky bottle outside to the water feature, where the rubber pustule had got even bigger in the heat of the last few days. And when the bottle was all empty I smashed the base against the brick step, thinking of Boru and Hon and Adrienne and Serena's faces, and I chucked it hard as I could against the pustule, and there was a hiss and the most astonishing honk, and someone shouting from one of the flats, so I ran off, through this crappy little shrubbery the developers have planted, and round the corner of the apartments to the little shingle beach by the river, where I could hide and wait until the voices had gone.

The joke is, you see, that there's no joke. I spend my career constructing right-on comedy which rejects all stereotypes, but the life I live is full of the bastards. There's no such thing in real life as the scheming, tyrannical, music-hall mother-in-law – except that I happen to have one. There's no such thing as the waspish, camping, treacherous homosexual – except one happens to be my best friend. Vampish, bitch-goddess women are figments of the male imagination – except that one of them happens to have fucked up my marriage. Scheming bitches; chinless wonders; Irish blarney merchants; hippy mercenaries; sexless wives; there was the cast of three third-rate sitcoms there – except they all happened to be squatting on my life.

I waded into the river then, without taking off my shoes, and stood there knee-deep, watching the constellation of lights that was only an oil refinery fade into the dawn that was sliding upriver from Chatham and the Medway towns, and the Isle of Grain. The river was turning slowly from black silk to brown sacking, detailed with driftwood and bobbing gulls and Evian bottles. It was a large creature, laden with sewage and litter, dragging itself effortfully and for ever, down between broken banks towards the sea.

My head was aching, and my feet were cold, and I wanted to piss, but I wanted to stand there too and watch the sun come up and light the new towers of London. I wanted to make a pattern out of this moment, but the sun takes a long time to rise in London, and I was very tired of making shapes out of the meaningless. My life was all tests and exams and jobs and conquests and patterns and schemes. Courtship and marriage, adultery and divorce and paternity and death.

Like a novelist I could feel the weight and tension of all the relationships in my life, taut and meshing, as if their structure depended on me alone to keep it there. My life was an intricate latticework, held up only by force of will, and I was tired of keeping it there. I was tired of holding on, I wanted to just let go and so, for a moment, I didn't hold on, and I felt the front of my trousers hot and wet where I had opened my sad bladder and pissed myself steaming into the cold and muddy Thames, that was dragging itself down between broken banks to the sea.

CHAPTER THIRTEEN

'Hello, this is Philip First speaking. Please leave your name and number after the beep, and I'll call you back.' (*Beep*)

'Oh Phil, this is Reg, calling at, umm, ten thirty on Tuesday. Just wanted to talk to you about this Body Positive concert at Drury Lane. Some people there wondered if you might like to do something, and I promised I'd ask. Give us a ring when you're in. Um, that was it I think . . . Byeee.' (*Beep*)

'Ah yes . . . no, it's one of those bloody machines . . . Mr First? This is Central Transport speaking, and it's, ah, Tuesday afternoon. Just to confirm that one of our drivers will be collecting you at eight thirty on Saturday. If there's any problem please call us on 071–348 0263. Ah, right . . . Byeee.' (*Beep*)

'Philip? This is Diana here on, ah, Wednesday morning. I thought you should know that Dewi's not been very well, and I wondered if you'd noticed anything on Saturday? I'm taking him to the GP at the health centre this afternoon, and I'll call you later . . . Um, but try and give me a ring before then . . . Byeeeee.' (*Beep*)

'*Philippe!* You 'ave *disparu* into ze depth of Dockland. Ow you say, *le fond du Londres*? This is Thursday morning, and Body Positive is itching to hear from you.' (*Beep*)

'Phil? Look, *can* you ring me back if you get this message. I've seen the consultant about Dewi, and he thinks it may be the kidney thing again, though they can't be certain until they've done some tests. I've tried the BBC and they can't – look, just bloody *call* me will you? I *can't* deal with all this on my own.' (*Beep*)

'Oh screw this thing. Mr First? Central Transport. Message as before. Over and out.' (*Beep*)

'Oh God, it's one of these tape things. Hello? Is it still going? Philip? This is Adrienne . . . Um, Diana's been trying to get in touch, and she's just rung from the hospital again to see if I can try you. They say there's nothing to worry about but they want to keep him under observation for a few days, while they do some more tests. I think that was all, but you must ring the Royal Free as soon as um . . . well I know you will as soon as you can . . . Byeee.' (*Beep*)

'Reg again, Phil, at six o'clock on Thursday evening. I had a call from Adrienne and Diana and I went to see Dewi this morning. Everyone's a bit worried about you, mate, and if you don't phone back I'm coming round with the plod to kick the door down, so stash the manacles and flush the grass down the loo.' (*Beep*)

A novelist I used to know was always threatening to write a book one day called *After The Tone*, which would be entirely composed of messages from telephone-answering machines. It would be a twentieth-century answer to the epistolary novel of the eighteenth: allusive, fast-moving and tantalizingly oblique, but I think the callers will have to brush up their technique. There are too many stunned pauses; too many repetitions; too many fluffs and falters; and why does everyone have to end up with that embarrassed squawk of a 'By-eeee'?

The recording is, in any case, the only evidence I have of whatever happened to me that week. White tapes have cordoned off the area now. Firemen equipped with breathing apparatus have returned to base. Forensic experts are still sifting through the debris, while sniffer dogs scour the rubble for further survivors, but hopes are fading fast.

I hadn't been able to think of anyone I knew to go to the party with me, so I'd phoned Lotte in the end.

'I don't know if you remember me. Philip First. You looked after my little boy one afternoon.'

'A nice liddle poy. To me all the words for *Neighbours* tune he is teaching. Henrietta says this week that not so good he is.'

'No, he's not very well.'

'So now you are phoning me for the first time in six months and wanting again for me some afternoon with him perhaps to sit?'

To hear Lotte embark on an English sentence was like watching an Alsatian dog disappear into the waters of a muddy pond, from which it would emerge, whole anxious minutes later, on the opposite bank, with tail wagging triumphantly, and a verb in its mouth.

'Well actually no. His mother's looking after him now. I wondered if you might like to come to a party with me this evening.'

And I waited for another of the Alsatian sentences, ending this time in a negative. But all she said, after the shortest of pauses, was, 'Okay.'

She turned up at my place in her Karmann Ghia at eight fifteen, wearing a bowler hat and long gaberdine tailcoat like a Stamford Hill Jew, over a bronze plastic breastplate and striped baseball breeches.

'Liddle present from Camden Lock market for you I have bought.' It was a small set of clockwork teeth which chattered when I wound it up.

'Dewi will like those.'

'For you not the liddle poy them I have found. But this is not meaning to bed with you I want to go.'

'What?. . . Well, no, of course not . . . I didn't mean for a min . . .' And she laughed loudly and punched me in the stomach. 'In your auto or in mine we are going?'

'I think they are sending a car to fetch us.'

'But who are these "they"?'

'I'm not entirely sure.'

'This kind of party I like,' said Lotte.

The car was an old black Daimler Sovereign with chipped

crystal vases in gilt brackets, and little roller blinds on the windows. The driver's name was Dave: a thick neck, earlobes like satsumas and a heavy aura of security consciousness.

'So what's the address we're going to then, Dave?'

'It's not normal policy to disclose addresses I'm afraid, sir.'

'So we draw down the blinds when to the pardy we are coming?' suggested Lotte with a giggle, but Dave answered gravely.

'Would you happen to be from Eastern Europe, ma'am?'

'Leipzig,' said Lotte.

'In that case it won't be necessary to draw the blinds,' he said, and firmly closed the glass partition behind his neck.

It was a long drive, nearly an hour, right over to the west of London, and on the way I told her about Dewi, and then about Hon, and Diana and my mother-in-law and Reg. And I don't know why I told her exactly, except that she asked me, and she listened hard, with now and then a bark of laughter and a poke in the ribs.

'So. It is a bad woman that you have married.'

'No, not at all. I think she's a very good woman. She's very kind to her mother and to the children. She's always been the sort of person who visits people in hospital and supports charities and school jumble sales and all that sort of stuff. And she doesn't have a nasty tongue like I do. Never speaks ill of anyone. Never sneers at the Labour Party or the NHS or state schools . . .'

'Boring liddle prig,' said Lotte.

And I thought then about all the times Diana had turned from me in bed, and of her incomprehension of my anger. Of the way her eyes and then her mind had drifted from us to the children. Of the way our life together had shifted from partnership to duty, to a minefield of petty responsibility that seemed expressly designed to find me always wanting, always guilty. And I said gratefully that yes, perhaps she was.

'We're here,' said Dave the neck.

'You are sure?' said Lotte.

It was a squat, red, Edwardian semi, somewhere around Hammersmith or Ealing to judge by the size of the sky, and the rumble of big jets in their holding patterns. A tiny front garden was carved into a grid of rose beds and turves, like a chocolate bar. Above the red painted door were hanging baskets of alyssum and aubrietia, and the black snout of a video camera.

In a small front room Bob Dylan was thinking very loudly about the Jack of Spades, and people were eating crisps from the arms of a heavy three-piece suite in knobbly oatmeal. I recognized the front-bench spokeswoman for social services in one corner, nursing a baby, and the political editor of the *Sunday Telegraph*, nursing another. A presenter from *Channel Four News* was arguing noisily with Alec Smith, the publisher who had once been a boyfriend of Hon's. 'Of *course* they wanted Gorbachev to go down the pan. The last thing a reactionary government wants is to see socialism with a human face. It's Dubček and Czechoslovakia all over again.'

'We had a Labour government when Czechoslovakia was invaded,' Smith protested.

'Like I said, *reactionary*,' said the Channel Four man.

I had lost Lotte somewhere in the hallway, and so I hovered, examining the plaster loving doves which decorated the chimneypiece and nests of tables.

'Sweet, aren't they?' said a voice at my elbow, and I turned to find Malcolm Rutherford in baggy black suit and Ray-bans. 'It must be the perfect political marriage – at least, we've not got anything on him yet.'

'Is that why you're here?'

'Oh, any marriage will do. How's yours, for instance?'

'Why don't you go and fuck yourself?' I asked him.

'Oooh, but I *do*,' said Rutherford.

I walked off into the kitchen where there was a table laid

with sandwiches and tandoori chicken pieces. In the corner I could see Lotte's bowler hat bobbing away in a huddle of theatre types that included the Labour candidate for Hampstead and the latest West End dame. I tried to catch her eye over the heads, but a stocky man with ginger hair and Rohan leisure trousers was bearing down on me through the crowd.

'Phil boy! You haven't got a drink. Hang on by here, love.' He seized a glass and a bottle of Veuve du Vernay from the tray of a passing waitress, and manoeuvred us a space behind a bulky pair of serge shoulders.

'Sorry I didn't see you by the door. Bloody madhouses these things, but smashing you could come. You're from somewhere down our way, aren't you?'

'Near Cwmbran.'

'Bloody next door. But you've lost the accent. I was just saying to your ... friend in the lovely hat how much we enjoy your programme. Shove over a bit will you, mun?' he said to the serge shoulders behind him, but they failed to budge.

'I haven't done a programme for a year.'

'Well when you do it's a proper scream. That one about the Prime Minister and Reagan trying to book into a hotel! Laugh! Did you ever hear the one about the English motorist gets lost in the valleys ...'

Lotte had left the theatre types and was standing on her own by the door to the garden, looking long and lithe and comical in her Chaplin hat. She gave me a wink across the room and I thought she wasn't nearly six foot after all, but more like five ten, and I wondered what her breasts would be like under the silly bronze corset, but there wasn't much point wondering about things like that with Lotte because –

'And when he woke up in hospital he told the doctor he was trying to find this bloody Taff place called Dan-ger-a-head.'

'Oh yes, that's very good.'

My host was wheezing into his wine glass, and fumbling in one of the pockets of his Rohans for a filthy old pipe.

'Oh, I love a good laugh. We need more laughs in the Party, I'm always telling him by here.' He pointed at the serge shoulders, which were deep in conversation with a pretty publisher from Virago. 'In fact, Phil boy, I was wondering if you might like to help me with the odd speech now and again. Not the whole thing of course, but the odd line here and there – you do have some crackers . . .'

'Well, you know I don't really do jokes . . .'

'Course you do. That one about the Prime Minister doing her smalls. Laugh! I nearly died.'

'Well that's very kind, Mr –'

'No Mister here. You make yourself at home and have something to eat, there's a good boy. It's only Marks & Spencer, mind, but they are very good when you haven't got the time, don't you think?'

'Good old M&S? Oh yes, anything you want these days. The one down the road from us is doing primary education off the shelf now, just past the Greek yoghurts. And there's minor surgery while you wait, next to the delicatessen counter – and I've heard they're doing babies at the Muswell Hill branch, though I haven't been myself. Both sexes and any ethnic mix. Take them back if you're not satisfied – up to the age of eleven of course.'

This was an old routine, and I was motoring through it without really thinking, but a look of concentration had stolen over my host's face and he had begun to shift in his Reeboks and glance uneasily at the serge shoulders behind him. But what the hell, I didn't want to write jokes for this loquacious little jerk-off with his Hovis socialism and bullying sincerity . . .

'I don't quite –'

'Good old M&S. If you go down to the Marble Arch branch, well . . . they've got weaponry now, same floor as gents' knitwear. Small arms, semi-automatics, search and destroy vehicles, right up to the latest heat-seeking missiles, though off the peg naturally . . .'

'I think I must be – '

'And lovely politicians you can get from the cold counter. Conservative, Labour, Lib-Dem, corn fed, free range, organic, whatever you like. We had a self-basting Roy Hattersley the other week, you wouldn't credit the flavour . . .'

And the serge shoulders turned ponderously around towards us in recognition of their name.

'Ah yes,' said my host. 'You haven't met Roy have you, Phil?'

When I crept from bed on Saturday morning to snuff the flashing green LED on the answering machine, there were three empty bottles of Bushmills in the kitchen bin and a lot of takeaway cartons. There were shredded copies of *Time Out* and *City Limits* all over the sitting-room floor, some lipsticked wine glasses, a Sony Trinitron TV, still in its box, and a child's tricycle, gift-wrapped by Hamleys.

In the shower I found there were long, thin scratches down my right arm and across my back, while the right side of my jaw had become purple and puffy. I had been dismantled some time in the last four days, and reassembled from cheap spare parts. The new arms and legs were still numb and sluggish from surgery: incapable of managing zips and buttons without careful instructions. Mismatched synapses fizzed and sparked in botched-up junctions. The tongue was far too big, and rested woodenly on my lower teeth. The brain was too small for my skull, and swung sickeningly in its gimbals. I tried traversing my head gently from bathroom door to basin and it took whole, swimmy seconds for my field of vision to catch up, while flakes of loose distemper rained gently from somewhere inside the occipital orbit.

I filled a bin-liner and dragged it painfully downstairs to the carport where I noted the Mercedes now had a long scrape down both sides. A flat tyre, ground down to rubber rags, sprawled pathetically from the battered wheel rim, like a squashed squid. The aerial and both wing mirrors had disappeared, and on the back seat was an apricot silk bikini brief with a label from Silver Rose on the Finchley Road.

'First?'

It was Clive Gorman, my downstairs neighbour, in the outfit he wears for cycling to his merchant bank in the City. Black Lycra tights, yellow plastic crash-pads at knee and elbow, and a yellow Bell helmet with smoked perspex visor. Gorman has the yuppie knack of spending huge amounts of money on things whose whole point is to be cheap. His carbon-fibre windsurfing board cost more than a four-berth family cruiser; his chrome-vanadium pasta machine would bankrupt a whole Italian village; and his Cannondale Omega mountain bike cost him a brazen two thousand pounds. He's a total berk, in fact, and he looked today like a cross between a comic-book stormtrooper and an intergalactic bee-keeper.

'Oh, hi Clive.'

'Don't give me fucking Clive. I've written a full report of the events of last week, which is going to the management committee on Monday.'

'What events?'

He seized me by the elbow and marched me around the corner to the communal gardens. He has long, clean, pink fingers, with polished nails and no trace of callus, but they gripped like Mole wrenches, and I had to scurry along at his side, my legs half-pedalling the air, in case they came away with a piece of my fragile new forearm.

'How about this for a start?'

The half-acre of the water feature was dry and empty except for a weed-draped fountain and an Asda trolley. Two men in waders and overalls were raking together piles of dead fish and dying water plants.

'You can count yourself lucky that nobody called the

police. And my girlfriend expects a full apology.' He climbed on to the Cannondale and snapped down the black visor.

'I apologize, but what did I do?'

'You can read the report,' said Gorman. 'It's only six pages long.'

The black girl at the Royal Free reception desk didn't want to meet my eye: 'He's in oncology on the fourth floor,' she said, and I found Diana there, sitting in a crowded waiting room with Serena Arum, who was wearing a white wool catsuit, with a crystal on a silver chain around her neck, and one of those disgusting studs stuck through her left nostril.

'God, Philip, you look terrible. Where have you been?'

The room was furnished with beige plastic banquettes, heavily scarred with cigarette burns. All the seats were filled by an enormous Cockney family called Pearson, who were arguing, weeping and scorching the banquettes with Rothmans king-size.

'Can we talk in the corridor?' I asked her, and Diana glanced at Serena.

'*If* it's all right with Miss Milky Way, of course,' I said heavily, and Serena looked away, erasing me from the sunlit snowfields of her mental landscape.

'Must get rather unpleasant when you take it out,' I told her, and she flushed.

'I beg your pardon?'

'Bit crusty on the inside.' And as her dainty finger moved involuntarily to her nostril, I gave her my brightest smile.

'Oh for God's sake, Philip, come outside then,' said Diana, and led the way into the corridor. There were signs for haematology, radiology, oncology. What was oncology? Diana looked terribly tired, with the snail trails of dried tears on her cheeks and a limp Mother Hubbard frock that had been slept in more than once. We edged into a radiator niche, away from the crashing trolleys and rumbling oxygen carts.

'Is that sick down the front of your trousers?'

'I hadn't noticed.'

'I've been trying to get in touch since Tuesday.'

'I've been away a bit. Working. Why's Dewi still under observation? Have they found anything?'

She twisted a strand of hair around a finger and glanced up and down the corridor. Outside the window a pigeon was pecking at a crust on the fire-glass skylight of a ward below. A staff nurse was barging past with that air of underpaid indispensability they like to wear. An old man in a plaid dressing-gown was creaking painfully through the door of the sluice room on a Zimmer frame. Then the world stopped working for a moment.

'He's got cancer, Phil.'

'And you said something about what he'd eaten on Saturday, but I told you he hardly had anything . . .'

'Phil . . .'

'So it may have been something he had the day before . . .'

'Phil . . .'

'But I was sure it wasn't anything very . . .'

'He's got cancer, Phil.'

The fast-moving staff nurse was still abreast of us, and the old man on his walking frame still inched through the door of the sluice room. I had a sudden memory of a dark room in my parents' house, where I lay on the floor once when I was small, stabbing tiny holes in the carpet with a stolen screwdriver. What was it I was so angry about that time? The pigeon picked up its crust from the roof outside and flew away with a sticky clatter, and I remembered what oncology meant, though I think I probably knew it all along.

She was talking some more about glomerulonephritis and Wilm's tumour and cyclosporin while I looked at my fingernails which were as long and filthy as Reg's once had been when we met at university and drank bitter with advocaat and a cherry on top. Reg the magician who hid his lights under a barber's gown and read *Liberté* upside down, turning wintergreen forwards into ruched, blind-side egg cups. Because down at the orgy bush with Sid the Skeleton it was nearly the first century AD where Reg and I performed on eighteen-inch boards of seasoned oak that launched a thousand chips Hélène Ma Belle. For crooks and cabinet ministers never smoked in the street of launderette crucifixions, first or last not knowing the treatment for fine silver was cyclosporin God its boring; chitter chatter, sticky clatter; not a glimmer Mr Zimmer –

'Philip? Are you listening? Can you hear what I'm saying?'

'Of course I can hear you. I just need to wash my hands.'

In the lavatory I let my head press against the tiles above the urinal to cool my forehead. There was something wrong with the tubes to his bladder when he was born, and he kept getting infections. Diana fussed a lot about it, but Diana always fussed, and you don't get cancer from infections, do you? The doctors had probably panicked; confused the symptoms; some junior medic who'd gone for the big dramatic disease he remembered from medical school. I watched my own rope of bright pee tumble into the urinal and tried to remember when I last checked Dewi's.

I washed my hands then, taking far too long over it, soaping them twice and rinsing them in hot and then cold water. I wiped the soap smears from the sink trays with a paper towel, and listened to the groaning and scurrying of water in the plumbing. Some compulsion was making me afraid to look up into the mirror above the basin. I think I had some idea that my face might be horribly changed. Someone else's features might be there, looking out at me. I might not even be there at all, and I didn't look in the end, turning for the door, with my head held low.

Dewi was in the side-room of a ward full of terrible old women whose fallen faces lusted upwards for air like dying mackerel. The skin of his body was yellow and puffy and bruised by the drips and drains and monitors. A perspex duct like an elephant's trunk had swallowed half of his face and I was glad I couldn't see it.

'He's swollen up.'

'It's oedema,' Diana said. 'He's not getting rid of fluid fast enough. They were going to try dialysis before the operation.'

'I didn't know you could get as bad as this in a week.'

'Things happen to children very fast.' Her shoulders were hunched forward, her hands clasped together tightly in her groin, and I wondered if I should put an arm around her, but I didn't. 'He wasn't too bad on Thursday. But they gave him a general anaesthetic for the kidney biopsy, and they lost heart function for a couple of minutes.'

'You mean they fucked up the biopsy.'

'They don't know what happened, Phil.'

'I thought they were supposed to be fucking doctors. And now they've done what? Given my son brain damage?'

'They don't know if there's any damage. They won't know until he comes around.'

So we stood there hopelessly, with a yard between us, this mother and father, looking at what we had made and couldn't mend.

'Where's your mother?'

'She was here earlier. There's a chapel downstairs, and she said she wanted to pray.'

'So God'll be popping around any minute then?'

'Do you want to try and talk to Dewi?'

'Is there any point?'

'People often say they remember being talked to when they've been in a coma.'

'People in third-rate American hospital dramas.'

But I sat down beside the bed anyway, and tried to knead his fingers, which were as inert and chill as candles. They were my own nails and skin and wristbone and thumb, but the messages they sent me were remote and impersonal as telegrams.

'Is there anything I could do? I mean if you thought we should ask another consultant or something. One of those private places like the Wellesley. I could afford that.'

'It's not money, Phil. He's getting all the right stuff: steroids, antibiotics, cytotoxins. There isn't anything else you can do. But I've been sitting with him the last few nights. You could take over tonight. That would be a help.'

I was instantly enraged at her assumption that I might *not* want to be with Dewi.

'There *was* something I was supposed to go to tonight, but I could cancel that.'

'Adrienne can stay until midnight. You could take over from her then.'

'But is there really any point if he's like this?'

'It would make me feel better.'

'And you're sure there's nothing else we could be doing for him?'

She hesitated for a moment. 'Serena has made up some arnica remedy –'

'Oh for fuck's sake. I meant medicine, not bloody voodoo. If that silly cow is slipping stuff to Dewi that the doctors don't know about . . .'

'They know about it. They're very sympathetic to alternative remedies at this hospital. It can't do him any harm, and it's always possible that it could do some good.'

'I'm not having that witless bitch standing over my son mumbling fucking Muswell Hill mantras –'

'I thought you said that you wanted to help?'

'I do.'

'Then sit with Dewi tonight.'

I got back to the hospital at midnight and found Dewi and my mother-in-law and a room full of Horsey Horsey impedimenta. There were two new Horsey Horsey dolls, in magenta and tangerine; a Horsey Horsey carriage; drinking trough; hitching rail; tack room; and set of brushwood jumps made from puce P-Tex bristle.

'What's all this about?'

'I telephoned the manufacturer's yesterday, Philip, and told them about Dewi, and they very kindly sent round all these toys to cheer him up.'

'He's in a fucking coma, Adrienne. He doesn't know they're here.'

'The marketing director came over as well, and he was very kind. He told me about a little girl who had polio last year who learned to walk again when they put her Horsey Horsey over the other side of the hospital room. Just a little bit further every day, he said.'

'I suppose he'll be sending over a team of photographers next to put Dewi in their next catalogue.'

'Oh no, they sent the photographer this morning . . .'

'They *what*?'

'And a very nice girl from the *Ham and High* who said it would be some lovely human interest for the Heathman's Diary . . .'

'So it will be all over the *Sun* tomorrow.'

'And the vicar of St Christopher's has said there'll be a special mention of Dewi at the Prayer and Care meetings all this week. All those people sending out their good thoughts to him.'

'Why don't you go home, Adrienne?'

And so I sat for a while in the room, watching the phosphorescent squiggle on the heart monitor, and listening to the purposeful squeak of nurses' shoes in the corridor outside. Just above his face the ridges of the plastic duct dewed and then paled in rhythm with his breathing. For a few seconds a tiny flush of water droplets, then clear again. Dewed, then clear. Dewed, then clear. Dewi here. Dewi not here. Dewi here. It was all he was. His fingers were still waxy and cool in my hand, and I knew there was nothing going on in his brain. He was suspended still at the moment three days ago when the needle had slipped into his arm, and the nurses' voices had cooed, and doctors' faces had grown watery above him. Dewi had stopped there, was still there. And he might be there for ever.

I walked out through the ward of mackerel women and found a grey-faced junior registrar in a slot of an office along the corridor. There was no change in Dewi's condition; they were doing all they could; he was sure it was helpful for the family to be nearby; there was a coffee machine by the lifts.

I went back to the room where the only light now was a blue glow from the cathode-ray tubes and a warmer saffron spillage beneath the door from the sister's office. The glow caught the edge of objects, turning spheres into crescents and solid cubes into isometric projections, so the room seemed to float after a while, like a blue-tinged hologram in space, a computer simulation of itself that I could rotate at will and view from any angle.

From the door I could see a clipboard, full of bad news, hung from the bedrail; then a CRT screen with the row of spikes marching steadily from left to right. Rotate the room to look down from the ceiling and I could see myself, my bald spot, my right hand holding the hand of the figure on the bed.

Rotate room again and I was looking up from the pillow through Dewi's sightless eyes: a Disney mobile, a teddy, a horse doll, a forest of get-well cards. A skinny man with hollow cheeks and a bald spot was sitting in the visitor's chair holding my hand. He was bored: playing head games with architecture and point of view.

I stepped out again – quietly, but I didn't know why. Along some sighing corridors I found the vending machine and punched chocolate, as the only vending-machine drink which does not taste solely of vending machine. In the buzzing beige squalor of the waiting room the Pearson family had thinned out to a mother and her husband who was fast asleep across the banquettes.

'It's your son in there, isn't it? My Pauline was in the same bed but they moved her now to Insensitive Care. 'Cross the corridor. I was talking to your wife's mother.'

'She's not my wife any more.'

'Nor he isn't my husband.' She waved at the sleeping figure. 'He ain't seen her in four years. His own daughter. Not till the accident.'

'What happened?'

'Driving my granddaughter to school she was hit by a car. The little one went through the window. Killed straight off. And my daughter, she lost the one she been carrying six months.'

'That's terrible.'

'Now my daughter, she's had three heart attacks since then. On a thread the doctors say she is. Our only one she was.' And she started to cry then in horrible dragging, mucosal sobs that shook her from shoulder to knee. She was a huge woman with a crumpled Les Dawson face and a bright blonde rinse. Her husband began to stir in his sleep at the crying.

'Look, why don't you come outside in the corridor. Walk about a bit. Make you feel better.'

It was after three o'clock and the hospital was as quiet as a hospital ever gets, with its sobbing air vents, and humming lights, and muffled cries. I got her a chocolate from the machine, and she dried her eyes, half perched on the same radiator where I had sat with Diana and where the world had stopped.

'I seen you on the telly, I told him in there, but he never watches nothing but the sport.'

'I haven't been on the telly for quite a long time now.'

'You're one of them new comics. My daughter she used to like all that; *Saturday Night Live* it was she used to watch with our Mike. She's tried to get me to watch but I told her

I like my Cannon and Ball and my Mike and Bernie and I'm too old to change now, though I do like a good laugh. You need a joke a day is what I always say.' And she looked at me expectantly.

'I don't really tell jokes as such, I'm afraid. You see –'

'Garn, everyone knows a few, I heard one the other day 'bout this nig-nog, opened a paper shop . . . no, it wasn't a paper shop. It was, well never mind, this blackie, see . . .'

Down the long corridor to the left I could see a pair of West Indian nurses approaching, so I stepped into her stumbling delivery. 'Okay, look, there's a few Irish jokes I used to know. Paddy walks into a building site looking for a job, y'know, and the foreman says, "Can you make tea?" And Paddy says, "Aye, that I can." So the foreman says, "All right then, can you drive a forklift?" And Paddy says, "Why? How big's the fucking tea-pot?"'

Mrs Pearson was still cackling when the two nurses passed us by, giving me an approving nod. Good lad, keeping his mum cheerful in troubled times. Nice to see a smile on someone's face in a hospital. And so I gave Mrs Pearson another one before she had a chance to straighten up properly.

'So Paddy goes off to another site, where the foreman says to him, "Okay mate, what's your name?" And Paddy says, very dignified, "Me name's Paddy Mulligan." And the foreman says, "Right, so how do you spell that?" And Paddy says, "Stick your job up your arse."'

It's so easy this stuff, like pressing buttons on a drink dispenser. Insert joke, extract laugh. Joke in, laugh out. And if you catch the stride and hit the rhythm, which is easy with one person, you can start them laughing in pulse, and quite helplessly: twitching like a puppet on the strings of their own conditioned reflexes, of assumption and prejudice. And they're happy, they're really happy, just to be suspended for a while from the duties of consciousness. To be nothing but a wheezing diaphragm, and a spastic larynx, and an autonomically driven set of tear ducts.

So I told her about the Irishman who breaks his glasses on a Friday evening and asks the optician can he have them boarded up until Monday. And about the Irish mystery tour where they have a draw to guess the destination, and the coach driver wins fifty-three pounds. And the Irish bank robber who saws the wrong end off his shotgun, and the Irish Muslim who tries to assassinate William Rushton.

And I went on to queer jokes, and lesbian jokes, and Japanese jokes and, yes, mother-in-law jokes. I went on for an hour or more, in the empty corridor of the deserted hospital, where my son and Mrs Pearson's daughter lay in darkness. And Mrs Pearson rocked and laughed and panted and choked. And she told me I was a devil and a caution and a bugger and she hadn't laughed so much since when. And I smiled at her red face, and pressed the buttons, and went on pressing the buttons, that made Mrs Pearson happy.

CHAPTER FOURTEEN

Funerals begin to accumulate in middle age. There was a time when I was eight or nine that my father seemed to be getting out his black coat every Saturday afternoon, and coming back after tea with red-cold ears and whisky breath. 'Where've you been, Dad?' I used to ask. 'Telephoning the Pope,' he would say, and I imagined him in his black coat at a phone box on a windy heath somewhere, trying to get through to Rome. I never made the connection with the bottle of Vat 69 in the kitchen cupboard, and it was years later, mindlessly screwing the optic on to a bottle at The Jar that I laughed, finally understanding his small joke.

His own father died when I was seven, an enormous man with white, muscular breasts and a black soupstrainer moustache. Sepia-coloured uncles with sock-suspenders died as well, and beer mates of his from the Labour club, with gurgling, catarrhal laughs and receding gums. They died of strokes and heart attacks and cancers and bronchitis and emphysema. Bred on beer, fags and chips they never lived long enough to develop sophisticated ailments, but their wives lived for ever. Spry, leathery old ladies who were still hopping over garden walls at eighty.

Women never went to funerals, since it was a South Wales tradition that burials were too terrible for womenfolk. They stayed at home preparing an enormous tea, it being another custom that the thing had not been done properly unless you were buried with ham. And I took that literally as well when I was small, imagining the wet pink ham with its crust of yellow crumbs and blanket of white fat and the paper ruff around its shank, being tucked tenderly into the coffin beside the corpse.

But there were women at this funeral, of course. My mother-in-law in her preposterous bird-of-paradise hat, and Diana in her old navy Burberry that was growing faded along the seams. We'd squeezed hands and said hello and how are you, but there didn't seem to be much else to say. I was walking with Reg beside me, and Saul a few steps ahead, just behind the coffin, which was on a sort of muddy barrow.

There were twenty or thirty people, strung right out across the field, which was mustard-coloured clay, some-where near the M25. Beyond an embankment and a line of bare poplars I could hear the Doppler shift of heavy trucks passing, and see the sluggishly synchronized scatter of feed-ing crows. Reg had done all the arrangements. He had tried to find space in a churchyard in Hampstead or Highgate: a few yew trees and mossy headstones; but you have to have a family plot for generations to get into that kind of place. It seemed that almost everybody gets torched these days.

So we had ended up in the great necropolis that stretches out from the northern fringes of London right into Herts. and Beds. I had glimpsed it from motorways and feeder roads sometimes; meshing perspectives of white headstones, suddenly gone again behind a factory, like a filing drawer slammed shut. But I had never grasped the scale of it until our funeral cortège began to wind its way through the cir-cular drives and avenues and access roads. Mile after mile of graves – millions of them – all shrouded in hogweed and briar; memorialized only on council microfiche. Nobody would know where this grave was in five years from now.

'I've been wondering,' I said to Reg, 'if you'd mind me staying on with you and Saul for a while longer. Until things have settled down a bit.'

'Course not, mate. Stay as long as you like.'

I had decided to sell the flat in Docklands. There'd been

Clive Gorman and the management committee brandishing writs, and all the travelling to visit Dewi, but I'd got fed up with it anyway. Stuck out there on the cold edge of London with new winds beginning to blow from the east. I would sell up, and make a few thousand, and buy a little place in Swiss Cottage or Camden Town, where proper people lived. Saul had made a hundred thousand on his Wapping warehouse, but something had happened in the last six months. The pile-drivers had grown silent along the river levees, and forests of To Let signs were sprouting on the yellow brick condominiums. The estate agents made sucking noises with their teeth when they tapped the walls of my flat, and inspected the dried-up water feature, and counted the encroaching graffiti in the car park.

They put it on the market for the same price I had paid two years before, but nobody came to view. They dropped it twenty thousand after a month, but still nobody came, and I abandoned it to the methane bubbles and graffiti artists. I moved into Reg and Saul's spare room, which had a pleated valance on the bed and an embroidered text on the wall, 'O Bog our help in ages past'. I lay reading it, pondering the *double entendre* and listening enviously to Reg and Saul in the kitchen below, where they made treacle sponge pudding and toad-in-the-hole from Reg's Mrs Beeton, and sang a song they had made up called 'Ninnies in Pinnies'.

By the time the tail end of the procession reached the grave the priest, who nobody knew, had almost finished his patter. We stood on the mats of greengrocer's grass that had been laid around the grave. Diana's face, on the other side of the hole, was wet with tears, but I couldn't squeeze any juice from mine. The priest pulled a small tin of John Innes potting compost from beneath his cassock, and scattered it on to the coffin. He was wearing oxblood Doc Martens, I noticed.

'Earth to earth. Ashes to ashes . . .'

'So they actually *say* that,' said Reg.

A few yards away a boy in a leather waistcoat sat waiting on a red dumper truck, smoking a roll-up. The pile of yellow clay from the grave was only sketchily camouflaged with wreaths. There was one in the shape of a pink triangle from the percussion section of the London Symphony Orchestra; another, of bronze chrysanths and beige gardenias, in the shape of a foaming tankard.

'From the brewery,' said Reg. 'Clive would have loved that. Those bastards spent most of the last year trying to get him out of the pub.'

'They knew what he died of?'

'I got Dr Dougal from the Gospel Oak health centre to look after him for the last six months. He's a pisshead, but he's a good bloke. The death certificate says double pneumonia.'

The mustard-coloured clay was seeping through the grass mats, on to polished pumps and tasselled loafers. We picked up token crumbs of soil and tossed them in the hole, but my mother-in-law had to find a spade and start shovelling down a rain of echoing clods.

'Adrienne!'

'People are far too squeamish about death,' she said.

Saul was gazing off towards the motorway, his hands buried in his coat tails. The breeze whipped my mother-in-law's black bombazine and she was a flapping Bedouin tent, smeared yellow about the hems with clay, her bird of paradise askew.

'Oh, Mum!' It was a despairing Diana.

'Embarrassed by natural process. In my beginning is my end.'

'Embarrassed by you, you old cow,' I said, but I said it only to Reg.

We washed our hands under freezing taps in an open-sided shed, and wiped the clay from our shoes with paper towels. I took a miniature cigar from Reg and swallowed it in half a dozen grateful drags.

'It was nice of you to fix all this for Clive.'

'It was good of you and Diana and Adrienne to bother to come. The poor old sod didn't have any family to speak of, and none of the useless dipsos from The Jar would have made it out here. Don't suppose they've got a valid driving licence between them. Anyway, Clive was very good to me when I first came to London.'

'Buggering the barman in the beer cellar.'

Reg smiled. 'I don't think old Clive ever buggered anybody in his life. He received, but he did not give.'

I tossed the cigar butt into the pyracantha that bordered the chapel of rest. 'There's a line from Sean O'Casey about going to his son's funeral. I was trying to remember it.'

'A sense of trespassing joy,' said Reg. 'I was wondering if you might give Adrienne a lift home. My car seems to be pretty full.'

I didn't really relish the idea of a half-hour car ride with Adrienne: chain-smoking, and fiddling with the stereo, and playing with the electric windows, and dominating the heater controls, and criticizing my choice of route – all of which was her normal method of repayment for scrounging a lift in someone else's car. But what can you say? You can say no, that's what, so I said, 'Oh, um, yes, of course . . . why not?'

I'd hardly seen my mother-in-law in the last six weeks. She'd phoned all her friends to tell them throbbingly that she was 'nursing her grandson', but she seldom appeared at Dewi's bedside except to soak the occasional hankie. She bought herself a dramatic new wardrobe of capes and snoods in black and red, like a medieval plague doctor. She spent her days praying noisily in the hospital chapel, and crossing herself in toe-curling fashion whenever we went in to talk to the consultant.

Was it ever possible I had liked this person? I was irritated by the way she spoke and the way she ate and the way she dressed. I hated her smell, of new clothes and unwashed armpits. I loathed the booming, actressy projection of her voice; the greedy way she ate, with her arms around her plate; the infantile attention-seeking of her public praying and weeping; the prattling vacancy of her politics and aesthetics; the contrivance of her eccentricity; and the calculation behind her candour. 'You run her down all the time,' said Reg, 'but what harm is she doing? She's not such a bad old girl. She's always been nice to me, and you.'

'Nice people are nasty,' I told him, but I couldn't be bothered to explain.

She had even developed an exotic new ailment of her own called bronchial spasm, which caused her occasionally to collapse spectacularly in crowded corridors, and which meant she had to carry a small oxygen mask and cylinder at all times. She organized a sponsored run across Hampstead Heath and sponged free samples from toy companies, until Dewi's room was stuffed with polyethylene junk. She appointed herself public relations consultant to Dewi's disease and was forever talking to the tabloids: 'Comic tot's cancer – by tragic gran.'

'She's only trying to help, Phil,' Diana said, when I showed a copy of the *Star* with the latest of my mother-in-law's garbled pieties.

'Like fuck she is. This is the best role she's had since her Oxo advert. She's got that silly bloody throb in her voice like Lady Gridlock used to do for train crashes, and she's even started to talk like a tabloid.' I recited from the grimy newsprint: '"I believe it has brought us closer together as a family," said Mrs Schondler, fighting back the tears. The glamorous former stage star says, "My grandson's plucky fight for life sends a message of hope to us all."' I screwed the thing up and stuffed it in a hospital litter bin. We were standing in the corridor outside Dewi's ward, Diana half sitting on the radiator again.

'It makes me want to puke. And so does that soppy Serena, with her bloody eye of newt and toe of frog routine.'

'It can't do any harm, Phil.'

'Of course it can do harm. Haven't you heard? These people with cancer who take themselves off to expensive feelgood places to drink carrot juice and to visualize space invaders zapping their tumours – they die off at twice the rate of sensible people who stay in bed with a bottle of whisky and a box of Milk Tray.'

Diana's face was stiff and grey with tiredness and I could see the little muscles under her skin flinching with the battering. She needed, for some reason, to believe in all this bullshit, but I needed just as urgently to stop her.

'And it's not just nonsense all this alternative medicine crap – it's *wicked* nonsense, because what they are saying is that you can *do* something about having cancer, because in some way or other it's your fault that you've got it in the first place. You ate the wrong stuff, or breathed the wrong air, or thought the wrong thoughts. And now you try to get better by thinking the right thoughts and eating the right stuff, but if you die then it's still your fucking fault because you weren't thinking hard enough. So the Serenas of this world have got it covered from every angle with no comebacks: they're right if you die, right if you don't, and they get paid either way.'

I was shouting now, but Diana was shouting back. 'Serena's making nothing out of this. And she's been a good friend to me, Phil.'

'It doesn't give her and people like her the right to try to put causality and morality into illness and death, when it isn't anything except cruel and pointless and stupid.'

'So what do you want us to do, Phil? What do you want?' She was red and crying now. There were people turning their heads in the hospital corridor. A nurse had appeared from the ward office and was hovering anxiously in a doorway.

'You think we should just give up, is that right? So Mum can go back to her drugs and cats and you can go back to your nice flat and get pissed again. The doctors should just pull out the plugs on my little boy and let him die. Is that what you want?'

And I just stood there and didn't say anything, because it was what I wanted. I didn't want my son to wake up from his sleep to face chemotherapy and radiotherapy, and pain and fear and humiliation. The bleeding gums and nailbeds and wigs and lies and then death in the end anyway, because all the figures for cancer are fiddled, and everyone knows that survival means five years, which is not a life for a little boy of seven. So yes, I did think the doctors should pull the plugs and let him die, but I didn't even have the courage to say it, much less do it, so I stood there and didn't say anything.

I just got on with the numbing routines of hospital life instead: sitting every other night beside Dewi's bed and watching the spikes march steadily across the grey phosphor screens. The time passed terribly slowly, even with a book to read, even with the routines of drip changes and catheter emptying and blood-pressure checking. His skin was always cold and waxy, and in the blue electronic light the fine down on his cheek became a rime of frost. When nobody was around I used to comb his lank hair, and trim his fingernails, and push down his cuticles, and moisten his dry grey lips with glycerine. I didn't ask myself at the time why I did it, but I suppose I'd have said it made him look more alive.

When I could not sit beside him any longer I patrolled the empty corridors and waiting rooms and concourses. I got to know the withered old volunteer ladies on the tea stall, and the night cleaners. I began to grasp the hierarchies of staff and sister; houseman, registrar and consultant. I fell asleep on sticky plastic banquettes and grew flatulent on canteen food and dispenser drinks. An oily film descended between me and the world and I would wash my face in empty lavatories, four or five times a night, scrubbing at the film with hard water and stinging hospital soap.

One day I stepped out of the lift outside Dewi's ward to find the corridor full of people. There were a couple of photographers and my mother-in-law, talking to two men in dove-grey suits, both carrying Cellnet telephones in leather holsters. A kid in burst baseball boots and Eraserhead T-shirt was gaffer-taping a thick wrist of rubber cables across the floor and into the ward. In the middle of a group of giggling nurses a yob with a keyring clipped to his belt and an ENG camera on his shoulder was pretending to shoot pictures. A bossy girl with a clipboard, and an arse too fat for her Lycra leggings, was pinning badges on people.

'What's going on here?'

'Oh Philip darling.' My mother-in-law's jewelled claw was on my arm. 'These are the nice gentlemen I was telling you about who sent Dewi all those lovely –'

'Ah, Mr First,' said the biggest suit. 'Can I say on behalf of Kids'N'Stuff how deeply we sympathize with you at this –'

'What exactly do you think you are doing here?'

He laid a gentle, sympathetic hand on my other arm. 'Mr First, we know exactly how you must be –'

'Get your wanking paddle off me, right, *wus*?' Fatarse had pinned a badge on my lapel, and I yanked it off and sent it spinning down the corridor. The Eraserhead kid was inside the ward, working his way down the ranks of dying mackerel with his wires and tape reel.

'Nurse!' I dived into the gaggle of primrose nylon overalls and found one with a brown stripe on the arm. 'What's going on here, staff? These people are not taking pictures of my son.' It wasn't one of the night nurses that I knew well. Some silly bitch from an agency, with a South Ken accent.

'It has all been arranged with the hospital administrator, Mr First. These gentlemen have been very kind with donations to the children's ward, and the patients are looking forward to it.'

'What do you mean "looking forward to it"?' I waved at the ward of mackerel women. 'They're all half dead. They don't have a fucking clue what's going on.'

'There's no need to swear at me, Mr First.'

'I wasn't fucking swearing at you, you silly bitch . . .'

My mother-in-law had produced her oxygen cylinder and was taking deep sucks from the mask, supported solicitously by the second suit.

'Mr First?' It was the first suit again. 'Kids'N'Stuff has a great deal of experience with the beneficial effects of play therapy, together with external enrichment of the usual hospital environment –'

I seized him by a lapel, and dragged his broad, clean-pored face to within an inch of mine.

'Listen, wus. My son is in a coma. He does not know what is going on. He is dying. Do you understand me?'

'I think you are really being rather negative here, Mr First . . .'

He had taken me soothingly by the arm again and I began to wind back my free fist to take a swing at him. But then there was a flutter in the crowd and the second suit was saying something into his Cellnet, 'Yes, yes that's right. It's just on its way . . .'

The Eraserhead kid flipped a switch on the gang socket on the floor and the ward beyond flooded with light from an unseen bank of softs somewhere behind the door. There was a wheeze from the direction of the lift and the squeal of opening doors. The second suit started to applaud, but he was on his own and stopped after a few claps. A nurse giggled and started to say something, but then fell into awestruck silence, along with the rest of the little crowd.

Clopping towards us down the corridor was Dewi's Horsey Horsey doll, with the usual headache-yellow coat and viscose mane. But it had grown to enormous size – five feet at least at the shoulder, with hooves the size of washing-up bowls and lips like Lilos. It stopped a few feet away from us, and batted its scrubbing-brush eyelashes. There was some scrabbling movement inside its viscose hide, then a mechanical whirr.

'*Horsey Horsey, don't you stop*
Just let your feet go clippety-clop
Your tail goes swish and your wheels go round
Giddy-up, we're homeward bound.'

'Ohhh, isn't he *sweet*,' my mother-in-law said behind me.

'You are not taking that bloody travesty into my son's ward,' I told the first suit. 'I am his father and I absolutely . . .'

But the ENG camera was whirring now and the suits were gently pushing the crowd to make way for the Horsey Horsey. A camera flashed and I made a grab for the horse's slippery viscose rump, but I tripped somehow on the wrist of rubber cables and went sprawling. A photographer knelt quickly to get the picture, and I swung both legs sideways as hard as I could, getting him square with both knees in the grinning pan of his face.

The door of the ward was jammed with people now, so I clambered over them, using ears and noses and hair for my toe and handholds.

'What's he doing?'

'Mr First!'

'Philip!'

'Hey, stop that!'

Inside the ward the Horsey Horsey was clopping along the lines of mackerel women towards Dewi's room. As I ran towards him I could see the second suit from the corner of my eye, talking urgently into his Cellnet.

'Yes, I've informed security.'

I grabbed the thing's rump as it reached the open door of Dewi's room and pulled hard at the viscose, which tore away in my hand to reveal a triangular section of straining blue denim backside. ''Ere, what's going on out there?' There was another whirring noise from inside the head.

'Horsey Horsey wishes you were well
Take your medicine and you'll feel swell
A positive attitude, a cheerful smile
You'll be going home in a while.'

People were pouring into the room behind me. Someone grabbed my elbow from behind and I lashed out backwards and the hand went away. I tried to seize the creature's head, but the thing went sprawling, half across Dewi's bed. The rack of electronic monitors behind the bed was rocking dangerously and a drip stand went crashing to the floor.

Everything inside the room now seemed to be happening in a ghastly slow motion, as if we were all swimming in a dense sea. There were whole minutes to study the falling arc of the drip stand, and the sluggish, anemone blossoming of glass fragments as it hit the floor. The first suit's mouth was opening and closing, slowly as a grazing whale, but I could not make out his words. My ears were filled with a white noise, the susurration of tropical surf. The ENG camera was swimming towards me, the black sucker of lens reaching for my face, and I picked up something and threw it hard, but it was only a Horsey Horsey doll, and it sailed slowly, so slowly on its submarine parabola, to bounce harmlessly off the questing tentacle.

With a glassy smile on his face the first suit was moving down the far side of Dewi's bed, holding a large parcel wrapped in Horsey patterned paper.

'Horsey Horsey thinks you're cute
Sittin' in bed in your pyjama suit
Mom beside you and your dad
Here's a gift to make you glad.'

I grabbed the creature's head and wrenched sideways hard. There was a muffled yelp of pain from inside, and then the head came off in my arms to reveal an angry red face. I threw the thing across the bed and it hit the suit hard this time, and he tottered sideways.

There was another commotion now in the doorway, white

coats pushing through the crowd of faces. The Horsey Horsey head was singing to itself in a terrible, drugged, slow-motion voice, but nobody was listening.

'Security . . .'

'*Horsey . . . Horsey. . . don't . . . you . . . stop . . .*'

'No, it's the defib. unit . . .'

'*Just . . . let . . . your . . . feet . . . go . . . clippety . . . clop . . .*'

'What are these people doing here . . .?'

'*Your . . . tail . . . goes . . . swish . . . and . . . your . . . wheels . . . go . . . round . . .*'

'Can you please clear this room . . . I'm a doctor.'

'That's right, they've lost reading . . . he's gone flat.' A nurse, calm and intent and oblivious, was loading a syringe beside Dewi's bed, and a doctor was bending over his chest, ear to his mouth. The defib. trolley with its ugly matt mushroom pads was being shoved through the crowd at the door. 'Get out the way please . . . we've lost . . . he's gone flat.' And I glanced over at the grey phosphor screen that I had stared at for so many nights, watching the spikes march from left to right, left to right, one after the other.

'Yes, he's gone flat . . .'

But the spikes weren't marching anywhere now, and the plastic respirator tube was clear, undewed. No dew, no Dewi. And I kicked the obscene banana body on the floor, but there was nobody in it now, and there was someone holding my arms: 'Mr First, Mr First.' And there were no spikes on the grey screen, just a flat line and a flat whine from the machine, saying nothing, nothing, nothing.

'Yes, that's right, he's gone flat.'

'He's gone flat.'

'Gone flat.'

'Gone.'

'Flat.'

CHAPTER FIFTEEN

'Has it gone, the flat?'

'What?'

'The flat. Has it gone yet?'

'Oh, sorry. No, it's not gone yet. I think I'm going to have to drop the price again.'

I hadn't really been listening to my mother-in-law in the half-hour since we left the cemetery. She'd fiddled with the heater controls, and blown smoke in my face. She'd messed about with the electric windows, and played the radio full blast – some Wagner bombast which she knows I can't stand. And she had talked non-stop. But I hadn't said anything much apart from yes and no, and hmmnn and really?

'I'm so pleased you're coming back to Diana and the children again, Philip.'

'I'm not coming back to them, Adrienne. I'm just borrowing a room from Reg and Saul for a while.'

'And isn't it lovely about Saul and Reginald being so happy together. It's going to be quite like old times with the three of you at home together.'

'It won't be anything like old times, Adrienne.'

'Did I ever tell you about Clive playing Pyramus to my Thisbe when we were at St Albans together?'

'Yes, you did.'

The traffic was moving quickly on the Hendon Way and I played for a while with the idea of crossing the central reservation into the path of the oncoming traffic. There was no crash barrier here, and if I got up to fifty miles an hour, say, and went straight for the jaws of a heavy truck, the crumple zones and seat belts on the Mercedes would be no good to either of us.

It would just mean a quick flip to the right on the power steering. My mother-in-law would glance suddenly sideways at me, jolted from her monologue. Her face would turn from disbelief to panic, as the car bucketed fast over the kerbs. She would start scrabbling across towards the steering wheel, but by then great chrome teeth would be gnawing at the front fender of the Mercedes. Chewing up the headlamp casings and starring the bonnet enamel with stress fractures; crushing the battery casing with a bite; clambering heftily over the manifold and cylinder head; reaching through the crazed windscreen towards the soft morsels of our belted bodies.

I flicked the right-hand indicator and steered gently into the outside lane for the traffic lights at Finchley Road. I was writing alternative endings like this all the time now. My life had become so untidy that there seemed a need for something dramatic and conclusive. It was Reg who always said I planned things too much, and I suppose he was right. O levels, A levels, degree, career, marriage, property, children. The scripts always typed and the gags always rehearsed. Like that Kraut Kleist, who wrote out his life plan and locked it in a steel drawer, ticking off his aims every year, as he achieved them. I had wanted things like that – life as narrative – and I had it like that for a while until it became messy, unplanned, painful.

So I experimented with killing people off: Reg with Aids perhaps; and Saul with suicide. I remarried Diana, and we lived happily ever after. I ran away with Lotte and we bought a flat together in East Berlin, overlooking the Unter den Linden, with a scratched green door and terracotta pots of red geraniums on the window-sill. I murdered Hon with an undetectable South American poison, and I resurrected Cahill, who had been living all the time with a banker's niece in Toronto. My career revived with a Channel Four chat show, and I wrote a novel that was respectfully noticed in the *London Review of Books*.

'I thought that was quite a good turnout on the whole,' my mother-in-law was saying.

'Yes.'

'D'you know when Clive first came to London he used to sleep in Green Park? He told me he used to practise his elocution outside the Ritz: "I saw from the verandah a mass of people eating salmon on the grass."'

'Hmmnnn.'

'I went to poor old Harold Ledbeater's funeral the other week, and there were only four of us there with the vicar.'

'Really?'

I hadn't thought about The Zombie in years; that hopeless, smelly, stricken old man who used to totter about the back garden after my mother-in-law. I'd never liked him, with his phoney military bearing, and his racism, and his constant sponging of cigarettes and booze and fivers for the bookie. He was always going on about swastikas raining from the trees, and how his bus conductor was Papa Doc – even his insanity was tediously predictable. But I couldn't help thinking all the same how terribly sad it was to die in London, with no wife or children to miss you, and nobody to come to your funeral but a potty old lady and a faggy old vicar.

'You're crying, Philip.'

'No I'm not.'

'There's no need to be embarrassed you know. Funerals can be very moving, and everyone was very fond of Clive.'

'Well I wasn't fond of him. I hardly knew him, and what I did know was a bitchy old queen. And I am not bloody crying.'

Nobody was going to impose niceness on me, least of all my mother-in-law. I had a little rant about niceness that I was working up for my act one day. About how niceness was such a flabby, evasive, unprogrammatic, conservative notion. Nice people bought Oxfam Christmas cards and campaigned against gypsy camps. Nice people got damp eyes over cardboard-box cities, and then voted Tory. Nice people believed in private gesture, and disapproved of public action. Something like that anyway.

And my mother-in-law was a nice person. She collected these incontinent old ladies and importunate old men – loonies, alkies, druggies and dossers – because they made her look so much less of a wreck in contrast. And it made her into a secular saint for the drippy old dykes who gathered around her in the church porch: the Madges and Joyces and Pennies with their pudding-basin haircuts and brogued walking shoes and Organiser handbags. Adrienne was *such a case*, but she did a *lot of good work* in the parish. My mother-in-law was a nice person, and nice people were nasty.

What was the joke about mothers-in-law anyway? Why were they one of those things that were *automatically* comical, like Purley, and en suite bathrooms, and gravy granules, and balaclavas, and candlewick bedspreads, and gaberdine, and luncheon meat, and Blu-Loo, and John Noakes, and lemon-scented intimate wipes, and Nevil Shute, and puncture kits?

It was because they were so prosaic, I supposed, and so explicit. You married in passion and romance, to start a new life with a new person, but you also acquired a mother-in-law. A battered, leaking carrier bag of history and obligation and banality and complication. The comic contradiction to any romantic illusion you might ever have of independence and new beginnings and control over your own life. The mother-in-law joke was a kind of acceptance of all that: a rueful nod to the inevitability of defeat and decline and death. And maybe that was the reason I didn't think they were funny, and didn't tell them, and never would tell them – because I wasn't done yet, oh no.

*

The back bar of The Jar was a roaring sea of blow waves and flat-tops and toupees and the occasional female bob. 'Twice as many for the wake as turn out for the fucking burial,' said Reg. 'These old spongers can smell free booze from Box Hill.'

The street door was closed to the public, with a black bow tied around the handles, and there was only one part-timer behind the bar. Reg ducked under the counter flap, slung his jacket over the Laphroaig optic and began pulling pints and tonging ice with all the old balletic brio, while I watched him fondly from across the bar. My old mate Reg, who I'd known for so long, and who'd always stayed so loyal.

'Something long and cool for the young man with the cheekbones?'

'A pint of stout with a cherry and a dash of advocaat,' I told him.

'Disgusting drink,' said Reg automatically. 'Looks like someone's spunked in the bathwater.'

Somebody giggled further along the bar, and a few heads in the crowd turned our way, looking hopefully for the free show. But this wasn't for anybody else.

'It's all right, I can't afford it anyway.'

'Can't afford it? But you've never wanted for anything.'

'I've been wanted for indecent exposure,' I told him. 'But never mind, I'll tell you what, I'll just have a haircut.'

'You don't think you're in the wrong place do you, sir?' said Reg.

'No no no. I've just come from there.'

'The hairdresser's?'

'No, the wrong place. I've just come from the wrong place. So your argument doesn't stand up, I'm afraid.'

The conversation had dropped around the bar now, and people were listening to us, but it still wasn't a performance. It was just little bits and pieces from here and there. Tiny fragments of old sketches and old dialogues, to fill a gap or pad out a scene. Pieces that were so well worn they could fit together almost anyhow, like Lego bricks.

'All right, all right, I'll just suck a lemon-scented hygienic towelette.'

'Can't do that I'm afraid, sir.'

'Can't do that. And you call yourself a pub?'

'Well no, I don't call *myself* a pub, sir.'

'So what do you call yourself?'

'Reg.'

'Of course. Reg. And how's your wife, ummm . . .'

'Henrietta.'

'Did he? Did he by God? That must have been bloody painful.'

And people had started laughing properly by now because Reg was just so funny, with his pop eyes and pastry face and reined-in derangement. And I was remembering how much I used to like doing this sort of thing with Reg: this kind of seamless, idiotic rambling through old jokes and old punchlines, like jamming together on a battered piano.

'So anyway, there's this man enters a bar,' Reg was saying. 'It was an iron bar . . .'

'No no, he *goes* into a bar . . .' I said.

'No, he *walks*, that's it. That's the whole point of the joke.' The crowd around us was all cackling now, but it was still each other we were playing to. The joke about how not to tell a joke.

'Now look here. A man walks into a pub. It was an iron pub . . . no, that's not it.'

'Henry Cooper used to do that joke . . .'

'No, no, it was Tommy Bar. Tommy Bar used to walk into that one . . .'

'No, that's not right either . . .'

But they clapped it anyway, and we took a little bow to each other, and when it was all over I ordered a Scotch for Diana and a Pimms for my mother-in-law and a pint for Saul and wandered off into the little walled garden, where I found them defending a corner table and five chairs. 'I don't think we'll need that other chair. Reg is recapturing his youth behind the bar.'

'Big kid,' said Saul affectionately.

'How *were* the kids this morning?' I asked Diana.

'Oh, I told them we were going to a funeral, and Megan said did we want a lolly stick to make a cross. They're fine.'

And they were fine, more or less, because Dewi hadn't gone flat at all that time of the Horsey Horsey visit. It was just some problem with the monitoring equipment, and when the doctors had cleared the room of all the lunatics and got it all working again, the spikes were still marching from left to right, only stronger and steadier for some reason, and there was a flush on his throat. And that evening he was stirring in his sleep, and twitching when they made noises in his ear, and by the next day his eyes were open and I was dribbling water into his mouth from a baby-cup. In all the chaos someone had kicked out one of the leads. It might even have been me.

And it wasn't Wilm's tumour he had either, but glomerulonephritis, which was nasty but wasn't going to kill him. There would be antibiotics every day for years, and possibly dialysis, and maybe even, when he was older, a kidney transplant, but he wasn't about to die. He was out of hospital in another fortnight, and gingerly riding his new bike along the pavement a fortnight after that. I'd left him with Lotte, outside Aberdare House, giggling as she rode his bike along the cobbles of the mews, with her fishnet knees up by her chin and her black weeds flapping.

'I'd quite like a walk across the Heath,' Diana said to Saul after her second whisky. Not talking directly to me at all these days if she could avoid it. So I asked her chattily if she remembered the first time I had walked across the Heath on my own, which was the first day I had met her mother in the Royal Free. And how I'd come across the black-magic hippy on Parliament Hill, and found the view over London, which had looked all new-minted that day, as if it had just been made for me.

But I'd got it all wrong, Diana said. I'd met her mother for the first time at Louis' Patisserie, where we'd had Scotch pancakes with honey. It was the year after that she'd had her ingrowing toenails done at the Royal Free. And she remembered the walk over Parliament Hill and the black-magic hippy because she'd been on that walk too, but that was another weekend altogether, when she'd come up from Cardiff to see me and Reg perform. So it seemed as if I'd got it all wrong again, and I didn't argue, because she's usually right about these things.

So she and Saul went off for their walk, and I drove my mother-in-law back through the evening traffic to Aberdare House, not listening to her chatter, rattling on the roof like rain, and thinking about the first night I had spent there with Cahill and Hon and Reg and everyone, and how strange it was that a tiny step on a road can lead so far. And it was getting towards twilight when I turned into the mews, so I steered carefully, around the clutter of Testarossas and Maseratis and Astons and the other millionaire skateboards, and pulled in close to the garden wall of the house.

'Why don't you come inside and say hello to Dewi and Megan for a moment, Philip?'

'No, it's okay. I'll be seeing them tomorrow, and they'll want me to stay and read stories, and I should do some work tonight.' And so she leaned over and gave me a squeeze on the knee with her ringed and wrinkled old claw, and I thought about the time I had seen her in the bathroom mirror all those years ago, and the oily nakedness of her bare skin. And about the other time when she had come to my room, intent and oily-breasted and tobacco-tongued . . .

When I checked in the passenger-door mirror I could see the heavy red Testarossa again, wheeled out of the garage now and with a mechanic opening the driver's side. I could have afforded something like that by now if it wasn't for this silly old cow, who was blowing her smoke in my face and dropping ash all over my lap as she waved her fag around and fussed over her carrier bags of pills and junk food and cat laxatives.

'Well it's very sweet of you, Philip, and I'll give a big kiss from you to Dewi and Megan. Mmmmmmmnnnnaahhh!' She sprayed the air around my ear with an aerosol of bronchial phlegm and California Poppy, and I reached over and popped the door lock for her and saw that the red blob in the door mirror was much bigger now, but there was still plenty of time. Plenty if she hadn't got so slow, of course, with her rickety old hips and tar-clogged lungs and drug-shot synapses.

And I checked the door mirror again and thought why do I have to play nanny to a 60-year-old woman that I'm not even related to any more, and she could do with a bloody good fright, might wake her up a bit, get her to take some responsibility for herself for a change, and it's hardly my fault if she's so slow it takes her three minutes to open a car door, and so thick that she doesn't read labels on bottles of drugs, and doesn't see the copper behind her when she shoplifts from Boots, and doesn't look left when she crosses the bloody road.

And when it began to happen I found myself remembering something my old games master told me in junior school, about the cricket bat, and it was the same with a golf club too, and tennis racquets. That there was one spot on the face of a bat where all the weight and energy were concentrated on the swing – where all the lines of mass and stress and energy intersected. And that if you hit the ball at the right moment on its trajectory, and the right moment on your own swing, and if you got it right there, on the sweet spot, that magic spot on the face of the bat – well, then the force was two, three times what you got with an ordinary stroke.

And I suppose that's what happened, with the red axe-blur swinging so hard and sweet down the road behind as my mother-in-law stumbled out of the car, and hearing the lion roar turned so slowly, and stepped so slowly out into the trajectory of the axe as it swung and took her, two tons of steel on the sweet spot, swinging her so fast through the first inch of air and whisking off the heavy door of my Mercedes like a magician's handkerchief, and leaving the doorhole there naked and stupid, as it swung on with a wild squeal, carrying her aloft into the evening air wrapped around its red blade like a soft rag against the sky.

So they were nice to me at first, of course, bringing tea to my chair in the corridor, and wrapping my legs in a blanket. Concerned policewoman faces asking me for names in baby whispers. And I remember a dark-faced man in overalls being hustled past very fast – feet practically off the ground – and that had to be the mechanic. And then Diana's face and Saul's floating by, Diana hot and red around the eyes, but neither of them saying anything to me. And then there was another policewoman driving me back carefully across London to the Isle of Dogs, and looking around there at the bourbon bottles on the floor, and the half-wrapped tricycle, and the half-full packing cases, and looking at me again.

And when I got back to the police station the next morning to make my statement I saw Jack of Diamonds there talking to an Inspector. The family lawyer who stitched me up on the separation agreement. And they both turned and looked at me, but didn't say anything. And when I went into the interview room there was this old fart of a sergeant who was playing TV detectives with me. Asking had I been drinking, and what was my relationship with my mother-in-law, and did I check behind normally when I let someone out of the car, and why didn't I help her out.

Then he went out to the corridor, where I could see him nodding heads with Diamond Jack, lawyer to the gentry, and he came back half an hour later with more stuff about wasn't it strange, Mr First, how your mother-in-law died just before your divorce from your wife was complete, meaning you are now a joint beneficiary to her estate, which is all very handy given that your career's not doing too well, is it, Mr First? And you're behind with your mortgage aren't you, Mr First? And the bank has been bouncing your cheques hasn't it, Mr First? And was it just possible as your mother-in-law got out of the car that you helped her with a teensy-weensy push, Mr First?

So I just laughed at him and said look, cunt, you think I'm fucking Bluebeard or what? You think it's so easy to kill someone by arranging for them to step out of your car into the road at the precise moment as some loony you've never met in your life drives past in a Ferrari, why don't you try doing it yourself one day? And if you still think it's possible then lock me up and charge me with manslaughter, and take me to court and let everyone have a fucking good laugh, and he stuck his strawberry nose right up my face and said I don't like you, Mr First. Not at all.

And I saw him talking to Diamond Jack again later in the corridor, and they both looked at me very dirty, and strawberry says now he's going to give me a hard time and take another statement and all that crap, but I know he's just whistling, and he knows I know. They've got nothing they can do to me, nothing at all, and if they do cook up some shit about due care and attention or wilful negligence they'll just be laughed out of court – because you can just imagine it, can't you? Comic kills mother-in-law. I mean, really. It's a joke, isn't it?

READ MORE IN PENGUIN

In every corner of the world, on every subject under the sun, Penguin represents quality and variety – the very best in publishing today.

For complete information about books available from Penguin – including Puffins, Penguin Classics and Arkana – and how to order them, write to us at the appropriate address below. Please note that for copyright reasons the selection of books varies from country to country.

In the United Kingdom: Please write to *Dept. JC, Penguin Books Ltd, FREEPOST, West Drayton, Middlesex UB7 OBR*

If you have any difficulty in obtaining a title, please send your order with the correct money, plus ten per cent for postage and packaging, to *PO Box No. 11, West Drayton, Middlesex UB7 OBR*

In the United States: Please write to *Penguin USA Inc., 375 Hudson Street, New York, NY 10014*

In Canada: Please write to *Penguin Books Canada Ltd, 10 Alcorn Avenue, Suite 300, Toronto, Ontario M4V 3B2*

In Australia: Please write to *Penguin Books Australia Ltd, 487 Maroondah Highway, Ringwood, Victoria 3134*

In New Zealand: Please write to *Penguin Books (NZ) Ltd, 182–190 Wairau Road, Private Bag, Takapuna, Auckland 9*

In India: Please write to *Penguin Books India Pvt Ltd, 706 Eros Apartments, 56 Nehru Place, New Delhi 110 019*

In the Netherlands: Please write to *Penguin Books Netherlands B.V., Keizersgracht 231 NL–1016 DV Amsterdam*

In Germany: Please write to *Penguin Books Deutschland GmbH, Friedrichstrasse 10–12, W–6000 Frankfurt/Main 1*

In Spain: Please write to *Penguin Books S. A., C. San Bernardo 117–6° E–28015 Madrid*

In Italy: Please write to *Penguin Italia s.r.l., Via Felice Casati 20, I–20124 Milano*

In France: Please write to *Penguin France S. A., 17 rue Lejeune, F–31000 Toulouse*

In Japan: Please write to *Penguin Books Japan, Ishikiribashi Building, 2–5–4, Suido, Tokyo 112*

In Greece: Please write to *Penguin Hellas Ltd, Dimocritou 3, GR–106 71 Athens*

In South Africa: Please write to *Longman Penguin Southern Africa (Pty) Ltd, Private Bag X08, Bertsham 2013*

READ MORE IN PENGUIN

A CHOICE OF FICTION

Changes at Fairacre Miss Read

'Miss Read understands and loves the country and can write tenderly and humorously about the minutiae of village life without distortion or sentimentality' – *The Times Educational Supplement*

Lucia Rising E. F. Benson

Outrageously funny and wickedly satirical, E. F. Benson's portrait of society in the glamorous 1920s is as endlessly entertaining today as when it was first published.

Travels with My Aunt Graham Greene

In *Travels with My Aunt* Graham Greene not only gives us intoxicating entertainment but also confronts us with some of the most perplexing of human dilemmas.

The Folks That Live on the Hill Kingsley Amis

'In this utterly entertaining piece, Kingsley Amis proves once more that no one can hold a candle to his blistering command of contemporary life – and letters' – *Mail on Sunday*

A Gentleman of Leisure P. G. Wodehouse

Redolent with the sights, sounds and smells of rural English life, *A Gentleman of Leisure* also contains all the wit and vivacity we have come to expect from the inimitable Wodehouse.